P9-DFM-881

LOST REPUBLIC

PAUL B. THOMPSON

SCARLET VOYAGE

Scarlet Voyage, an imprint of Enslow Publishers, Inc.

Library of Congress Cataloging-in-Publication Data

Thompson, Paul B.
    Lost republic / Paul B. Thompson.
      pages cm
    Summary: "In 2055, eight teens board the S.S. Sir Guy Carleton, the world's last steamship on its final voyage. Once far out in the Atlantic, all modern technology fails. Each teen must rely on their own special skills to survive on a strange island that should not exist and escape the Lost Republic"—Provided by publisher.
    ISBN 978-1-62324-000-4
    [1. Science fiction. 2. Shipwrecks—Fiction. 3. Survival—Fiction.] I. Title.
    PZ7.T3719828Lo 2014
    [Fic]—dc23   632 4553
                2013048978

Future editions:
Paperback ISBN: 978-1-62324-001-1
EPUB ISBN: 978-1-62324-003-5
Single-User PDF ISBN: 978-1-62324-004-2
Multi-User PDF ISBN: 978-1-62324-015-8

Scarlet Voyage
Box 398, 40 Industrial Road
Berkeley Heights, NJ 07922
USA
www.scarletvoyage.com

Cover Illustrations: Shutterstock.com: Aleshyn_Andrei (4th portrait); Anastasios Kandris (man on bridge); Couperfield (6th portrait); diversepixel (temple); Julia Zakharova (7th portrait); Monkey Business Images (2nd and 5th portraits); Nolte Lourens (1st portrait); ollyy (3rd portrait); Piotr Marcinski (8th portrait); pixelparticle (star).

In memory of my brother
Robert Wayne Thompson
1952–2014
Chi mi a-rithist thu

CHAPTER 1

The ship stood out like a crisp French flag—red hull, white superstructure, with a peerless blue sky above. It didn't look like a relic about to begin its last journey. The old ship looked as good as it must have the day of its maiden voyage, eighty-two years ago. It looked solid, like it was carved from a single block of steel. Only a thin gray ribbon of exhaust from the streamlined funnel spoiled the image. Though the ship was far away, the onshore breeze carried the odor. It smelled old, toxic, and forbidden.

François Martin set down his bag and adjusted the Info-Coach in his ear. A warm voice filled his head.

"Cherbourg harbor is the largest artificial roadstead in the world. Even after two centuries, no other port has exceeded its size, though the Chinese 'Super Hong Kong' project is predicted to surpass Cherbourg when completed in 2089 . . ."

François shook his head to fast-forward the Coach. He looked again at the ship, stared at it to make the device recognize what he was seeing.

Without a slip the woman's voice said, "S.S. *Sir Guy Carleton*, a steam turbine cargo vessel of 15,412 tons. Canadian registry, the ship is operated by a Panamanian company, Conejos SpA." François continued to stare at the ship, but the Info-Coach had nothing more to say.

Standing on a street overlooking the Darse Transatlantique in Cherbourg's inner harbor, François Martin saw his father advancing up the gentle hill toward him. The company car, a graphite-colored Mercedes, waited at the curb behind him like a patient dog.

His suit was the same color as the Mercedes. Not similar, but exactly the same color. This was the latest executive style. François thought it made his father look like a Lego man.

"There you are," said his father.

François looked past his father to the *Carleton*. Streams of water poured from drains at the ship's bow. They were trimming her for sea.

"I came to ask you one last time: will you come with me on the *Sunflyer*?"

Sunflyer was the new solar-powered supership about to make its maiden voyage to Canada and America. It was anchored in the outer harbor, beyond the Jetee des Flamands. Serge Martin's company had installed most of the sunship's environmental systems—heating and air-conditioning—thus earning Monsieur Martin a berth on the *Sunflyer*'s much-heralded first trip.

François shook his head no. By doing so, he woke the Info-Coach at skull-blasting volume. It roared something about the weather in Nova Scotia until he flung it from his ear. It tinkled off the curb into the gutter.

Serge Martin picked up the little silver bead. He smiled at his son until he put the Info-Coach in his own ear. Dialing down the volume with twitch of his eye, Serge removed the device.

"Why did you choose that voice?"

François put the bead in his pants pocket. "Why shouldn't I want to hear my mother's voice?"

He hadn't seen his mother in three years, since the divorce. She lived in Montreal now. Serge Martin invited François to go with him to Canada on the *Sunflyer,* with the unspoken promise he would see his mother on the other side. When François found out the *Carleton* was going on its final voyage along with the sunship, he hacked into his father's travel account and changed his berth from *Sunflyer* to the old steamship.

His father said nothing. He beckoned, and the Mercedes crawled up beside him. Silently the door opened. Serge Martin leaned in and brought out a second soft suitcase, which he set on the walk by his son's feet. He got in the car and said to the machine, "Jetée des Flamands terminal."

The car door slowly closed, sealed. With only the sound of its tires crushing loose grit on the pavement, it rolled away. François picked up his bags and started for the Darse docks.

Ten meters away, Leigh Morrison was also headed for the *Carleton* dock. He saw François and his dad, or more accurately, he saw the smooth sedan lurking behind the well-dressed man. He knew from the contours and the color it was the latest model. People said the 2055 Mercedes had the most advanced guidance system in the world. In a missile it could take you to the moon if you told it to. Leigh liked the color, too. He had a pair of shoes that shade. He envied the guy, not only because his old man had stylish wheels but he had the latest model Topkapi PDD, personal data device. It fit in one ear, and you could adjust it with a simple head or eye movement. Leigh had a two-year-old Quipu model, the twin-ear kind joined by a hair-thin wire. Old stuff now, but at least it allowed him to tune out Julie when he needed to. She was going full blast now.

"Gala, what do you mean he won't go? He's got to! Do you see what Pam van Zant is wearing? What trash! God, who picks clothes for that show? He has to go, Gala! Is it raining again? You must be swimming to school, Miki!"

Julie Morrison, two years younger than Leigh, walked about half a step behind her brother. She was talking to friends in Dallas and Jakarta while the video feed from Your/World covered half her gold-tinted shades. Her parents couldn't understand how she could carry on two conversations, watch a program, and walk at the same time. All it took was practice, Julie said. She'd been practicing for sixteen years.

"'Scuse me!"

The stranger's voice cut through their ear traffic. The Morrisons stepped apart and a tall bronze figure flashed between them. Leigh and Julie stopped in their tracks and gawked. In a silver tank top and electric blue silk shorts, the runner practically glowed with energy in the fresh morning light. The appliques on her feet glittered as they rose and fell.

"Hey!" Julie called, putting her friends on pause. "Are you in training?"

The running girl glanced back over her shoulder. "Yeah! For 2056!" Her English had a Caribbean lilt.

"Good luck!" Leigh called. The Summer Olympics in Montreal were a year away. He watched the girl overtake the slow-moving Mercedes and pass it. The car turned right, but she kept straight for the Darse Transatlantique.

"Too much sweat," Julie said, starting Your/World on her glasses again.

"You can't be an athlete without sweating," Leigh replied.

"Who wants to be? I mean, she's all toned and everything, but she must have to shower five times a day. And being that tall, where does she find shoes?"

"Runners don't wear shoes." Competitive athletes—and those who wanted to look like them—wore nylon soles glued to their feet.

"That's what I mean! Appliques are smooth at the beach, but you can't wear 'em to a—"

Leigh turned up his old PDD. It was better than listening to one of Julie's rants on style.

His translator software converted local news to English.

"All eyes are on Cherbourg's Grande Rade, awaiting the departure of the all-solar powered ocean vessel *Sunflyer*," said the bland news voice. Leigh asked for a deeper translation. Grande Rade meant "Great Roadstead." What the hell was a road doing in a harbor?

"A roadstead is a place outside a harbor where a ship can anchor. It's an enclosed area with an opening to the sea," the PDD explained. It reverted to news.

"Almost lost in the furor over *Sunflyer's* debut is the final voyage of the world's last steam-turbine ship, the Canadian freighter S.S. *Sir Guy Carleton*. Once the old steamer reaches its final destination, Boston, U. S. A., it will be scrapped. Fossil-fueled, carbon-emitting transportation will soon be part of history." The PDD said nothing about there being any passengers on the *Carleton*.

Sea travel of any sort was new to Leigh. Since enrolling at the University of London last year, he'd been back and forth from the U. S. to Europe half a dozen times, but always by air. He didn't know anyone, not even his ancient grandmother, who'd ever traveled by ship. Leigh was taking final exams when he heard about the last voyage of the *Carleton*. The idea of going home on the last steamship in the world appealed to him in a way he couldn't quite explain. Julie, visiting him on the excuse she might also want to attend the university, had a major tantrum over the idea.

"Ships sink!" she cried. Had Leigh ever heard of the *Titanic*?

"Planes crash!" he snapped back. "So do airships! Ever heard of the *Hindenburg*?"

"Ships are slow!"

"Ships are romantic," he countered.

She snorted. "Like there'll be anybody on board but Forties and nostalgia freaks!"

In the end, she had to give in because their parents transferred money for the trip to Leigh's account. He bought two one-way passages on the *Carleton* from Cherbourg to Boston. The *Carleton* started its voyage in Britain, at Portsmouth, but Julie had to shop in Paris before going home, so that put them on board at the steamer's last European stop. Leigh ended up carrying four bags of stuff Julie bought in Paris in addition to his own luggage. Julie, as usual, carried herself. As they trudged down the hill, boarding was already underway. *Carleton* was due to depart Cherbourg at 1400 hours today.

Loping past the Americans, Jenny Hopkins instantly classified them. Football player. Cheerleader. She had watched the Your/World series *CampUSA* long enough to know the types.

The street ahead was almost empty. A three-wheel Vivo truck rattled by with a bed full of seafood crates on ice. Jenny watched for spilled shavings on the road. It wouldn't do to slip now and break an ankle before tryouts in Canada.

She'd been seriously training since spring. British weather being what it was, Jenny hadn't had many field workouts. She'd run indoors all winter, lap after lap in the Southampton Sports Hall until she knew every rivet in the rail, every scuff in the rubber-paved track. Working harder than the next girl was like breathing for her. Not being a college student, she had to train on her own where she could.

People did help. The sports hall let her run when the gym was supposed to be closed. Local shopkeepers who knew her parents donated running gear and sometimes free meals. Jenny was known as the Running Girl of So'ton (which was what local folk called Southampton). If she made the cut in Canada, Jenny would run for Britain in the 2056 summer games.

Time was short. She had no time to waste even on a flight to Canada. Her father heard about the old ship crossing the Atlantic and thought it would be a perfect way to get to the tryouts. Jenny could run all through the voyage.

The ticket wasn't cheap, so they had a block party to raise money for her. So'ton's West Indian community turned out for barbecue, and Jenny got a berth on the last steamship to America.

Ahead, a guy was walking down the hill with a suitcase in either hand. Trudging, really, with slow, heavy footfalls. As she flashed past, she gave him a sideways glance. Euro, no doubt, about her age. Not an athlete. He had the clothes and posture of *le geek*.

She wasn't pushing hard, just keeping her tempo up. As the hill flattened out, more people appeared. A bus squatted by a blue stop sign, heat shimmering from the drippy fuel cell on its tail. Families filed off with lumpy travel bags attached to their clothes. To Jenny they looked burdened and slow, like crabs on the beach at Nassau, where she was born.

More cars entered from side streets, and she reluctantly slowed to a walk. The fire of her own exertions caught up with her in a rush. Sweat trickled down her neck, behind her ears, and pooled in the appliques on her feet, making each step squish and squeak.

A black limousine ten years out-of-date turned ponderously into the lane, halting by the river of bus passengers flowing through the street to the Security and Customs office. Inside, Emile Bequerel peered through the severely tinted windows. He did not see tropical crabs, laden with their lives. The travelers headed for the *Carleton* seemed happy, carefree. They looked much alike, wherever they came from—shorts, light shirts in intensely artificial colors, sunhats. Older people wore tinted sunscreen, the blues and oranges Emile remembered from childhood trips to the beach. Children looked more natural. They used SPF pills to protect them from the sun.

Behind him, his three older sisters were all talking at once, as usual. Catharine was giving him advice again (he didn't listen), Jeanne was correcting Catharine, and Michele, loudest of all, was urging the chauffeur to drive through the crowd. *Les touristes* would get out of the way when they saw the blunt nose of the limo pushing toward them. Dirk the driver said, "Ja, ja, madame," but he didn't obey.

"I'll get out here," Emile declared quietly.

"No, you won't," Michele replied.

"Why not? The booth is right there, and we're stopped."

Before the Bequerel sisters could unite in their disapproval, Emile pulled the door handle. He stepped out of the chill air of the limo into the late spring sunlight and slammed the door before anyone could follow.

A window slid soundlessly down.

"Where are you going?" Jeanne demanded.

"Canada and America."

"I know that! What about your luggage? Your PDD?"

"I don't need them. I don't need any of it."

Emile slipped into the crowd of brightly dressed travelers. The last thing he heard behind him was Michele's shrill cry, "What will Papa say?"

He'll say, good for you, son. Get away from those harpies. At least that's what Emile wanted him to say. Emile saw his father at breakfast. They parted with a firm, manly handshake and no words at all.

Emile fell in line behind a woman and a girl wearing matching hats. The girl, about Emile's age but annoyingly taller, wore a white sundress that showed off her smoothly tanned shoulders. Her mother, also clad in white, had sleeves down to her wrists and slacks down to her ankles.

"Nellie, do you have the tickets?"

"They're e-tickets, Mum."

The woman checked the PDD attached to her wrist. It was an uncommon style on the continent. The woman and girl spoke to each other in English, but they did not sound American.

"Oh yes, I see," the woman said. "I feel like I've forgotten something—"

"You forgot to not call me Nellie," said the girl with forced patience.

"Yes, yes, now you are so old, I must call you Eleanor?"

The girl smiled a bit. Then she noticed the boy dressed in black trailing close behind. Too close.

"Nosy," she said, frowning. "Watch your valuables, Mum."

Being mistaken for a thief pleased him. Emile dropped back a step and tried not to look innocent.

Check-in for the *Carleton* was funneled through four gates. Agents of the shipping company and officers of the Securite Maritime stopped each passenger and scanned them for ID and properly paid fares. Emile followed Eleanor and her mother through gate 2. The girl glanced back at him, still frowning.

"Madame Margrete Quarrel? Your passage is paid. Eleanor Quarrel? Paid." The agent dabbed the backs of the hands with an invisible dye. Mrs. Quarrel moved on to the security check. Eleanor lingered behind her.

"Monsieur Emile-Bertrand Baptiste Bequerel?" Emile nodded, looking right into Eleanor's eyes. "Your passage is paid. Pass on, if you please."

Emile sauntered past Eleanor. Though tans were long out of fashion, he decided hers looked good on her, scowling or not.

At the security station, Mrs. Quarrel was nearly in tears. Eleanor hurried to her side.

"My passport has expired!" her mother said. "They will not let me board the ship!"

"How can that be?" asked Eleanor.

"There must have been confusion between Cape Town and here." She took Eleanor's hand. "Check yours, Nellie."

Eleanor ignored the childish nickname and held her left hand under the scanner. The chip under her skin read out perfectly. Her virtual passport appeared on the monitor. The security agent shrugged.

"Mademoiselle is in order. But you, madame, cannot board," he said.

Mrs. Quarrel began to cry. "After all our planning and saving!" Eleanor bit her lip and tried to console her mother. The nosy Euro kid who followed them into the station stepped up.

"May I offer a suggestion?" Emile said.

"No," Eleanor said.

"Be nice, Nellie! Yes, please," her mother countered.

He concentrated on making his English perfect. "The *Carleton* is not so fast a ship. It may be possible to correct your document and join the ship at sea." He turned to the security officer. "There are helicopters for hire around here?"

"True—but expensive" was the reply.

Emile passed the security check easily. He took a small plastic card from his wallet and gave it to Mrs. Quarrel.

"When your passport is fixed, use this to hire a helicopter. They will fly you out to the ship."

Mrs. Quarrel blinked away her tears. "Sir—monsieur—I cannot accept."

Emile withdrew his hand, leaving the iridescent card on her open palm. "It's nothing, madame." He eased past and started down the quay to the ship.

"Hey!" Eleanor called after. "Where's your luggage?"

He spread his hands wide. "Somewhere in Ghent!"

Mrs. Quarrel looked at the credit card in amazement. "What a strange, wonderful boy!"

"It's probably phony!" Eleanor muttered. She grabbed the card and held it out to the security man.

"Can you scan this? Is it any good?"

The Securite Maritime officer laid the little square of plastic on the station's PDD. A long series of numbers scrolled across the screen.

"*Mon dieu!*"

"Stolen?" Eleanor leaned in to him, trying to see what he saw.

The officer quickly removed the card and pressed it into Mrs. Quarrel's hand, closing her fingers firmly around it.

"Not stolen, mademoiselle. With the limit on this card, you could buy the *Carleton* outright, much less hire a helicopter to chase it!"

CHAPTER 2

The first passenger on board the old steamer was already below deck when the rest of the voyagers started up the canvas-walled gangplank. Hans Bachmann managed to get aboard early because his parents, owners of the antiques firm Bygone Age, had been hired to outfit the ship's dining room with dishes and cutlery for the passengers. The old *Carleton* was not a cruise ship, with accommodations for hundreds or thousands. Conejos SpA, operators of the ship, had her freshly painted and her limited cabin space spruced up for the final voyage. The Bachmanns brought on board place settings for 200 (there were, according to Your/World News, 133 actual passengers). The plates and cutlery came from the old *Queen Mary 2,* last of the great ocean liners.

Gottfried Bachmann left his son on board with their property. "Every broken cup or plate comes out of your allowance," he joked.

"I'll wash and put them away myself every night," Hans vowed with a straight face.

His mother and father were extremely proud of their collection of nautical relics, of which the *QM2* china was only a small part. Hans was, too. Though he joked about it, Gottfried and Elke knew their son would keep an eye on the collection during the voyage.

"Where will you go first in America?" his mother asked.

"To see the *Constitution*," Hans said.

She looked puzzled. "In Boston? I thought they kept it in Washington?"

Hans smiled. "Not the document, the ship! The wooden frigate in Boston harbor."

"More old ships!" Elke said. "You and your father—if it's old and damp, you love it!"

Gottfried put an arm around her waist. "Is that why I love you?"

She laughed and whispered to her husband in English, which she still thought Hans did not understand. Six years studying English, and his mother still thought he was eleven and innocent.

Back to business. His father reminded Hans for the fifth time not to miss his flight back to Europe.

"Delag Flight 5737," Gottfried said, emphasizing each number.

"Yes, sir." With his eyes, Hans appealed to his mother, but in this case, she was as obsessive as her husband. She repeated the date and time and made him recite it back to her.

"Very good." Gottfried shook his son's hand. Elke put a hand behind Hans's neck and kissed him hard on the cheek.

"Text us!" she said. Hans held up his PDD and smiled.

The first passengers were filing on board when the Bachmanns left. Looking down from the boat deck, Hans waved to his parents. In their sober, turn-of-the-twenty-first-century clothes, the Bachmanns were soon lost in an inflowing tide of vivid greens, yellows, and reds. The passengers were greeted at the top of the gangplank by Captain Viega and Purser Brock, decked out in their best white uniforms. Farther down the deck a winch whined, hauling up passengers' luggage. The cargo net was designed to handle whole pallets of goods, so it looked nearly empty bringing up several dozen suitcases and backpacks.

Out of the stream of brightly dressed travelers, Hans spotted a lone shadow. A boy came aboard alone, wearing a stark black suit over a bone-white shirt. His hair was almost as dark as his clothes. At the top of the ramp, Captain Viega not only shook the boy's hand but he bowed to him.

VIP, Hans thought. At that moment, the boy in black looked up at him. The captain and the purser were going on about nothing important. The boy stared up at him awhile and then moved on, leaving the *Carleton's* master talking to his back.

There were a few other noteworthy characters Hans saw: a tall girl in running clothes who broke out into a sprint once she cleared the captain and the purser. There was an old lady, unable to walk, in a lifter chair. Hans had seen these on Your/World, but he'd never seen one in real life. It glided along, held off the ground by powerful magnets. He saw four men in American naval uniforms, a group of Chinese tourists with holographic hats (one had a short and flickered), and an entire Irish football club in striped jerseys and shorts.

There was a break in the line, and Hans thought the boarding was over. He started to leave the rail when he noticed Captain Viega wasn't leaving. He could see down the covered ramp, so there must be someone else coming.

A lone girl appeared out of the canvas tunnel. She was tall and thin, with black hair bobbed at her ears. Clasped in her hands was a simple carpetbag. Her jade-colored skirt came down to her ankles. Pausing at the top of the ramp, she exchanged courtesies with the purser and captain before moving on.

She was the last. Captain Viega held up a hand and called out, "Vamos!" The purser held a finger to the PDD in his ear and issued rapid orders. It was time. The *Carleton's* last voyage had begun.

The boarding ramp was cleared. Lines, hoses, and data cables dropped free and were reeled onto the quay. The steamer's turbines, idling since daybreak, surged, sending vibrations throughout the steel hull to every deck. A ship the size of the *Carleton* did not simply pull away from a dock like a speedboat. Two electric tugs, unimaginatively labeled *109* and *73*, approached the *Carleton's* free side. The massive magnets on their bows, encased in peeling rubber bumpers, pulled hard on the old ship and with a deck-shaking thunk-thunk locked onto the steamer.

Many passengers flocked to the port side to watch the action. Seawater boiled at the tugs' sterns as they reversed engines.

François Martin was at the *Carleton's* bow, as close to the water as he could get. Tug *73* was below him, straining against the bulk of the old freighter. He could smell ozone from the tug's electric motors. No one was visible on the tug's deck. In the lofty pilothouse, *73's* master sat in a high chair wearing an enormous pair of dark glasses, guiding the tug with a simple joystick.

Stale green water swirled around the *Carleton's* hull. Up close, the ship was not nearly so fine as it looked from the streets of Cherbourg. François bumped the toe of his shoe against a line of rivets thickly crusted with new paint. The owners had decided to send the old ship off with a fresh coat, like sending a dying man to the hospital in a new suit.

A droning overhead and a broad shadow drew François's attention skyward. A Eurochannel blimp drifted over at low altitude. Clusters of cameras raked up and down the *Carleton,* sending images live through Your/World. The American girl must have been watching the feed on her glasses. She punched her brother on the arm and yelled something about being on TV. She wasn't the only one watching the ship's departure through Eurochannel's eyes. All around the deck people stared into their PDDs instead of looking around for themselves.

Captain Viega must have rung for more RPMs from the engines. The deck trembled. *Carleton*'s bow turned left (Port, Leigh Morrison reminded himself. On a ship you say port.) Tug 73 churned backward, sending foaming green water over the tug's stern.

Leigh was at the rail amidships. Julie was behind him, watching the TV feed of their departure. In addition to the Eurochannel blimp, there were drones overhead bearing logos from China Star TV, Al-Tayr Networks, NHK, and Your/World News. The drones hovered and darted like giant dragonflies. A silver-sided one with a Russian logo swept over the deck so low, everyone ducked.

Tug 73 detached and drew away. *Carleton* moved ahead, slowly. Cherbourg's inner harbor was full of small craft. Securite Maritime boats herded them away. Hundreds of personal cameras soaked up the steamer's image. When Leigh mentioned that, Julie went to the rail and began waving to them.

"Bon voyage! Bon voyage!" she shouted.

"That's what they should say to you."

A kid dressed in an ugly black suit stood by Julie's elbow. He was not waving.

"What?"

"We are the ones leaving. It is for them—" he pointed at the swarm of small boats—"to wish us a good trip, a bon voyage."

"Oh." All the fun had gone out of waving. Julie backed away from the rail and the weird boy.

Hearing the exchange, François said to Emile in French, "Don't tease the Americans."

"Was I teasing? I thought I was helping her understand," Emile replied.

The boy's accent was different. He was not French, François decided.

"Are you Swiss?"

"Belgian."

François introduced himself. Emile gave his first name only, then pointedly turned away to watch the pageant around them.

As the ship crossed the inner harbor, the tugs kept pace on either side, like guard dogs. Ahead lay the two jetties that enclosed the Little Roadstead. The right hand one was the Jetee des Flamands. Beyond it, the new solar-powered vessel *Sunflyer* was waiting. Already the abstract upperworks could be seen, looking more like an artsy new office building than a seagoing ship. According to news reports, *Sunflyer*'s departure was to be synchronized with the *Carleton*'s. Invited guests, VIPs, and celebrities had been boarding the sunship since last night. A big party was thrown on the vast, open paraplane deck—all broadcast live on Your/World, of course.

The white wave curling back from *Carleton*'s bow got bigger as the ship passed between the jetties into the Grand Roadstead. Off to the right (starboard, Leigh reminded himself), the *Sunflyer* crouched on the water. Fully visible, the solar craft resembled a vast glittering insect. It was a catamaran—it had two long, slim silver-green hulls—joined by many wide decks. *Sunflyer* was about as wide as it was long and built entirely of carbon and glass fiber. High above the highest deck were many thin, airfoil-shaped towers. Solar panels sprouted from them like iridescent wings. Though *Sunflyer* was three times longer and six times wider than the *Carleton,* it contained far less steel and no petrochemicals at all.

"Looks like a bug." The American teenager with the noisy sister had joined François at the bow. He agreed. "It doesn't look sturdy enough to cross the Atlantic."

"Think about the explorers who crossed in little wooden ships," François said. "*Sunflyer* is the strongest and fastest commercial vessel ever built."

Leigh shaded his eyes with his hand. "How fast is it?"

"With a half-million horsepower, in hydrofoil mode it can reach fifty knots."

Tugs and Securite Maritime craft were clearing the hodgepodge of small craft out of *Sunflyer*'s way. As Captain Viega put *Carleton*'s wheel over to port, tugboats *73* and *109* left her. A fresh breeze whirled down the steamer's cluttered deck. Then *Sunflyer* spoke. A weird, high-pitched siren blasted from it. François thought he could see the calm waters of the Grand Roadstead ripple from the roar.

Julie caught her brother's arm. "Come inside, the *Sunflyer*'s going!"

"What do you mean?" Leigh pointed at the gossamer giant. "It's right there!"

"Your/World has coverage. They're showing it on the big screen in the ship's lounge," Julie said, tugging at Leigh.

He looked at the French guy, still leaning on the steamer's rail. He wasn't going anywhere.

"Why go inside? You can see everything right here," Leigh complained.

Julie groaned. "It's big-screen HD! Come on, it's better than outside. We'll see everything at once!"

Leigh let himself be dragged away. François was almost alone on deck. Most of the passengers rushed in to see *Sunflyer's* departure in high definition. His only companions were the running girl (on her fourth lap), the old lady in the lifter chair, the Chinese tourist in the blinky hat, and the Belgian boy in black.

François took out his PDD and shot some quick video of the chaos around the sunship. The Eurochannel blimp and drones had forsaken the *Carleton* for the solar wonder. Naval and security helicopters hovered near *Sunflyer*. The authorities struggled to get the sightseers out of the way. Boxy ferries and elegant yachts, pleasure boats and hired cruisers, churned the green waters, trying to make way for the stirring giant. Two charter boats collided, prompting police boats to charge in with lights flashing and sirens wailing. Compared with the monster blast of *Sunflyer's* horn, the police were guppies before a whale.

The *Carleton* drew away, picking up speed as she passed the length of the Jetee du Homet. Other cargo vessels had been cleared out, sent to sea last night or held at the docks until the passage of the two historic ships was done. When the steamer was halfway down the roadstead, *Sunflyer's* horn sounded again. François, Emile, the lifter lady, and Mr. Blinky Hat trailed down the ship's side, keeping the sunship in view.

Sunflyer seemed to rise up out of the water. The old woman asked in English, "Is it going to fly?"

"No, madame," said François. "It rides on hydrofoils, which lift it out of the water to increase speed and lower drag." Blinky Hat said something in Mandarin. Emile answered him.

A cloud enveloped the *Sunflyer's* hulls. Over the flat waters of the Grand Roadstead came a rushing sound, more like a waterfall than a seagoing ship. The fleet of small craft around the sunship parted. Every horn, siren, and klaxon in Cherbourg began to bleat. François looked back at the *Carleton's* bridge. The tinted glass concealed Captain Viega and the bridge crew, but alone of all the craft in the harbor, the *Carleton's* horn did not sound. Why should it, François thought. *Carleton* was going to its demise. Why scream about it? The old ship had its dignity.

The strange, insectlike shape of the *Sunflyer* grew larger. Spray and water vapor trailed behind it. François knew the sunship had another system to reduce drag and make it faster and more efficient. The lower hulls were electrically charged to repel seawater. Between this and the hydrofoils, *Sunflyer's* imprint on the water was about the same as a medium-sized yacht.

"Here it comes!"

For the first time, the Belgian boy sounded excited. He and the Chinese fellow grabbed hold of the old lady's chair. François gripped the rail, bracing himself.

In a flash *Sunflyer* was past them. It was so overwhelming, it took longer to remember what it looked and felt like than the actual event. The sunship towered over the *Carleton* many stories, the shining green and blue solar panels tracking the sun even as the vessel moved at high speed. The hulls, half-hidden by spray, looked like knives thrust into a powerful jet of water. In between the hulls and solar panels, the multideck center of the ship was out of place, like a luxury hotel on a pair of giant jet skis. In the days that followed, François often tried to call up any trace of human faces at the portholes, but they were as blank as a row of silver coins. To the people on *Sunflyer*, the *Carleton* was an unremarkable object it passed on its way to North America.

Sunflyer whooshed on toward the eastern harbor exit, between the old forts de Chavagnac and de l'Ouest. The news blimp and drones followed, but the sightseers in small boats fell back. A few approached the wake of the steamer, wallowing in the mist raised by the sunship. François saluted the nearest ones, but no one waved back. On the pitching foredeck, people struggled with handheld PDDs, looking at the video footage they had just shot of the *Sunflyer's* departure.

The deck diehards gave up and entered the main deck lounge. There were giant screens set up at opposite ends of the long room. Everyone was watching aerial views of the sunship as it skimmed out to sea.

"Can you imagine?" Julie Morrison was saying. "The view from up there must be gorgeous!"

"If you could see anything through all that spray," her brother replied.

"I heard New Man was on board with his whole band," said a young woman. "Along with the entire cast of *Chances They Take!*"

New Man was a Norwegian pop star, very big in Europe. *Chances They Take* was an American Your/World show about a team of professional daredevils who traveled the world trying every kind of dangerous challenge.

"The only danger on board *Sunflyer* will be overeating," said a tall Asian girl in impeccable Parisian French.

François smiled. "And papercuts from their napkins," he said in the same language. The girl smiled a little.

Many passengers filed out of the lounge after *Sunflyer* disappeared out to sea. Eurochannel switched to commentary about what the maiden voyage of the sunship meant, further thinning the crowd.

François decided to find his cabin. It was below deck, a shared berth. For what his father was paying for luxury on the sunship, François could have had the most deluxe cabin on the *Carleton*. It suited his mood to choose the cheapest accommodation he could get. He wondered who he would be with. Not the weird kid in black, oh please . . .

He found a guy about his age unpacking an antique leather suitcase. He was neatly stowing his socks and underwear in drawers under his bunk.

The guy stood up and smiled. "Ah, hello!" he said in English, but he wasn't English or American. His clothes were quite old-fashioned, with many buttons and strips of leather here and there.

"Hello," François said. "François Martin."

The guy took his hand and shook it firmly. "Johann Sebastian Bachmann—but call me Hans."

CHAPTER 3

The ship rolled slowly through the Atlantic swell. Early morning rays of sunlight pierced the low clouds that veiled the French coast. Leigh Morrison walked out of the *Carleton*'s lounge (now serving as the dining room) onto the boat deck. The sea air was cool but damp. He sipped coffee and gazed at the northern horizon, still gray from dawn.

A soft thump-thump-thump announced Jenny Hopkins. Clad in electric blue sweats from neck to ankle, she jogged by Leigh, whose head was wrapped in coffee steam.

"Morning," he said. "How many laps?"

"Thirteen, so far," she replied. Jenny meant to do thirty before breakfast. Forty would have been better, but the deck was hard on her ankles and knees. It was wood planking laid down over steel plates and had no resilience at all. The first evening after they left Cherbourg, she had shin splints from running too long on the hard deck.

She followed the slow curve of the ship forward, keeping clear of doors, vents, and hatches. Her mother warned about such obstacles. Her mother had trained for the 2032 games on a cruise ship in the Black Sea and knew a Senegalese runner who broke an ankle and wrist by tripping over a hatch coaming.

Rounding the bow, she started running along the port side. The rising sun was in her eyes. Jenny liked it. Living in Britain for ten years made her appreciate the sun more than she ever had growing up in the Bahamas.

Some other walkers were out. A lean, dark-eyed man with a white ship's towel around his neck was earnestly working on his morning 5K. He was trailed by a few plump women, the American teenage girl, and the youngest of the Chinese tourists, without his holographic hat. The American girl—Julie—was wearing her PDD shades and talking to friends via Your/World. On an earlier lap, Jenny asked in passing why she was up so early.

"I promised my friend Miki in Jakarta I'd be up for her link. She's having trouble with her boyfriend," she said. The deck was quieter than the lounge and walking let her talk better, she said.

As she passed the clump of walkers, the dark-eyed man sped up to a race-walk. As Jenny was only jogging, he kept pace a few steps behind until she quickened her stride. He did the same, breaking into a jog.

Ah, she thought. You want to try me, do you?

Without looking back, she upped her pace slowly until she hit her 1500-meter stride. Jenny circled the stern and started up the starboard side. To her surprise, the dark-eyed man was still in sight, though a dozen paces behind. She watched how and where he held his hands. He moved like an athlete all right.

Grinning, she kept up her speed past the American guy leaning on the rail with his coffee. Leigh was startled to see Jenny pass at such a clip. Then her pursuer whisked by, and he smiled, too. The *Carleton's* Olympic hopeful had a rival.

He watched the two runners pass out of sight forward. The little group of walkers appeared, chattering among themselves. Julie was with them, waving her hands and declaiming something to the world about stupid boyfriends who were too cheap to buy a girl a decent graduation present . . .

The lounge door slid back and the French guy emerged with a softly steaming mug in both hands. It was one of those heavy, handleless ship's mugs that were weighty yet satisfying to hold.

The walkers trampled by. Julie cocked her head and said brightly, "Hi, France!"

François crossed to the rail after the morning exercisers went by. Leigh nodded a greeting and said, "'France?'"

"She finds it easier to say than 'François.'"

"Julie doesn't need people to make things easier for her," her brother remarked.

"I don't mind. It sounds friendly."

Leigh told him a story about Julie when she was fourteen and decided she wanted to be called Nova. She wrote Nova on all her possessions and signed everything Nova for months. She even managed to get her teachers and friends to call her Nova, though her family resisted.

"What made her stop using it?" France asked.

"Our grandmother left us a trust fund, which we could draw on starting at age fifteen," Leigh said. He blew steam off his coffee and sipped it. "Not a fortune, but it was legally assigned to Julia Diana Morrison and Leigh Ellis Morrison. The bank would not issue payments to anyone named Nova."

"So, given the choice, she chose money over her special name?" Leigh nodded.

Jenny rounded the deck again, still in medium-distance stride. Her rival kept up, though he was a full two paces behind. Leigh saluted with his cup and urged them on.

"Do you know who that is?" France said.

"Jenny Hopkins, she told me her name was—"

"No, I mean the man." Leigh had no idea. "That's Kiran Trevedi, the cricketer." Leigh knew next to nothing about cricket. France knew about cricket from his school friend Sanjay. Trevedi was not an Olympic class runner, but he was a considerable athlete.

"Do you think he'll catch her?"

France drained his mug and said, "I don't think he means to." He watched Trevedi's steady lope. "Looks to me like he's just having fun."

On the port side, Julie slowly dropped out of the walkers' group. Her connection to Jakarta was going bad. Noise bars broke up the image, and the sound blipped in and out like a rhythm-buster video.

"Hello? Miki, hello?" she shouted. The view in her Your/ World glasses went blue—the Blue Screen of Death. "Lower your rez," she pleaded. "I'm losing you!"

She kept to the rail and walked slowly. Maybe if she was clear of the ship's superstructure, her signal would come back.

There was a girl there, a little younger than Julie, sitting on a piece of deck equipment, looking out to sea at the *Carleton*'s wake. She had too much tan but nice clothes. Julie stopped a few steps from her, shaking her contrary PDD glasses.

"Broken?" said the girl.

"I hope not!" Julie said. "I've only had these a couple months. I got 'em before I left the States."

"American?"

"Yeah." She put the glasses on and pulled her eyes open as wide as possible. The gesture was supposed to reset the PDD to Your/World specs. Julie saw a few color bars, heard static, and that was all.

"Damn it!"

"Maybe there's a satellite problem," the tanned girl suggested.

"Can't be that. The feed would just switch to the next satellite in orbit." Julie wasn't a techie, but she knew about Your/World. She looked up at the sky. It was wide and blue, with only a few stringy clouds clinging to the horizon. She whipped off the PDD.

"I ought to throw 'em in the ocean!"

"Don't do that."

Both girls turned to see who spoke. It was the kid in black. Two days at sea and he was still dressed like the star of some vampire flick. The tanned girl frowned and resumed her study of the ship's swirling wake.

"It's under warranty, isn't it?" he said. His English was accented, more than the French guy's. Julie sighed and admitted it was.

"Bring it by my cabin and I'll check it for you."

"Check it? How?"

"The TV in my cabin has jacks for plugging in PDDs. Do that and you can use the TV controls to test your glasses."

Julie liked the idea, but she said warily, "Your cabin? Who are you, anyway?"

"Emile Becquerel," the tanned girl said. "Weird rich boy." Julie stared at her and then at Emile.

"How rich?" she said bluntly.

"His family owns the largest chocolate company in Belgium," the girl said. "Isn't that right?"

"The largest in Europe devoted only to chocolate. Nestle is bigger, but they are more diversified," Emile said. He looked unhappy saying so.

"How weird?" was Julie's next question.

"Don't ask me, ask him."

"Miss Quarrel resents me. I'm not sure why. I helped her and her mother in Cherbourg, and she has resented me ever since."

"My name is Eleanor!" she snapped, jumping to her feet. "If you helped so much, where's my mother?"

Julie learned of Mrs. Quarrel's visa problems and how Emile loaned her a credit card so she could charter a helicopter and rejoin her daughter at sea. Eleanor had been watching for two days. No helicopter had come.

"That's not my fault," Emile said mildly.

"Maybe it is, and maybe it isn't." Eleanor turned first one way, then another. Fists clenched, she said, "It's all too weird!"

She stalked away, almost blundering into the path of the runner. Now blotched with sweat, Jenny was beginning to open up. Trevedi, her shadow, was only a pace behind.

"Hey, uh, Emile? Can we check my PDD now?"

Wind got under the boy's black jacket, and it billowed around his thin frame.

"Are you afraid I'll be weird?"

Julie laughed. "Nah, I'll kick you in the balls if you mess with me!"

Emile watched her go. He wasn't sure if she'd made a threat or a promise.

In the dining room, the wall screens were banded with black lines. The forward screen, tuned to the BBC, had its sound go in and out. The screen at the rear of the room had better sound, but the picture kept breaking up into stray pixel patterns. Passengers complained over their breakfast until the stewards went to fetch an officer. The purser returned, dressed in a navy blue blazer and baseball cap.

"I'm sorry, ladies and gentlemen. We seem to be experiencing communications difficulties," he said. Someone asked if the ship's systems were being affected, too. Brow furrowed, the purser admitted they were.

"What could it be? The weather's fine," said the old woman in the lifter chair.

"Solar flare, perhaps, or a magnetic storm in the upper atmosphere," suggested the man in the tweed cap.

"There's no danger to ship's operations," the purser said. "It's just an inconvenience."

One of the Irish ballplayers said, "At this rate, we'll have to break out the shuffleboard gear!"

Some of the passengers laughed. Others did not. And as the day went on, more and more PDDs failed. By nightfall, there was no Your/World access at all.

CHAPTER 4

Dinner was subdued. Without the constant background chatter of the lounge TVs and people's personal data devices, the dining room was remarkably quiet. To France Martin it was like the quiet that fills a room after someone had died.

Hans Bachmann, for one, did not mind it at all. He was one of only four passengers who took the offered tour of the *Carleton's* engine spaces. He admired the turbines, the diesel auxiliary motors, pumps, injectors, and Gorgonian mass of pipes, large and small. The chief engineer, a Panamanian named Pascal, knew his engines and plainly loved them.

"After this trip, it's no more," he said, speaking loudly over the deep hum of the turbines. "No more steam."

"And no more pollution," said one of the tourists, a Canadian woman in her forties.

Pascal shrugged. "With our modern stack scrubbers, my engines' emissions meet current UN levels," he said. "We're not carbon-free like *Sunflyer,* but we impact but little the air."

"Then why are they shutting you down?" Hans asked.

A bitter smile creased the old engineer's face. "Don't you know? The company, they sold the ship to the *Sunflyer* people, to take us out when the sunship sailed."

"You mean, this whole last voyage business was arranged?" asked the Chinese man. His name was Chen. He and his brothers were from a shipping company in Shanghai. Hans wondered if they were on board because they were interested in buying the old *Carleton*.

"Por supuesto!"

The Canadian woman said there was nothing wrong with that. Why shouldn't the *Sunflyer*'s owners hail their success by arranging the retirement of the last polluting vessel at sea?

Engineer Pascal's face darkened. "Polluting?"

"Burning is death," she said.

Hans interrupted a budding fight. "Are the boilers gas-fired or oil burning?"

Pascal said something in his native tongue. It did not sound nice. Turning to Hans, he said, "As built, they burned fuel oil, but we converted to natural gas in 2029."

Later, at dinner, Hans sat alone in the corner of the lounge reading about Parsons turbines on his PDD. Like everyone else, he had lost his Your/World connection, but he had over two hundred terabytes of print on his device, more than enough for ten trips across the Atlantic.

A shadow fell across the screen. Hans looked up and saw the American, Leigh Morrison, standing over him.

"Excuse me, my sister wanted me to ask if you had an outside connection." Hans's eyes flicked back to the screen, where Parsons' experimental speedboat, *Turbinia*, slashed through a slow-moving line of British warships in 1897.

"No. This is stored data."

Leigh sat down. His voice dropped. "I knew you didn't, but she made me ask." In a room full of bored, nervous people, Hans seemed to be the only one with something interesting to do.

"What are you watching?"

"Reading."

"Oh. What are you reading?"

"About the history of the nautical turbine." He spun his notebook PDD around so Leigh could see the screen. Seeing all the lines of printed text made his eyes quickly glaze over.

"Are you into machinery?"

"'Into—?' I am not inside machinery." Leigh laughed and explained his expression. "Yes," Hans said, "I like anything old."

He held up a piece of tableware. "This is from the *Queen Mary 2,* the last of the ocean liners. My parents are dealers in antiques. Since the *Carleton* did not have plates, forks, and things for so many passengers, the company rented these relics from my family."

Suddenly the ship's horn blared a deep bass blast that rattled Bachmann's antique plates on every table in the room. Half the passengers present stood up, twisting this way and that to spot the cause of the alarm.

Someone shouted, "Out there! Look!"

There was a rush to the starboard side. Sliding doors slammed open, and the passengers surged out.

It was fully dark and easy to see the lights of the other ship, a big one, and close. Leigh felt Julie slip in close beside him.

"What's up? What's happening?"

He didn't know. It was just another ship cruising through the calm sea. Patchy clouds allowed stars to shine through. The moon had set, so it was not easy to see any detail on the other vessel, just a lot of navigation lights and the black outline of the hull.

The horn blasted again. The passengers shrank from the punishing wail.

An officer—not the captain or purser, but a woman with gold stripes on her sleeve—hurried by. Some of the more agitated passengers blocked her path.

They bombarded her in several languages, but they were all saying, "What's going on?"

"It's all right! We're sounding the horn to warn off the other ship," she said. She tried to get by, but some men refused to budge.

"Why use the horn? Can't you radio them?" one asked.

Another said, "Is their radar out?"

"How close are we?"

"Ladies and gentlemen!" Captain Vlega appeared, hatless, in his shirtsleeves. "There is no problem. Please return to the dining room. Allow Ms. Señales to go about her duties!"

Slowly the passengers filed back into the lounge. Trapped by the crowd by the rail, Eleanor Quarrel had been recording everything on her PDD. She was about to turn it off when she caught the captain and Ms. Señales exchanging hushed words in Spanish. She slipped by, avoiding their gaze. Inside the lounge, she quietly shut off the recording app.

What did they say? Eleanor knew a little Spanish, tourist phrases, but not enough to follow the officers' urgent conversation.

The big, well-lit ship drew away from the *Carleton.*

"She's moving off," a man said.

Danger averted, everyone went back to their tables. The hard questions were unanswered though. In this day and age of radar, satellite tracking, and instant communications, how could two ships almost collide in the wide waters of the North Atlantic?

Eleanor scanned the room. She didn't know any of her fellow passengers well enough to know who spoke Spanish. Most of the crew did, but she didn't want to share her eavesdropping with them. She'd met the French fellow, the German guy, the American brother and sister—and the creepy kid in black. For some reason Eleanor decided to ask him. He probably spoke all sorts of languages.

Just her luck, Emile wasn't in the lounge. She circled the room and didn't see him. Jenny Hopkins was there, eating dinner with the cricket player and some of the football team. The French girl, Linh Prudhomme, was by herself. For that reason alone, Eleanor slipped into a chair across from her.

"Hi," she said. "How's the food tonight?"

She didn't speak much English, apparently. Linh smiled and said, "Not so good. Everything is cooked too much."

Eleanor made nervous small talk for a short while, gradually bringing up the subject of language.

"Where did you learn English?"

"I have not learned it."

Eleanor's eyes widened. "But you're speaking it to me!"

Linh put a hand to her ear. "I have—what is it—*un entraîneur*, a teacher?"

She removed the pink bud from her left ear. It was an Info-Coach, a nice one. At Linh's quiet urging, Eleanor put the device in her ear. Linh said something in French. After a very brief delay, Eleanor heard her words translated in her ear.

"This allows me to speak," she said.

The Info-Coach formulated likely responses, and all Linh had to do was repeat her choice aloud. Eleanor wanted to try it. Linh asked in her native tongue where Eleanor was born?

38

"Je suis né en Afrique du Sud," which meant "I was born in South Africa."

"Dijjy!" Slang baffled the Info-Coach. "Dijjy" meant "cool, neat, novel."

Eleanor returned Linh's device and leaned close. "Can it translate from a recording?"

"Certainly."

She tapped the PDD on her wrist. "I caught the captain and the officer on deck talking about our situation. They seemed worried. Will you help me translate it?"

Linh stood up. "Come with me."

No one paid them any notice as they took the inside stairs to the deck above. It turned out Linh had a stateroom in the superstructure, a suite in fact, with a sitting room, private bath, and paneled bedroom.

"Oh, posh!" Eleanor said as the lights brightened.

It took some fiddling to link the PDD output to the Info-Coach. The usual wireless connection would not work, probably due to the same interference that had cut the ship off from Your/World. Linh had to hard wire a connection using the earphone jack.

Eleanor played the recording. In a low voice, Linh repeated what she heard her device translate.

Captain Viega said, "Why are you away from your post?"

Ms. Señales replied, "All communications are out. Am I to sit and stare at empty screens?"

"The blockage may clear at anytime!"

"I was on the boat deck signaling the bulk carrier," Ms. Señales said.

"How?" the captain demanded.

"By flashlamp."

Señales said the other ship was a bulk carrier out of Gdańsk, *Dzien Kolyska*. They apologized for the near miss, but claimed they couldn't see the *Carleton*'s lights.

Linh put a hand to her lips. "Here the captain says a crude word."

"Couldn't see our lights?" Eleanor was puzzled by that. The *Carleton* was at least as brightly lit as the Polish freighter, if not more so.

Señales warned the captain Eleanor was near. He said, "The English kid won't understand us. Go back to the communications center until relieved." Sullenly, the signals officer obeyed.

"That's all."

Linh disconnected the Info-Coach from Eleanor's PDD. "Nothing new here," she said. The slight delay in her speech made her seem thoughtful, reserved. "Everyone on board knows communications are out."

"But why couldn't the other ship see our lights?"

Linh had no idea. With the recording done, there suddenly felt like there was nothing else to say. Eleanor got up to leave.

Linh looked lost in the spacious sitting room, scuffing her feet on the newly laid carpet. Why was she alone, Eleanor wondered?

At the door, she said, "I guess my mother's helicopter will find us in daylight."

"I hope so."

Her hand rested on the unopened door handle.

"If you're not doing anything, you can come down to my cabin. Your/World is out, but I have a deck of cards and some print books."

Linh smiled. "Cards?" Eleanor nodded. Linh wrapped a fine lace shawl around her shoulders. "That sounds fun. What do you play?"

"Oh, hearts, spades, bridge if there's four—"

"Poker?"

Being asked by the slender, dark-haired girl if she played poker was almost as odd as the Belgian boy loaning her mom a high-value credit card.

"I know how to play some types of poker," Eleanor said. Linh went to the dresser beside her bed and took out a slim, stainless-steel case, too flat for makeup and too thick for a laptop.

"What's that?"

Linh popped the latches and opened the case. Nestled inside were rows of shiny disks in different colors.

"You have your own poker chips?"

"It's my hobby," Linh said with a gleam in her eye.

I've made friends with a card shark, Eleanor decided. At least Linh did not give off the creepy aura Emile Becquerel did.

They played until two in the morning. Linh taught her several new games, and for a while Eleanor forgot the *Carleton* losing all communications, the mystery of their near collision, and the fact that with every hour the coast of France fell farther and farther behind, making any rendezvous with her mother more and more unlikely.

CHAPTER 5

Who was crying?

France opened one eye. It didn't help. The room was black. For a second he thought he'd dreamed the sound, but then he heard the sobbing again.

He was in the lower bunk. Hans Bachmann was above him, thoroughly asleep. France rolled out of bed and crouched in the dark. The deck moved up and down beneath him. The old *Carleton* was pitching up and down like a carousel horse.

Who was crying?

The sound was fainter, more muffled than before. France realized he had been hearing it through the wall. He crept to the wall and listened. Someone was sobbing in the next cabin.

He was wearing pajamas. His parents always insisted he sleep in pajamas, winter or summer. Anything else was disreputable.

France opened the door. It was a light wooden panel with louvers in the bottom half. The corridor outside was dimly lit and completely empty. He stepped out. Just as he did, the ship staggered sideways, throwing France against the facing wall. Was there a storm? He didn't hear thunder or pouring rain.

The *Carleton* righted herself. France went to the door of the cabin next to his. He tapped lightly on the painted wooden panel.

"Hello? Hello?" In English he said softly, "Is everything all right?" When no one replied, he repeated the question in French. To his surprise, he heard a choked reply in his native tongue.

"Va-t'en, connard!" More of the same followed, a gasped torrent of curses and abuse.

That was more than rude. France hit the door with his fist.

"What's the matter with you?" he demanded. "Come out here and say that to my face, *lâche sale!"*

Silence. All sympathy gone, France noted the number on the cabin door, B14. He'd find out who was in there.

Back in his own cabin, he dressed with angry haste in total darkness. Hans never stirred, not even when France stubbed his toe and cursed aloud. France stalked up to A deck, then to the weather deck. Along the way, he passed a wall clock that read 03:22.

Out on deck, wind was blowing. The old steamer plowed steadily ahead, pushing her bow against rough seas. Overhead, stars flitted between gaps in the clouds and a brilliant moon washed everything in pale light.

There were people in the lounge. France ducked in and saw they were crew members eating dinner, having come off their watch. He asked how he could find out who was in the cabin next to his.

The men smirked. Was she hot, *une bébé?*

"No, he's a loudmouthed bastard!" The crewmen laughed.

The fellow with a closely trimmed gray beard said, "Go up to the signals room on the boat deck. There's always an officer there. Don't bother the bridge watch, though." France thanked him curtly and left.

Higher up on the ship, the motion of the seas were worse. Climbing the steel steps to the boat deck was actually hard.

Once there, there was nothing above him but *Carleton*'s massive streamlined smokestack, some pole masts with antennas, and assorted ventilator hoods. Forward was the ship's extensive bridge. France found the signals office at the rear of the structure. He didn't knock but simply threw open the door.

It was dark inside, with no light visible but the glow of a dozen thin monitors. Most of them were blank and blue. One played a snowy scene of static. Another was covered with marching lines of random letters and numbers.

"Hello?" he said. The blank silence of the place took the anger right out of him.

Someone stirred in the shadows.

"Who's there?" the voice challenged in English.

"François Martin. I-I am a passenger."

"Passengers aren't allowed in signals."

"I know. I'm sorry. I'm having a problem with my neighbor."

A woman in the blue jacket of the merchant service emerged from the darkness. She was about forty, pale, with eyes shot with thready blood vessels. Her name badge read Señales.

"What problem?"

"He's making noise." Mad as he was, France couldn't bring himself to accuse anyone of crying like a baby.

"Did you ask him to stop?" France admitted he had and was insulted for trying.

"I'm too busy for this," Señales said, waving him off. "Find the chief steward. He'll help you."

She turned away. France said, "What's going on here?"

"Go back to bed. Everything will be fine ... "

That's what they told people on the *Titanic*. France came two steps into the room.

"Is every computer on the ship out?" he said, gazing at the empty screens.

Her voice came from the shadows. "No, the systems on the ship are old, but they work. It's the outside connections that have failed. We're cut off from everything—satellite navigation, Your/World net, telephone, radio . . . radar is out, too."

France's complaint suddenly seemed very childish. He said, "How are you steering the ship?"

"By the sun and stars. At least they haven't left us."

"Will we make it to Canada?"

Officer Señales gave a weary sigh. "If we don't run into Ireland or Greenland first!"

France left her surrounded by blank screens and a wall of electronic silence. By the time he descended to the lounge, the crewmen had finished their meal and gone to bed. The ship felt deserted.

Down on B deck, he paused in the passage outside his door. The door of the cabin next to his, B14, was ajar. France tapped on it firmly.

"Hello?" he said. The door swung inward halfway and stopped.

The cabin was weirdly lit by a lamp fallen to the deck. Half the LEDs were out and the shade was bent, throwing what little light that was left at an odd angle from the floor up. The lower bunk was a tangle of stark white sheets.

France stepped in. "Hello?"

Something crackled under his shoe. He picked it up. It was half a Globus chocolate bar. The gold wrapper was folded back, exposing the chocolate. France saw more candy bars scattered around the cabin, wrappers torn open and stomped into the carpet. Milk chocolate and crispy rice covered the floor.

He checked the washroom. No one was there. There were no bags or cases in the room, no stray clothing, nothing. Nothing but ruined candy bars, all by the Globus Company of Ghent, Belgium.

Belgium? France had a revelation. He set the broken lamp upright and sat down in an armchair, facing the half-open door. There he waited. Before long, he fell asleep. In his light, undreaming state, he easily heard soft footsteps enter the cabin.

"What are you doing here?" Emile Becquerel demanded. His voice was low, but his tone was not friendly.

"Trying to get some sleep," France replied, yawning. "Someone was crying."

"You were dreaming. Go back to your own room!"

France remembered the insults shouted through the closed door. He was half a head taller than Emile and obviously stronger. He was no bully, but the Belgian kid had been really insulting. He could have knocked the smaller boy down, or blasted him with all the insults he'd learned listening to his father's underlings. But no.

He stood close, too close. Emile did not back away. France slapped a broken candy bar against his chest.

"Here. Eat your family's junk more quietly next time!"

He pushed Emile out of the way and went out. A moment after he passed through the door, half a Globus bar hit the corridor wall behind him.

"You're welcome!" he called out. The door of B14 slammed shut.

Back in his bunk, he heard Hans Bachmann grunt, "What's the matter?"

"Nothing. Go back to sleep."

"Are systems still out?"

"Oui. Ja."

"Don't worry," said Hans, rolling over to face the wall. "I have the answer."

"You do? Are you a systems expert?"

"No. My folks sell antiques . . . "

Soon he was asleep again, breathing deep and slow. France tried to sort out the strange mix of events in his late night wandering. He couldn't, gave up, and joined his cabin mate in slumber.

When day came, the sea was much calmer. Without the diversion of their PDDs and Your/World, the passengers spent a lot of time on deck. Jenny Hopkins and Mr. Trevedi led a band of hopeful joggers around the *Carleton*. Julie Morrison was among them, much to her brother's surprise. She'd never been into sports before, but she did love celebrities, and an Olympic hopeful and a professional cricket player were the most the *Carleton* offered in that line.

Not long after breakfast ended, Hans Bachmann went to his cabin and returned with a flattish wooden box. It was heavy, whatever it was, and he carried it in both arms. France saw him take the steps up to the boat deck. He caught Leigh Morrison's eye, and they got up together to follow. Eleanor and Linh saw them go and started after them. Mr. Chen, the lady in the lifter chair (her name was Mrs. Ellis), and other passengers joined the parade.

Hans went up the bridge deck. He was stopped by the purser before he reached the bridge. Leigh stopped on the steps below them, waiting to see what happened. Curious passengers piled up behind him.

Hans and the purser had a quiet, earnest conversation. Finally the ship's officer raised the lid of the box and peered inside. He reached in and took out a gleaming triangular brass instrument.

"What is it? What are they doing?" Eleanor called from several places behind Leigh.

"It's one of those ship-thingies from the old days," Leigh said. He struggled to recall its name. "A compass?" That wasn't right.

"An astrolabe?" Linh suggested. Leigh had no idea what an astrolabe was, but the name didn't spark any recognition.

"It's a sextant."

Everyone turned to stare at Emile. Looking rumpled and red-eyed, he was by the ship's rail, out from under the overhang of the bridge deck.

"Sextant!" he repeated crossly. "For navigation!"

Hans came down with the empty box. He was surprised at the crowd waiting for him.

"What's all this?"

"We were wondering what you were taking to the bridge," Leigh said awkwardly. He couldn't believe the weird kid knew what the instrument was, and he didn't.

"It's a sextant, once used on the great sailing ship *Preussen*," Hans said. It was from his parent's antiques inventory. The Bachmanns thought it would increase interest (and value) in the old instrument if it crossed the Atlantic on the last steam-powered cargo ship. Captain Viega was old-school enough to know how to use it. Soon enough, he was seen by the rail outside the bridge, aiming the brass sextant at the sun while a mate stood by to record his readings. At lunch, the captain appeared in the lounge to share his findings.

"Ladies and gentlemen! I know you've all been concerned since we lost communications yesterday. First, let me assure you everything on the *Carleton* is working as it should," Viega said.

"Then the problem is out there?" said a woman, pointing vaguely out to sea. "Is the world system down?"

Viega laughed. "No, I don't think so. Ms. Señales has found traces of the usual carrier signals, but they are too weak to reach us."

"What does that mean?" France Martin asked.

Viega rubbed his hands together. "Something is blocking the signals. They're not getting through to us."

From the lounge door, Jenny Hopkins said, "What would cause that?"

The captain had no answer. After a long silence, someone called out, "Sunspots?"

Viega spread his hands wide. "Sunspots! Who knows, it could be! Be assured, my friends, that the ship is well and on its way. Thanks to young Herr Bachmann, I have been able to fix our position this morning."

He snapped his fingers and a waiting crewman stepped forward with an old paper chart pinned to a large sheet of cardboard. Captain Viega pushed a pin in a spot in the open sea, southwest of Ireland.

"This was our position: 49 degrees, 21 minutes, 13 seconds North by 13 degrees, 47 minutes, 55 seconds West."

Tension in the room seemed to evaporate like dew on a hot morning. They were not lost. The tiny pin in the map was reassuring. It gave them a place to identify and understand.

Not everyone was comforted. Eleanor Quarrel tucked her hands into her armpits. A red pin on a paper map? She shuddered.

Standing close by, Jenny saw her and said, "It's all right. We're not lost. It's the Atlantic! There must be hundreds of ships nearby!"

"Yes, hundreds," Eleanor said. "Are their electronics jammed, too? Maybe next time we see a ship, it will crash into us."

Those around her turned to stare. "Don't mind me!" she said, shaking her head. "It's just sunspots, after all!"

CHAPTER 6

Julie Morrison kicked the footstool away. It was heavy, chrome steel and fell over with a loud thump. If she could, she would have thrown it as far as she could.

It was the sixth day out from Cherbourg. Overnight the air-conditioning had failed, leaving everyone belowdecks sweltering in their sleep. Julie, who usually slept in an oversize man's T-shirt, woke before dawn with her shirt stuck to her and her sheets damp with sweat. She went to the bathroom and flicked on the light. She looked like a girl in one of those nasty frat-boy movies her brother used to like before he was old enough to go to college.

The LEDs around the rim of the light were dim and red. Even Julie knew that meant not enough electricity.

She had a tepid shower and put on some dry clothes. There was a porthole in her cabin, but opening it didn't improve anything. A strong ocean smell crept in. It reminded Julie of trips to Kure Beach in North Carolina when she was a kid, when everything smelled moldy and faintly rotten, but you didn't care because it was the beach. Funny. She thought it only smelled this way at the coast, not hundreds of miles at sea.

Her cabin mate slept on, sprawled out with her arms and legs splayed wide, seeking coolness even in the depths of sleep. Julie looked over the useless hardware on her dressing table: PDD, Your/World glasses, pocket phone, Info-Coach. She hadn't gotten a peep or gleam out of any of them in three days, so she kicked the footstool and decided to go up on deck.

The overhead light in the passage flickered and buzzed. All else was quiet. What an ugly old tub this ship was. Why couldn't her parents have booked her on *Sunflyer*? She could be going to New Man concerts every night and enjoying carbon-free air-conditioning...

It was then Julie realized the usual constant vibration of the engines was missing. Nor was the *Carleton* bobbing up and down in the waves. The ship was so still, it was like being in a not-so nice hotel, one with riveted steel walls and no piped in music.

Wind, warm and damp, wafted down the open stairwell. The light above was gray and colorless. Julie emerged on deck and saw the Atlantic was dead calm, like a lake of glass. Where sea and sky met was an indistinct gray zone. Whether there was mist the color of the sea rising, or the sea had gone pale as the sky, Julie couldn't tell. It gave the horizon a strangely flat look, like a painted backdrop. Julie felt like if she could lean out far enough, she could touch the featureless place where sky and sea met.

She went aft and found other passengers leaning on the rail or talking in small groups on the *Carleton*'s quarterdeck. Julie looked for someone she knew. The German guy, Hans What's-his-name, was standing at the far end of the ship, writing in a notebook—actually writing with an ink pen in a paper notebook, something Julie had only seen her grandmother do.

She walked up, hands clasped behind her back.

52

"Hey," she said. Something about the situation made her keep her voice low.

"Hello."

Hans didn't look up from his writing. Julie peeked over the top of the notebook and saw columns of figures.

"What are you doing?"

"Trying to estimate our position, based on our speed, elapsed time, and our location yesterday," he said.

"Oh. Where are we?"

He met her eyes. Hans' hair was mussed, and he looked like he'd slept in his clothes.

"I can't tell! It would be easier if the sun was out—"

Julie smiled. "It should be up soon."

Hans shook his head. "It was supposed to have risen ninety minutes ago."

That didn't make sense. The sky was uniformly light, but in a soft, diffuse way. Gray horizon slowly melded into blue sky overhead, with no distinct clouds anywhere—and no sun.

"That's just weird!" Julie went to the curved stern rail and looked down. The usual turbulence of the ship's screws was little more than a swirl. "We're hardly moving!"

"Yes, power is out to many of the ship's systems," Hans said. He came to the rail beside her. "The captain has not told us why."

He was good looking, in a clueless sort of way. His constant lost-in-thought manner was not Julie's favorite look in guys, but his enthusiasm was rather cute. She noticed Hans chewed the end of his pen when he was thinking and had long, expressive fingers. Musician fingers, Julie thought.

The purser, Mr. Brock, walked briskly 'round the stern, greeting each passenger by name. When he came near, Julie didn't wait for pleasantries.

"What happened to the air-conditioning?" she demanded.

Mr. Brock smiled, not showing any teeth. "Utilities are out on B and C deck," he said. "There's been a loss of power from the generators. Repairs are being made."

"This old ship is falling apart," Julie went on. "No Your/World, no TV, now no A/C? What's next, no toilets?"

Purser Brock eyed other passengers nearby who heard the American girl's complaints. He said, "The *Carleton* was never intended to carry so many passengers. Too many demands have been made on the ship's systems. As for the loss of communications, that is hardly our fault."

"I bet they have Your/World on the *Sunflyer*!"

"I'm sure they have many amenities on the sunship," Brock said carefully. To Hans he said, "Captain Viega wanted me to thank you again for the use of your sextant, Mr. Bachmann. It's a magnificent instrument."

"It was made in Wetzlar in 1899," Hans replied. "They made the best lenses in the world."

"I wish they made our air-conditioning," Julie grumbled.

Breakfast was cold that morning—fruit, yogurt, cheese, and cereal. The bread was leftover from the night before. The chief steward apologized. The electrical stoves in the galley were not working. So far, the ship's refrigerators were still cold, but power was slowly failing throughout the ship.

"Why?" France Martin asked. "The engines are still running, aren't they?"

The chief steward said, "Yes, but I am told the dynamos are down and storage batteries are barely holding any charge." Mr. Chen wanted to know his source of this information. "I have this from Engineer Pascal."

Sullen silence fell. One of the young kids started to cry about the tasteless breakfast and got a sharp reply from his mother. France didn't care much about the food, but he wondered where all the power generated by the *Carleton's* engines was going. They were turning, but the dynamos weren't putting out electricity. Even the batteries, which ought to have lasted for days, were malfunctioning. But why?

His question went unanswered. In that moment, the *Carleton* shuddered violently from end to end. A loud, crushing, crashing sound filled the air.

Leigh had a stale biscuit in hand, about to bite, when the deck flew wildly to the right, throwing him right over in his chair. An empty chair fell on top of him, which hurt, followed by the Belgian kid, Emile. That really hurt. The back of the chair rapped Leigh across the nose. Emile's weight drove the fallen furniture into him.

Jenny Hopkins was frowning at the breakfast buffet. There were too many carbs on the menu and not enough protein. Then the deck lurched under her. She caught the edge of the buffet in both hands, and tray after tray of canned peaches, muesli, biscuits, and jam packets hit her. She held on through the barrage until a pitcher of orange juice started to slide at her face. Jenny let go one hand and swung out of the way. The pitcher smashed to juicy bits against the starboard wall.

Eleanor was standing, too. She was tired and feeling ill from a sweaty night in her cabin. All she wanted for breakfast was yogurt and a little coffee. The *Carleton* always served good coffee (the Panamanian crew demanded it), but she had hardly filled her heavy mug before the ship creaked over on its side. Hot coffee poured over her hand and bare leg.

Linh Prudhomme was in her suite when the *Carleton* suddenly keeled over. She was thrown against the couch. Her case of poker chips hit the floor and burst open, spilling red, black, and gold disks everywhere.

On the boat deck, Hans had been trying to find the sun. He'd gotten the *Preussen* sextant from the navigator and was quartering likely parts of the sky for a glimmer of sunlight. He was so wrapped up in his task, he had no chance to brace himself. The impact half-flipped Hans over the rail. His feet went up and his head went down. His first act was to try to grab the thickly painted rail, but he misjudged the distance, and his hand closed on air. Hans's chin hit something hard, and his PDD, now useless, slipped from his shirt pocket and vanished over the side.

The ship lurched again, not as hard as the first time. Hans jammed a foot between the rails. Steadied, he finally managed to avoid being thrown thirty feet into the sea. The antique sextant was not so lucky. Hans saved his own life, but the 150-year-old instrument splashed in the water far below after his personal date device. Both sank without a trace.

Julie sat down so hard when the ship tilted that the shock ran right up her spine. It was like a jolt of electricity, and for a moment she was paralyzed. Plates and flatware rained on her. Mrs. Ellis glided past in her lifter chair, eyes wide with terror. She smacked into the wall just behind where Leigh and Emile Bequerel struggled under a pile of tumbled chairs.

The ship's whistle shrieked, followed closely by the bellow of the steam horn. Everyone was yelling, screaming, or crying. After a long, deafening concert, the ship stopped screaming first. The passengers quit when it slowly became clear they weren't all going to die in the next two seconds.

The chief steward, the cook, and the cook's assistants went through the slanted lounge, helping people stand. Eleanor's burns were painful, but not serious. Leigh had a black eye. Emile was untouched.

"Of course he is," Leigh snarled. "He had a cushion to land on!"

Hans used his foot hooked in the railing to lever himself back on deck. Looking at the slanted superstructure, he estimated the ship's list at ten degrees. When the horn fell silent, he groped his way forward to the steps up to the bridge. Other passengers felt their way out of the lounge and started that way, too. On the walkway just past the signals room, Hans heard Captain Viega shouting in Spanish. He didn't sound frightened, just mad as hell.

He emerged from the wheelhouse, red-faced. Seeing Hans, he cried, "What are you doing here? Passengers are not allowed on the bridge!"

"What's happened, Captain?"

"Can't you see? We've run aground!"

"Aground? In the middle of the North Atlantic?"

"It's insane, I know, but what can I tell you? Now get below!" To the crowd climbing toward him, he shouted, "All of you, return to your cabins or the lounge! There is nothing for you to do! The crew and I will deal with this emergency!"

Hans backed down the steps. He leaned out far enough to see the ship's stack. A ribbon of gray smoke from it rose straight up in the still air. The engines were still running, it seemed. Some of the ship's masts had been damaged by the collision. One of the aft stacks had broken off and was only held up by its wires. The spinning radome atop the wheelhouse had stopped. There was the sharp smell of ozone in the air.

Carleton's crew crawled all over the ship, inspecting every nook and cranny. The captain, Purser Brock, Signals Officer Señales, and the chief steward took up positions on deck and received breathless reports on the ship's condition. Gradually, some facts emerged. They didn't make much sense.

Carleton had experienced a slow loss of propulsive power over the previous twenty-four hours. Her speed had been down to about three knots when she ran into—whatever she had run into. Several compartments at the point of collision were slowly filling with water. Those compartments had been sealed off.

"We're not sinking, are we?" asked Kiran Trevedi.

"We are not," Captain Viega said gravely. "That is the good news—"

"What is the bad news?" Emile called out.

"We can't get off this—this obstruction."

The passengers took this news with puzzled calm. Mrs. Ellis, the only person not affected by the list, asked if they had hit an underwater object, like a submerged wreck.

"We are dead in the water," said the captain. "Apparently we've struck something solid."

Hans ran a hand through his sweat-damp hair. "But there's no dry land in the open sea!"

The closest land, as of their last-known position, was still the south coast of Ireland. Greenland was still a long way off, and Canada even farther away.

"Maybe there's been an earthquake," Mr. Chen said. "This bar could have risen from the bottom of the sea."

France didn't believe this. The North Atlantic was very deep. Even the closest undersea mountains, the Mid-Atlantic Ridge, were hundreds of miles away. How could an earthquake, even a monumental one, raise the sea bottom hundreds of yards?

Chen's earthquake idea caught on. The woman from the engine room tour said a big quake could explain the loss of communications.

"How?" said Julie.

"Ground stations and power plants are wrecked," she said.

With an air of growing understanding, Leigh said, "And that's why we can't see the sun—dust raised by a quake is blotting it out!"

Everyone began talking at once, loudly. Some people thought the whole world must have been destroyed, and they, the crew and passengers of the *Sir Guy Carleton*, were the last people on earth. Others, more skeptical, believed only Europe or North America was damaged. Disgusted by the growing hysteria, France worked his way to the low side of the room and tried to get out of the lounge. Emile followed him.

On deck, they peered over the side at the turbulent water below. They couldn't see any rocks or sand, but the ship was stuck hard on whatever was down there.

"Do you believe this earthquake business?" Emile said, watching the swirling green water.

"No. It makes no sense."

"Then what did we hit?"

France could not answer. He pushed away from the tilted rail, scanning the horizon. Not expecting to see anything, nonetheless he glimpsed something through the haze that made his heart beat faster.

"*Merde,*" he breathed. "Do you see?"

Emile braced himself against the rail and followed the older boy's pointing hand. In the pearl-colored haze he saw nothing, nothing, nothing—then he saw it, too.

"Land!" he cried. "I see land!"

France took up the cry, and soon the passengers were slipping and sliding out on deck with them. The boys thrust fingers at what they saw: a strip of sandy beach, backed by a dark shape, either trees or a rocky headland.

Captain Viega elbowed his way to the rail. Through binoculars he scanned the thinning mist. He uttered an old Spanish word under his breath.

"My God," he barely said aloud. "It is land!"

With agonizing slowness, the veil of haze dissolved, revealing more details as it faded. The beach was real, lapped by small, calm waves. The dark objects beyond were trees, although hints of lighter-colored hills farther inland teased their eyes.

A call from Chief Engineer Pascal took the ship's officers away. The passengers set up regular positions along the listing deck, padding the deck and rails with cushions borrowed from the lounge. Near noon (by the ship's clock; the sun was still not visible), Linh Prudhomme spotted land off the ship's bow. Shortly after that, a matching peninsula was seen astern. Everyone marveled at the scene emerging around them. Somehow, the *Carleton* had steamed into an unknown bay and run herself hard aground.

Captain Viega tried various measures to free them. He ran the engines full reverse. Shallow water barely foamed around the propellers. Engineer Pascal reported maximum revs from the turbines, but somehow the power was not reaching the water.

After watching the helpless frothing of the propellers, the captain and engineer faced each other.

"What do you mean power is not reaching the screws?" Viega demanded.

"Just that, Alessandro! How many times must I say it? The engines are running, but power is not reaching the screws, just as it is not reaching the ship's dynamos."

They were stuck, and when night fell, there would be no electricity. Furious, Viega ordered water pumped to the high side of the ship, to counteract the list. The pumps worked for a short while, then the flow of seawater petered out. Captain Viega stamped the deck and cursed.

Finally Mrs. Ellis, the oldest person on board, made the suggestion no one wanted to hear.

"Captain, should we abandon ship?"

Viega stared at her. "Why, madame? To go where?"

She indicated the mysterious land with a nod of her head.

"The ship is intact! We will stay on board!"

"For how long, Captain? All communications are out. We have no power."

"We have food and water for weeks!"

"Food will spoil without refrigeration. And how will we get to the water without pumps?" said the old lady.

"What is out there?" the captain countered. "Do you know? I have no idea."

"It's dry land. I see trees growing, so there must be water. Maybe there are people out there who can help us."

The captain looked ready to weep. "It is impossible! There is no land in the North Atlantic!"

"Then we must be far off course," said France. The land they saw must be the south or west coast of Ireland.

Captain Viega curtly cut off any suggestion of abandoning ship. The *Carleton* was sound, he said. Depending on the tide, they might yet float free.

CHAPTER 7

There's no night like night without electric light. Two hundred years of artificial light made people forget how profound darkness can be.

No sunset warned the *Carleton*. The peculiar gray-white atmosphere simply lost light. Almost before anyone realized it, shadows had grown so long, it was hard to see. The crew broke out battery-powered lanterns. They worked—for a short time. Within minutes their beams began to go orange, lose power, and fade. All the lanterns had come from recharging wall brackets. There was no reason they should all fail so quickly.

Captain Viega ordered the use of hurricane lamps. These burned butane. There were only a dozen on board, and most of them went to the bridge and engine room. The passenger lounge got just two. The remaining four were hung on the ship's bow, stern, and masts, in case another ship came along in the night.

Something about darkness made people speak in hushed tones. The younger children went to sleep wedged in place on the slanting deck. The stewards distributed what food could be salvaged from the now useless kitchen.

On the boat deck, France heard a crinkle of paper. He was lying on his back gazing up at the sky. Hearing the crackle, he smelled the soft, buttery aroma of chocolate.

"Emile?"

He was standing a meter away, one arm hooked on the rail. Emile unwrapped one of his family's chocolate bars, brought it to his mouth, but stopped short. He couldn't eat it. Hungry as he was, he hated chocolate so much, he couldn't make himself bite the bar.

"Here," he said in French, tossing the chocolate at France.

The hefty bar landed on his chest. France caught it before it slid off.

"*Merci.* How many of these do you have?"

"They're not mine," Emile replied. "There are cartons of them in the ship's store."

France took a bite. Crisp without being too hard, it melted like butter on his tongue.

"Why do you hate your family's product?" he said to the Belgian boy.

"The Becquerels are bourgeois exploiters. From the cocoa growers in Africa to the factory workers in Ghent, they exploit them without mercy for the sake of profit."

France could not imagine anyone exploiting workers in the European Union in this day and age. In Africa, maybe, but Belgium? The EU Parliament sat in Brussels. Anyone truly exploited could take the train and picket the parliament hall before lunch.

"Is that why you're on board alone?" asked France. "Running away from your bourgeois family?"

"Why are you here, the son of a Société Brise Mondial executive?"

He knew a lot for a snotty kid in bad clothes. France managed a chuckle and ate more bourgeois chocolate.

A shout from the deck below made France bolt upright. From what he could gather, a light had been seen onshore. Sure enough, a dim, yellowish dot of light wavered in the distance. It looked like fire—a torch perhaps? Whatever it was, a torch meant a torchbearer.

France heard Captain Viega on the deck below, his voice hoarse from shouting.

"It doesn't mean a thing! It's just a reflection!"

"Of what?" a man's voice challenged. "There's no moon, and I can't see any stars!"

The captain stomped away. The rest, crew and passengers, stood in silence watching the far-off glimmer of light. Was it some fisherman trying his luck in the bay? Or some beachcomber following the line of flotsam left by high tide in hopes of finding some treasure from the sea? The distant flame flickered and shivered. Several times it seemed to go out, only to reappear farther down the black shoreline.

Linh shuddered. She felt like she was doing something wrong, watching an innocent, vulnerable stranger go about his or her business.

Julie felt cold. To her the bobbing light was like a ghost— intangible, untouchable, and perhaps a warning. She turned away. A moment later, a murmur went through the *Carleton*'s people. The light had gone out, and this time did not reappear.

Most everyone slept on deck that night. The air was mild, and it was stifling below deck without any air-conditioning. Engineer Pascal and his crew abandoned the useless engine room and went outside, too, tying themselves to the rail so they wouldn't roll overboard.

Jenny was in the lounge. Sleeping in the open air was an invitation to an upper respiratory infection. That could knock her out of the running even before they got to Canada. She had no doubt they would get there. The weird problems with the ship were a pain, but the Coast Guard or the Royal Navy or somebody would soon find them. Where they were and how they got there were questions she didn't bother with. Her goal was in Canada, and it was gold.

With her head resting against the paneled wall, she relived her victory in the 800-meter race in Coventry a month ago, the win that won her a place in the Olympic tryouts. Another win and a few good showings in Montreal and her spot in the games was assured.

She didn't win with a fast final kick or anything like that. Jenny closed her eyes and saw her feet pounding on the track as she ran away from the rest. She kicked out front from the start and never lost her lead. The Scottish girl made a move on her in the last two-dozen meters, but Jenny had more than enough to outstretch her. She broke the tape a good three strides ahead of her rival and finished out with a triumphant jog into the sunlit end of the stadium. Sunlight on her face felt so good, she just stood there, soaking it in. The cheers of the crowd filled the rest of her with warmth.

The cheers melted into individual voices, but the sunlight remained. Jenny opened her eyes. Sunshine was streaming into the slanted lounge. Her fellow passengers were clustered at the doors and windows like they'd never seen daylight before.

Eleanor, the South African girl whose arm got burned when the ship ran aground, knelt in front of Jenny. Her right arm was bandaged at the wrist in white stretch wrap.

"Wake up!" she said. "The sun's out!"

Jenny worked her sleep-cramped shoulders. "So? The sun's out. Why all the noise?"

She understood when she stood up and looked out the lounge window. The beach, which had been a ghostly vision yesterday, now stood out clear as a Your/World video. It was an ordinary white sand beach, flat and without dunes. Behind the wide strip of sand was a line of dark trees, and beyond them, pastel hills in blue and gray. One of the Irishmen said it didn't look like their coast—not rocky enough.

Carleton lay stranded about two hundred yards from shore. The water level hadn't changed. They were just as solidly aground as before. Captain Viega ordered soundings made to find out how deep the water was. Sailors took a bright yellow nylon rope with a lead weight on it and dropped it over the side. On the port, or high, side of the ship, no bottom could be found. When dropped to starboard, the lead quickly came to rest within plain sight of the surface. Then something strange happened. As the crew and interested passengers looked on, the lead weight slowly sank out of sight.

Hans Bachmann and the navigator exchanged what-the-hell? looks. Captain Viega was summoned. They hauled the lead up and repeated the procedure. As the larger crowd looked on, the yellow line slowly wound out of view, attached to the sinking weight.

"It's not solid at all!" Hans said.

The captain had seen enough. He simply turned his back and went to argue with Engineer Pascal about how to free the ship. Barely had the captain started talking when a distant booming sound echoed across the water from the land. It wasn't thunder—the sky was bright and blue—it sounded almost mechanical, like a giant door slamming shut.

66

Clouds of dust rose from the hills and hung in the still air.

The sea around the *Carleton* rippled like a pool with a pebble dropped in it.

Wham! The deck heaved up and fell back hard enough to throw everyone off their feet. Windows shattered and portholes cracked. One of the *Carleton's* weakened radio masts gave up and came crashing down on the boat deck.

At once, everyone was talking, yelling, screeching. Leigh Morrison struggled to his feet in time to see a second cloud of dust billowing up from unknown hills. The unseen force flashed over the water. It struck the ship, heeling the *Carleton* almost upright before letting it crash back at a worse list than before.

Crew members boiled out on deck, most of them soaked to the skin. Some of the ship's seams had split open. Water was pouring in belowdecks, into every compartment along the starboard side. Without power for the pumps, there was no way to stop the flooding.

As one, the terrified people swarmed to the boat deck where the lifeboats were stowed. Captain Viega, Purser Brock, and Signals Officer Señales appeared between them and the starboard-side lifeboats.

"Where are you going?" Viega demanded.

"To the boats! The ship is sinking!" several people replied.

For a moment, the captain stood between the frightened passengers and the lifeboats. He could not speak the words. At last he stood aside, and with a curt wave of his hand allowed the people to abandon his ship.

Dirty white nylon covers were peeled off the boats. Julie was glad to see they weren't just empty wooden rowboats. Each lifeboat had a deck, collapsible awnings, engines, emergency rations, and battery-powered satellite phones. There was no power for the electric winches, but enormous steel cranks turned by three or four men, raised the lifeboats from their blocks. With much cursing and many bruised knuckles, the boats were swung out over the side. The list, now close to twenty degrees, made pushing the heavy boats even harder, but at last they had four boats ready to launch.

Just like in an old movie, Mr. Brock shouted, "Women and children first!" It was still the law of the sea.

Julie, Linh, and Jenny found themselves shoved into the same boat. Mrs. Ellis was there, too. Two crewmen hoisted her out of her chair and set her in the boat. Her lifter chair went in next. Mothers and kids piled on, most of them crying. When the boat was full, there were thirty-eight people aboard, all children or women.

"Lower away!"

Down they went, swaying side to side as they descended. Julie was pale with fear, not so much from the motion as the horrible idea the boat would flip upside down and dump them all into the sea.

It didn't happen. The boat squatted heavily in the water. One of the Panamanian crewmen came hand over hand down the ropes to the boat. He cast off and took his place at the engine controls. The electric motor whined, but the sound quickly faded away.

"The battery, she dead!" called the sailor to the officers above.

More cursing. The lifeboat batteries were constantly charged by solar panels on the ship's superstructure. How could they be dead?

The lifeboat wallowed against the *Carleton*'s high steel hull. Screams of alarm from the boat were matched by shouted advice from Brock and Engineer Pascal. The sailor left the motor controls and broke out four oars. Jenny and several fit women volunteered to work them. After a few clumsy tries, they got the bobbing boat clear of the ship.

A third shock wave spread out from the land and hit the *Carleton*. Fittings broke loose and tumbled down the deck. A sailor who had climbed onto the second lifeboat crane to rig the lines was shaken loose. He plummeted head first into the water, just missing the stern of the launched lifeboat.

"Ramundo!" his friends cried.

Three life rings hit the water where Ramundo disappeared. More were on their way when Captain Viega stopped the barrage. The sea was writhing around the ship. The lifeboat full of women and children made an awkward half-circle and came back. Viega and the officers shouted for them to stay clear.

Everyone waited for Ramundo to surface. He didn't.

A fourth shock arrived. There was a heavy thud under the deck. Smoke began to spill out of the ventilators. With a massive groaning of tortured steel, *Carleton* listed further to starboard. Hans asked Mr. Brock how far the ship could tilt before they couldn't launch lifeboats.

"The book says twenty-five degrees on these old davits," he said. "One way or another, we'll get them in the water!"

The women remaining boarded the second lifeboat. The young male passengers were next. Leigh shouted to Julie down in her boat and climbed in. France was in this group, and, reluctantly, Hans. He kept asking if he could bring up the silver or china his parents had sent on board. Brock coldly ordered him into the boat.

At the last moment, Emile slipped out of line and backed away. Everyone was too focused on getting the boat away to notice his departure. He ran to the door of the lounge, now flapping with every shudder of the ship. Emile ducked inside. Not seeing what he was seeking, he went to the inside stairwell and rattled down to A deck. The air stank of burnt insulation and an oily smell like diesel. He made his way down the tilted hall, calling a name. No one answered.

It was dark below deck without electric lights. A few battery-powered emergency beams shone in the stairwells and corridor corners. By this weak light Emile read cabin door numbers until he came to one he was seeking. It was open.

"Eleanor! Eleanor!"

She was fighting to close a hefty suitcase and failing.

"Forget it!" Emile said. "It's time to go! We're abandoning ship!"

"I've got to get my things and my mother's!" she protested.

"It doesn't matter! The ship may capsize at any time!"

He tried to drag her away, but she was easily his size and just as strong.

"Leave me alone, rich boy! You don't care about your things, but I want mine!"

He put his face inches from hers. "You're going to die! What good are 'things' to you then?"

To underline his words, the *Carleton* gave a savage lurch. The distinct sound of flowing water reached them. Eleanor lost all the color in her face.

"Oh my god," she gasped. "We're sinking!"

Emile grabbed her by the wrist and dragged her toward the door. At the last instant, Eleanor grabbed a photo from the stubbornly open suitcase. It was an LCD picture of her and her mom, taken outside the Parliament building in London.

In the corridor, they discovered the water they heard wasn't the sea filling the ship; it was from the fire extinguisher system overhead. They groped along the crazy, slanted corridor to the steps and started up. In the lounge they ran into Ms. Señales and a pair of worried sailors.

"What are you doing here? Get to the boats!" she said.

Emile nodded and kept going, dragging Eleanor by her unburned arm. On deck, Brock berated them both for leaving during an emergency.

"I went to find Miss Quarrel," Emile replied. Eleanor had never heard him sound so humble. "No one missed her but me."

The second lifeboat was in the water. Leigh, Mr. Chen, Kiran Trevedi, and France pulled on the oars. Their technique wasn't any better than the first boat's, but by sheer determination they managed to get away from the dying *Carleton*.

They put Eleanor and Emile in the third boat first. More passengers filled in behind them. The fourth was hung up on its crane. Crewmen swarmed over it, hammering and tugging to free it.

There was a lull in the terrible blows striking the ship. Eleanor slumped low in the boat. She didn't like seeing that they were dangling a dozen meters above the ocean. While there, she cast a secret eye at her rescuer. Emile risked his life to bring her up on deck. He was weird, but maybe he wasn't so bad.

The third lifeboat rode the waves at last. Some of the men got them under way. The fourth lifeboat, freed of its snag, came screeching down behind them. It held the last of the passengers.

The ship's list was so severe now, the boat cranes wouldn't work. *Carleton*'s crew launched an inflatable life raft. Sailors began leaping into the water to swim to the raft until Brock and Captain Viega stopped them. Their comrade Ramundo had gone into the water and never come up. There must be rocks or shoals down there, holding the ship and transmitting the awful shocks from shore. Diving in was a good way to break your neck.

The first boat, laden with women and kids, crawled to the beach. Fortunately, the surf wasn't high, and the boat washed up with a gentle bump. Linh and a woman at the bow leaped into the water with lines and dragged the boat higher onto the sand.

"Everyone out!"

The boat emptied. The sailor on the rudder and the four rowers remained.

"Back to the ship?" asked Jenny. The sailor nodded.

With much grunting and yelling, the women on the beach pushed the boat back into the surf. Getting used to their task, Jenny and the other rowers turned about and slowly paddled back to the *Carleton*.

CHAPTER 8

Wet from the waist down, Julie pushed her hair out of her face and gazed at the stricken ship. Leaning way over, with smoke and steam leaking from every vent and port, the *Carleton* looked like a set from a disaster movie.

"Doesn't look so bad from here," said Linh quietly. Julie almost laughed.

Some children tried to head up the beach, exploring until their mothers called them back. They made them sit down on the sand facing the ship. Surprisingly, they all did as they were told.

Linh looked up and down the wide band of sand. It was a remarkably empty beach. No driftwood. No drying strands of seaweed. No salty scrub growing out of the sand above the high tide mark. Linh rubbed the toe of her shoe into the sand.

No shells. Not even broken bits of shells. The sand under her toe was as clean and pure as if it had been sifted and washed.

The second lifeboat beached, and the passengers spilled out. Leigh found Julie and gave her a huge hug.

"Let go!" she groaned. "People are watching!"

"You're all right!"

"I was until you cracked my rib."

The rowers in the second boat called Leigh to join for a return trip to the ship. He kissed Julie on the forehead and told her not to go anywhere.

"Where is there to go?" she said. "The Hotel Bermuda Triangle?"

When Eleanor's boat reached shore, she wondered if Emile would leap into the surf and help her to dry land, but he didn't. He stood at the bow, eyeing the green water with distaste. Tired of waiting, Eleanor pushed past him and swung a leg over the side.

"Are you afraid to get wet?"

He peered down his nose at the foaming waves lapping around the boat.

"I don't like the sea," Emile said.

"Then you picked a damn funny way to travel!"

Eleanor slid off the gunwale into the surf. The landing, even in squishy sand, made her burned arm throb. More than disappointed, she slogged ashore alone.

Going back and forth, the lifeboats and inflated raft ferried most of the *Carleton's* people ashore. At last, the only ones left on board were the officers: Captain Viega, Purser Brock, Engineer Pascal, Signals Officer Señales, and the bridge crew.

Two boats bobbed below the battered ship. The lifeboat lines hanging down were a convenient, if strenuous, way to climb down. Braced against the slant of the ship, the officers debated who should leave now and who would be last.

"I don't believe this," Jenny said, waiting below. "Come on! Hurry!"

Señales took hold of a rope. In the boat beneath her, Leigh held tight to the other end to make it easier for her to climb down. She descended slowly. Señales was not as fit as the young sailors who had come down before.

"You're doing fine!" Leigh called. "Hurry!"

As he said this, the water began to boil around the *Carleton's* hull. Leigh knew what this meant: air was escaping from the ship. She was sinking for sure.

Instead of the *Carleton* slowly submerging in the roiling sea, something far stranger happened. The sea began climbing the red steel hull, clinging to it like viscous oil or gelatin. It did the same to Leigh's lifeboat. Jenny's boat, a few meters away, was not affected.

Everyone in the lifeboats screamed for the officers to jump for their lives. Señales halted her descent halfway to the boat when she saw the sea rising. She stared, eyes wide, as the unnaturally thick water flowed up the sides of Leigh's lifeboat. Leigh and his companions grabbed their oars and tried to free themselves from the grip of the green water. Señales' rope fell into the sea. The viscous water began climbing it.

Jenny's boat glided in. They threw a line to Leigh's boat, and eight oars flailing, they pulled free of the clinging trap. By now, the water had risen half the height of the *Carleton's* hull. It flowed upward over Signals Officer Señales. She kicked and screamed, but there was nothing any of them could do. In seconds, she was cocooned in a translucent mass of shimmering green water.

The weight of the water pulled the ship over. Leigh saw the masts and smokestack come whistling down. They rowed for their lives. Facing backward as they were, the rowers in both boats clearly saw the *Carleton's* officers flung over the rail into the sea. Only Captain Viega kept his grip on a davit. In the next awful moment, the ship rolled over on its starboard side. When the superstructure hit the sea, the strange, clinging water instantly turned into plain water again. A massive wave caused by the impact of the superstructure heaved the lifeboats away. In the boats, they could do nothing but hold on for their lives.

From the beach, the passengers and crew saw the *Carleton* roll over. A shout went up from all their throats, but the ship went down in a rush of boiling, frothing water. Then it was gone. Nothing remained on the surface but a great whirlpool as long as the ship. When it died out, there was nothing left but two forlorn lifeboats floating free, without any hand on the rudder or oars in the water.

The sailors dragged their raft into the surf, ready to search for survivors. Before they cleared the beach, a new shout went up. The lifeboats had recovered and were coming in.

Jenny's boat scraped land first. Men and women, passengers and crew, grabbed the gunwales and dragged the boat onto the beach. Everyone in the lifeboat was utterly stunned by the sudden loss of the *Carleton* and all the officers.

"Should we go back?" asked Mrs. Ellis. Her chair was not floating, but resting on the sand.

"There's no reason," Jenny gasped. Her arms burned from the frantic rowing. "They all went down."

Leigh's boat was also hauled up on the beach. No one said anything. There was nothing to say.

Minutes passed. The sea calmed, and half an hour later by Emile's Patek Philippe wristwatch, there was no sign anything had ever happened. Crying for the lost ones and their own fate went on a lot longer.

The chief steward was the senior surviving member of the crew. For the first time, Linh learned his name—Bernardi. At his direction, the boat and raft were drawn up beyond the high-tide line. He made an inventory of supplies. The list wasn't impressive.

"We have water for all for twenty days," he announced. "Food for fifteen." Some of the emergency supplies had been contaminated by seawater.

"It doesn't matter," said one of the American navy men. "This isn't a desert isle, and we're not named Gilligan."

"I am," said one of the Irish footballers.

A few laughed. Linh didn't understand what was funny.

"What I mean is," said the American, a petty officer named Clarke, "we're not marooned. This is Ireland, isn't it? If we go inland, we'll find help."

"Doesn't look like any part of Ireland I know," Gilligan said. "How 'bout you lads? Is this Eire?" The footballers all agreed— they were not on the Ould Sod.

Where were they? There weren't many choices—Canada? They hadn't sailed far enough to reach Newfoundland. Iceland? Iceland was mountainous, volcanic, and rocky. There were no mountains to be seen.

"Wherever we are, there's bound to be people around," Clarke said. "Let's go find them."

It occurred to France that the *Carleton* had been stuck offshore almost two days, and no one onshore had noticed. They saw no other boats, no planes, helicopters, or airships. Aside from the single torch they saw that night on the beach, there had been no sign of life here.

Mr. Bernardi insisted on making a head count. No one had a working PDD to check the passenger or crew list, but by checking and rechecking with everyone on the beach, it became clear all the passengers had survived, and all the crew except the captain, chief engineer, purser, signals officer, crewman Ramundo, and the three bridge officers.

Talk went on about this option or that plan, and nobody moved off the beach. The weather was mild, but they had no protection from the elements. France grew impatient with all the talking and talking. When the sun was almost overhead, he jumped to his feet and started inland. Mr. Bernardi called after him.

"Where do you think you're going?" he demanded.

"To find something!" France called back through cupped hands.

"What?"

"Anything!"

Leigh and Julie Morrison, Hans Bachmann, and four sailors followed him. France waited for them to catch up. They quickly decided to divide the unknown territory ahead into sections. Two people would explore each section. They agreed to strike inland for half an hour and then return to the beach.

"How long's half an hour?" asked Julie. None of their electronics, including watches, worked. Emile's watch, being mechanical, was the only working timepiece they had.

"Estimate," France said tersely.

The *Carleton* sailors paired up. Two went west, toward one headland. Their comrades took the next area, northwest. France wanted to head straight in, north. Hans offered to go with him.

"Hey," Julie said, "What about me?"

"Go with your brother," said France.

"I always have to go with him." She looked to Hans. "Can I go with you?"

He looked as though someone had just dropped one of the *Queen Mary* plates. "Ah, I do not mind, but—"

Leigh grabbed Julie's hand and dragged her away to the southwest. She protested all the way to the line of scattered pines that bordered the beach. Even after brother and sister disappeared among the trees, France and Hans could hear Julie's voice still complaining.

At last France said, "Let's go."

They climbed the gentle sandy slope up to the tree line. Hans noticed the sand continued, though there were boulders dotted here and there. Wiry grass and some sort of thorny vines sprouted around the rocks, leaving the space between the pines open, an easy walk. Hans paused to examine a car-size boulder half-buried in the sand.

France asked him what he was doing.

"The kind of rock this is could tell us where we are," Hans said. Volcanic rock might mean they were near Iceland, if not actually on it. Eroded sedimentary rock could mean they were on a continental landmass, like Ireland.

He pulled aside an armful of vines. The stone beneath was milky colored, fairly smooth on top but with deeply notched sides. Hans frowned. He got out his pocketknife and scratched the boulder a few times.

"What is it?" France asked.

"It's not right."

"Why? What is it?"

Hans folded his knife and tucked it away. "Looks like marble."

He didn't bother to explain what was wrong with a marble boulder, and France did not ask. Frankly, he didn't care. It could have been papier-mâché. All he wanted was to find help.

They walked along, close at first, but gradually drawing farther apart in order to cover more ground. The first mile or so was quite desolate. They stirred up a few common shorebirds, and a cloud of black flies swarmed Hans, but that was all the life they found.

The trees got taller the farther they went. Pines, cedars, and balsams were all they saw. France called a halt to answer nature. He stepped behind a pine. While there, he got the distinct feeling he was being stared at.

"Hans," he called. "Where are you?"

"About ten feet behind you . . ."

"What are you doing?"

"Same thing as you."

France turned his head suddenly. There was nothing there, but for the briefest instant, he thought there was—something that darted away between the trees. It wasn't low and animal shaped. It was upright and two-legged.

He zipped his fly and ran wide around the pine, trying to cut off whoever had been spying on him. He made a complete circle, returning to where he started just as Hans walked up, squirting sanitizer from a tiny squeeze bottle on his hands.

"Want some?"

"Did you see him?"

Hans's hands stopped rubbing. "Who?"

France turned in a slow circle. "Someone was watching me," he said in a low voice.

"What did he look like?"

"I didn't see clearly."

Hans went to the tree France claimed the spy had passed behind. He squatted in the stiff grass, studying the ground.

"I don't see any footprints." Their own shoes left plain marks in the sandy soil. France's path was clear, but there was no sign anyone else had walked here, ever.

I am seeing things, France thought. He said nothing more about it.

They walked on. Even though it wasn't hot, both boys were thirsty. France had set out so suddenly he'd forgotten to take a bottle of water along. When they saw a low embankment ahead, France and Hans assumed it was a stream. They hurried forward, pushing through brush and thorns. Hans had an easier path and reached the bank first. He halted atop it, staring down at what he saw.

France twisted through the brush and saw it, too. A road.

It wasn't much of a road, just a sandy dirt path with a strip of brown grass growing down the center. It curved away to the west and east, completely empty.

Hans jumped down and ran a hand over the trail.

"No tire tracks," he said. "There are some ruts made by hard, narrow wheels." He stood, dusting his hands. "Bicycles, I guess."

"Roads lead somewhere," France replied. "Let's tell the others. We can follow the road wherever it takes us."

They started back the way they came. Hans, who was taller than France by a couple inches, pulled ahead.

"I wonder what the others have found?"

"I hope an Orangina stand," France muttered.

"Make it Coke, and I'm there!"

They argued good-naturedly about the virtues of their favorite drinks a while. Then a high, far-off scream cut off all thoughts of a nice cold soda.

CHAPTER 9

Leigh and Julie had the sun at their backs as they wended their way through the sparse upland forest. Sea breezes had twisted many of the trees and made little drifts of brown sand on the seaward side of the trunks. Julie bitched a long time about being dragged off with her brother. Why did he have to throw his weight around? She would have been fine with the German guy.

"I did him a favor," Leigh said. "Now he owes me one."

"What does that mean?"

"Figure it out!"

Stomping along, arguing, they were the loudest things around. They had left behind the soft sound of the surf. A mile from the beach, the air was still. Though it wasn't hot, Leigh began to sweat.

"Stay where I can see you," he told Julie. She was leaning against a boulder, scratching her ankle where mosquitoes had bitten her.

"You can see me," she countered. "What's the big worry?"

Leigh surveyed the way ahead. All he could see were pines, sand, and blue sky. Anything could be out there—or anyone.

Sweat formed a drop on the end of his nose. It fell.

"Let's go back," Julie said. "Bugs are eating me up. Unless there's a guy peddling samosas and mango lassi nearby, I'm ready to go back to the beach."

Leigh was ready, too, but he didn't want to seem too eager. "A little farther," he said.

Julie grimaced and followed.

The woods ended not a hundred yards on. A low wall made of loose rubble stood there, separating the pine barren from a large, open meadow. Seeing it, Leigh smiled. He paused with one foot resting on the wall. Muttering about malaria, yellow fever, and West Nile virus, Julie caught up with him.

"What?"

He held out a hand. "It's a meadow!"

"Big effin' deal."

She sat down on the wall. A lizard covered with electric blue scales scampered into a dark crack in the wall to avoid her.

"Don't you get it? Meadows mean cows, or sheep, or something. And that means people."

"There're some people over there."

Leigh stepped back. He spotted who Julie meant: topping a low hill in the meadow came a group of men. They carried long poles. Sunlight glinted off their heads.

Metal helmets? They must be soldiers.

A cold sensation spread over Leigh's sweaty frame. He took another step back.

"Stand up," he said quietly.

"Why? We came here to find help, didn't we?"

Julie stood up, waving a hand over her head. "Hey!" she shouted. "Over here!"

Leigh dragged her hand down. She tore free of his grip, using the worst language she knew.

"What's the matter with you?" she demanded.

"They've seen us!"

"Wasn't that the idea?"

Leigh backed up more steps. "There's something not right about this." They looked like they were definitely wearing shiny metal helmets. Julie shrugged. Maybe they were a rescue party, looking for people from the lost *Carleton*?

The men stopped, pointed at Julie and Leigh, and then broke into a trot. They held onto those long poles, resting on their shoulders. It made no sense. Why run carrying a big pole?

"We gotta go—now!" Leigh said. Julie stared at the oncoming men and did not argue at all. She turned and ran, leaving her brother flat-footed.

They tore through the brush and pines, shielding their faces with their arms as they ran. They heard voices—loud, coarse voices—on the right and left and knew their unknown pursuers were trying to surround them. Leigh quickly lost any sense of direction in the sameness of the pinewoods. He tried to keep within a step or two of Julie, but she veered off to her right, and he had to follow.

"Wait!" he called, not too loudly. "We've got to stay together!"

Too late. Julie ran right into the arms of a band of six men. In addition to steel pot helmets, they wore metal breastplates and heavy, quilted trousers. The poles were not just sticks. At the end of each was a wickedly pointed, leaf-shaped head.

Two of the men dropped their spears and grabbed Julie. She screamed. Leigh ran up on them and threw one man aside before a third clubbed him across the shoulders with the shaft of his spear. Leigh's vision went red. He fell to his knees. Julie screamed again when she saw her brother fall.

France and Hans ran toward the screams. By the time they arrived, they saw the American teenagers being manhandled by a large group of strange men dressed like medieval foot soldiers. Hans skidded to a stop when he saw their steel helmets and armor. France blundered into his back, cursing in French at his companion's sudden stop.

"Schauen Sie!" Hans gasped. "Look!"

They did, but the strangers saw them, too. Several fanned out and started after France and Hans.

"Get away!" Julie cried. "Get help!" Leigh seemed stunned. He was being carried by the arms by two of the soldiers.

"She's right," said Hans. "We'd better tell the others—"

"We can't leave them," France protested. "What will happen to them if we go?"

Hans thought of several things, none of them good. The men were rough looking, with dirty faces and long, matted hair sticking out from under their helmets.

Back to back, Hans and France backed away as the soldiers advanced.

"Can you fight?" France muttered.

"Fight? I've never been in a fight in my life," Hans replied.

France abandoned any idea of heroics and bolted, dragging Hans along by his shirt. He almost stumbled over his own feet in surprise when he heard one of the soldiers declare, *"Après les avoir!"* ("After them!").

French? His accent was terrible, but why were their attackers speaking French?

Hans asked no questions but ran as fast as he could. They dodged the soldiers trying to hem them in and broke free. For a while, they kept ahead of their pursuers, but they never lost them. It occurred to France the men weren't trying very hard to catch them—they were following them. And he and Hans were leading them right to the beach, where the rest of the *Carleton* survivors waited unaware of this strange new peril.

What else could they do? The boys ran until their chests ached. Ahead, the trees thinned, and then disappeared. It was midafternoon, judging by the sun, and the passengers and crew were still squatting in the sand, passively waiting the return of the scouts.

"Alarm!" Hans shouted as he cleared the trees. "Alarm! Look out!" France joined in yelling warnings.

The Irish footballers and the American navy men were first to respond. They formed a ragged line between the children and old people. *Carleton* crewmen joined them, along with fit and ready passengers like Kiran Trevedi, Jenny Hopkins, and the Chen brothers.

Out of the trees, the soldiers halted, deterred by the numbers they faced. They formed close ranks with spears shouldered and stood off some distance. Hans and France rejoined the *Carleton* people. They gasped out their story, how Leigh and Julie were captured, how the strange men chased them, and how France heard at least one of them give orders in crude French.

"French?" said Chief Steward Bernardi. "Are we on the coast of French Canada?"

"Insanity," said Gilligan, the footballer. "Nobody in Canada runs around wearing bassinets and carrying spears!"

Jenny thought bassinets were something you put a baby in, and the men didn't look like fatherly types.

"Maybe we should rush 'em," said Clarke, the American petty officer. "There are only ten or so of them and more than a hundred of us!"

"Go right ahead," said Bernardi. "While they're busy spearing you, the rest of us can get them, yes?"

In the end, they just stood there, fifty yards apart, watching each other. Before long, another quartet of soldiers emerged from the woods with Leigh and Julie. Brother and sister stumbled along, hands tied behind their backs.

Cries went up from some of the *Carleton* people. Eleanor worked her way forward and demanded they do something to help the Morrisons. They had spears at their backs. If the *Carleton* people charged, Leigh and Julie might be dead before they ran five steps.

The standoff continued until a column of men appeared out of the east, marching along the high side of the beach. With them were three men on horseback. The riders wore more armor— polished steel plates on their arms and legs, closed visors on their helmets. Pennants fluttered from their lance tips. They looked like extras from a movie about Joan of Arc or the Crusades, only there were no cameras, no soundtrack, and no audience.

The *Carleton* survivors backed away from the oncoming men, concentrating into a tight circle. The soldiers who caught the Morrisons and chased Hans and France joined their comrades, dragging their captives with them.

Gilligan and his teammates flexed their hands into fists. Clarke and his Navy buddies muttered tactical advice to each other in jargon no one else understood. Bernardi hung his head. He was a service professional, not a fighter. His men were game, but the chief steward was horrified by the thought of bloodshed, and said so.

The soldiers stopped as one forty yards away. One man on horseback continued forward until he was quite close. He raised his visor. He had a young face, clean shaven, with expressive black eyes.

"*N'ayez pas peur! Je suis chevalier Armand de Sagesse. Vous êtes maintenant prisonniers du roi d'Ys!*"

Everyone looked at France, or Emile, or any of the other French speakers in the *Carleton* group.

"What did he say?" Bernardi asked.

"He's crazy. He makes no sense," Emile said, shaking his head.

"He says his name is Sir Armand de Sagesse," France said. "We are prisoners of the king of Ys—whatever that is."

"It's a lost city," said Emile. "A medieval city lost under the sea hundreds of years ago!"

Jenny said, "A real place?"

"No. Just a legend."

"Well, the 'legend' has sixty armed men behind him," Clarke said in a low voice. "So I'm not calling him a liar."

"*Rendre pacifiquement! Vous ne serez pas lésés!*"

"He says, surrender peacefully, and we won't be harmed," Emile added.

"They always say that," Trevedi said. "But what do we do?"

Bernardi pushed through the crowd and presented himself to the chevalier de Sagesse, who sat haughtily on his horse six feet away. Remembering he didn't speak French, he waved France forward to translate for him. The footballers and Navy men protested. Bernardi had no right to speak for them.

France joined the chief steward. Up close, something smelled terrible. It wasn't the horse, who was a fine, clean animal. It was the noble knight. He smelled like he had never bathed in his life.

"Tell him, I want guarantees for these people." Bernardi rubbed his sweaty hands together. "Tell him, we are unarmed, and are only here because our ship wrecked offshore. Tell him we're peaceful—"

France repeated the chief steward's message. The chevalier's lip curled in disgust.

"Dommage! J'avais hâte d'un bon combat!"

So saying, he lashed out with his ironclad foot, kicking Bernardi in the chest. The chief sprawled in the sand. When France helped him up, blood was running from his nose.

Gilligan, Clarke, and the others shouted at the knight's brutal treatment of Bernardi. In reply he lowered his lance and shouted a command to his troops. The soldiers broke ranks and jogged forward, spears and shields ready.

This is madness, France thought, holding up the stunned steward. I'm about to be killed by medieval soldiers in the middle of the twenty-first century!

The heavily armed men found it slow going through the beach sand. They were only halfway to the *Carleton* party when an arrow flicked through the air, striking the chevalier de Sagesse on his breastplate. There was a bright flash, a loud crack, and the smell of ozone. The chevalier dropped his lance, threw up his hands, and fell to the ground. His horse collapsed after him. Astonished, France and Bernardi staggered back to their friends.

The soldiers stopped short when their commander fell. They shouted among themselves, eyeing the *Carleton* people with fear and anger. Many threw down their spears and drew swords. Screams rose from the passengers. It looked like a massacre in the making.

More arrows hissed in the air, sprouting in the sand ahead of the furious soldiers. They hesitated, throwing their small round shields up over their heads before coming on. The next volley of arrows arrived. Some found their way past the shields. More bangs and intense flashes, like cameras going off, and several soldiers were left motionless on the sand.

At last the unseen archers appeared out of the pinewoods. They wore small metal helmets, light metal breastplates, and short kilts instead of the heavy trousers the French-speaking soldiers wore. They dashed out of the trees, aiming and loosing arrows at their foes just a hundred yards away. The soldiers shouted in alarm. They obviously knew who their enemy was. Packing close together, they held their shields high to ward off arrows. Two more knights on horseback trotted up, waving their lances and bellowing orders.

"What the hell?" Clarke said for most everyone. "What the hell?"

Behind the two dozen or so archers came more men—foot soldiers in gray armor and big, pot-shaped helmets with flaring neck guards. They carried large rectangular shields trimmed in brass. Short swords gleamed in their hands.

"*Wahnsinn!*" Hans Bachmann declared. "Insanity." The newcomers looked for all the world like Roman legionnaires.

Unarmed and helpless, the *Carleton* people shrank from both sides. The legionnaires deployed in close formation with their archers out front. The medieval French soldiers clustered together nervously. They had no bows, and they had seen the strangely powerful effect the arrows had.

A mounted officer in a gilded helmet appeared among the Romans. He rode out front of his men, ignoring the cowering *Carleton* survivors.

He boomed, *"Abscede! Vos es in Res publica tractus!"*

"Don't ask me—that's not French!" Emile said to all inquiring eyes.

Hans said, "It's Latin, I think. He's telling the French to go away."

"I could have told you that," said Gilligan.

One of the knights replied in an insolent tone. At that, the Romans advanced. Their archers showered the French with arrows. They stood up under the fire until a second knight was felled. With that, the last rider ordered his men away. He trotted off, peering nervously over his shoulder. His men paused long enough to pick up the bodies of the chevalier de Sagesse and the other knight and backed away in a tight mass, leaving several of their comrades sprawled on the beach.

Like a many-legged machine, the legionnaires churned past the amazed *Carleton* castaways. At a stately pace, they chased the retreating medieval soldiers until they were out of sight. The officer and a squad of twenty men and twenty archers remained.

He rode up quite close to the *Carleton* survivors. When he removed his helmet, they saw he was a rather rugged, handsome man of forty, clean-shaven, with short, curly gray hair.

Clearing his throat, he said, *"Vos es iam captus of Latium Res publica. Ego sum Titus Macrinus, tribus of XVII Legio. Vos mos pareo mihi, quod totus ero puteus."*

Hans struggled to understand. One of the Irish team members, Shannon, knew some Latin, too. Together, they pieced together what the officer said.

"We're prisoners," Hans said unsteadily.

"Of the Latium Republic—whatever that is," Shannon added.

"His name is Titus Macrinus. We won't be harmed if we do as he says."

"Damned if we will!" said one of the Navy men. "Bunch of geeks running around playing Roman! Who do they think they are?"

Just then, two legionnaires dragged a fallen French soldier past by his heels. His face was dead white save for a bright red welt in the center of his forehead where the arrow struck. It didn't penetrate his skull but killed him by touch alone.

"I think they've made their point," said Kiran Trevedi. "We'd better do as they say."

Everyone got up. Mrs. Ellis, whose lifter chair was not working, had to be carried. Mr. Chen and one of the Navy men carried her in their arms, fireman-style.

They formed a long double line, flanked on either side by stern legionnaires. Titus Macrinus sat on his horse, watching the *Carleton* people file past with an appraising eye. Linh Prudhomme, like everyone, wondered why they were being held prisoner. As she passed the mounted officer, their eyes met.

Who was he, this mature man in the garb of an ancient Roman tribune? An actor? Some kind of cultist, or a crazy survivalist? Linh had read about people who secluded themselves in some remote part of the world in order to live according to the deranged rules of a cult. She'd never heard of anyone choosing to live like Romans—or medieval Frenchmen, either.

He had a cool, measured glance. She wanted to speak up, to say, "Stop this, people have gotten hurt. What kind of game are you playing?" But she didn't. Looking into those exacting gray eyes, Linh realized something surprising and really terrifying.

Titus Macrinus was not a cultist or an actor. He believed he was just as he appeared to be—an officer in the army of ancient Rome.

CHAPTER 10

Not far away, Julie Morrison was flat on the sand, keeping her head down. One of her captors shoved her there roughly, and then he ran to join his comrades when the other party of armed men turned up. Leigh was beside her, still loopy from the blow he'd received. Poor guy, first he got a black eye when the ship ran aground, then he got whacked with the biggest baseball bat Julie had ever seen. He was not having a good couple of days.

There was a lot of noise, shouting and the clatter of metal, then the sound—and smell—of the armored men faded. Julie dared to lift her face from the sand. To her relief, the dirty soldiers were gone. Her joy was short-lived. Her companions from the wrecked ship were marching away, guarded by a bunch of guys in short skirts with more funny helmets on their heads.

"Hey," she said, shaking Leigh. "Hey, get up!" He just grunted.

Julie grabbed handfuls of his shirt in both hands and hauled him to a sitting position.

"Get up, quarterback! The team needs you!"

"Give it a rest, will ya?" he groaned.

"We're leaving! You want to spend the rest of your life on this ugly beach? Get up!"

"Leave me 'lone . . ."

Julie shook Leigh as hard as she could. She was not very big or strong, but she was mad. Her big brother was not giving up.

She kicked him as hard as she could, right in the butt. Julie was wearing nylon Snappers, trendy deck shoes, so the blow hurt her toes as much as it hurt Leigh.

He yelled. Some of the Roman types heard him and pointed the pair out to Titus Macrinus. At his command, two archers trotted over, pointing drawn bows at them and jabbering in some language Julie didn't understand.

"Yeah, yeah," she said, warding off the two bowmen with swats of her hands. "Don't stick those things in my face!"

Leigh's head cleared enough to see the danger they were in. He staggered to his feet.

"Don't shoot!" he said. "We'll come." To his angry sister he hissed, "Shut up, dingy, before they put holes in us!"

"Dingy" was a childish insult at their house. Julie slapped Leigh smartly across the face. The archers grinned and prodded them toward the others.

They fell into line with Eleanor and Emile.

"What is this, Mardi Gras?" asked Julie. Taking turns, Eleanor and Emile tried to explain the confrontation on the beach and how the "Romans" had driven off the "French."

"This is like one of those geeky Your/World games you used to play five or six years ago," Julie said. Wincing from his hurts, Leigh only nodded.

They trudged through the pines closely watched by their captors. France studied them as they went. The soldiers were all mature men, ranging he guessed from their late twenties to their mid thirties. He recognized the centurion, who was sort of like a sergeant, by the fact the plume on his helmet ran crosswise, while

Titus Macrinus's crest ran front to back. France was pleased he remembered so much about Roman soldiers. It all came from watching that series on the BBC ten years ago.

The soldiers wore breastplates, helmets, and metal plates on their shins. Their kilts came down halfway on their thighs, with strips of thick brown leather covering what looked like white cotton underneath. Each man carried a sword, knife, and shield. The archers wore less armor and were generally more lightly clothed. They didn't speak among themselves. Only Titus and the centurion spoke when they gave their troops orders.

Though the woods broke up the soldiers' line, there was not enough cover for the *Carleton* party to break and run. There were too many children and elderly people to worry about. Any attempt to escape might result in a bloodbath.

Before long they reached the same road France and Hans had found. Titus guided his horse to the side of the path and pointed east. The centurion snapped an order, and everyone filed off to the left.

It was late afternoon. None of the *Carleton* people had eaten or had any water since first arriving in this crazy place. Kids began to whine they were hungry and thirsty. The complaints became general. The column of prisoners slowed and stopped.

Titus rode up. What is this delay? Hans understood him to ask.

"*Nos es ieiunium,*" he stammered, trying desperately to remember his vocabulary from Latin Level VII. "We are hungry. How did you say 'thirsty'? *Nos es . . . es . . .*"

"*Siccus?*" Shannon suggested.

"*Nos es siccus!*" Hans declared.

Titus took this in stride. He had his men share canteens with the captives. They weren't insulated plastic, but leather bags of liquid the legionnaires wore around their necks.

The children drank and promptly complained about the weird taste. Chief Bernardi took a swig. He grimaced. The skins held a mixture of vinegar and water.

"Yuck," said Julie. She drank it anyway. So did Emile, while he remembered from the Your/World series *Imperator* that Roman troops often drank vinegar and water on the march. It was less likely to spoil than plain water.

No food was offered. The canteens were torn from thirsty hands, and the march resumed.

Hans spent a long time trying to form the words of a question. Declining Latin verbs while surrounded by men armed with swords wasn't easy, but at last he struggled to say, *"Tribus! Quare es nos ligatio? Qua es nos iens?"*

"Captus, non ligatio."

He was correcting Hans's Latin! "'Prisoners,' not 'imprisoned'!"

Hans repeated his questions properly. Titus said, "You arrived from the sea. We were told to collect you."

Another long interval and Hans managed to figure how to ask, "Who wanted us collected?"

"The First Citizen of the Republic." With that enigmatic reply, Titus spurred his horse out of range of Hans's questions.

The empty, featureless landscape above the beach slowly gave way to new vistas. Early landmarks—a plain dirt path, a simple stone wall—gave way to signs of regular life. Rusty brown cows lounged under the shade of an ancient oak tree. On distant hilltops, the *Carleton* people saw little earth-colored cottages with pale thatched roofs. Children herded squawking geese with willow switches. At the sight of the strange column of legionnaires and prisoners, they stopped and stared. Boy or girl, their clothing was the same, simple bags of cloth pulled over their heads and tied at the waist with a thong.

What was missing was any sign of the modern world. As they trudged along, Eleanor saw no PDDs, motor vehicles, antennas, or signs of electricity being used. The farms they passed smelled of cow manure. Most of the people they saw in the fields and lanes, young or old, were barefoot.

"I think we've gone back in time," Emile said.

"Ridiculous," Eleanor replied. She cradled her burned arm. When it didn't itch, it throbbed. The pain meds had worn off long ago.

"Where are we, then?"

She said, "I don't know. Why don't you quiz someone who cares?" She walked faster to get away from him.

A lot of people from the ship were talking time travel now. They'd all grown up watching science fiction on Your/World—*Deadly Moon, The Harriers, Things to Come 2200*—so the idea they had gone back in time to the Roman Empire was easy to embrace. Gilligan even used the words time warp to describe the strange demise of the *Carleton*. They had sailed into a time warp. All they had to do now was find out where in the Roman Empire they'd landed—where and when.

France was not convinced. Time warps and time travel were fiction, and bad fiction at that. If they were back in Roman times, where did the medieval, French-speaking knights come from? No, they had run into some kind of weird reenactors colony, where everyone took their parts far too seriously . . .

"Bermuda Triangle," said Ms. Martinez, a member of the *Carleton* crew. "We're lost in the Bermuda Triangle, and so are these poor fellows." She meant the legionnaires and Tribune Titus. "It's a kind of limbo where time stands still."

Utter crap, Leigh Morrison thought. All these theories were bogus and unnecessary. None of it would matter when they finally found someone in authority. Once they could explain themselves, they were bound to be set free.

Far back in the line, Emile shed his jacket. It was warm and balmy, more so than anyplace in the North Atlantic had a right to be. It was more like southern Italy here, or springtime in Greece. Weighed down by the impossibility of it all, his tired hands dropped, trailing his expensive designer jacket in the dust. Another mile and it slipped his fingers for good.

The sun was sinking. Jenny wondered if they'd be forced to walk all night. She was surprisingly tired. They'd only come three miles inland (she kept track of her steps; it was habit), so the distance was not so great, but the stress of the shipwreck and the unfamiliar strain of rowing so much had taken its toll. Her legs felt like lead. A lot of the others were feeling that way, too. Talk had died as the *Carleton* party dragged itself along. Any attempt to sit down or rest attracted soldiers with swords drawn.

The sandy beach road came to an end at a nicely cobbled road that led off in three directions: east, north, and northwest. Filling the land between the east and north lanes was an extensive farm—two-story house, lots of stone and rail fences, barns, and other out buildings. Titus Macrinus crossed the paved road and summoned his centurion. They conferred. The legionnaire put a ram's horn to his lips and blew a long, steady note.

Scattering squawking chickens as he went, the farmer appeared to greet the tribune. They exchanged words, with the farmer waving his hands and bowing a lot. Titus barked an order, and two hard-muscled soldiers found Hans and dragged him to their commander.

"You understand me?" Titus asked.

"If the tribune speak careful," Hans struggled to say.

"Tell your people we will pass the night here. Men and women will be separated. Children will stay with their mothers."

"What is they going to happen?" asked Hans. His Latin was not up to this.

"We rest here tonight. In two days we will reach Eternus Urbs, capital of the Republic."

"What to us happened there?"

Titus ignored the question and dismissed Hans with a wave. He went back to the others and told them what the tribune said.

"Eternus Urbs, eh? Even I know what that means," Chief Bernardi said. "'Eternal City.' We're going to Rome!"

France just didn't believe it. He'd been to Italy with his parents before their divorce, and even allowing for the difference in time, this place was not at all like Italy. The climate and terrain were wrong, and there were no French knights or men-at-arms in ancient Italy. He kept his thoughts to himself. Most of the *Carleton* crowd had come to terms with the situation by swallowing the time travel idea, and he didn't want to stir things up—yet.

All the adult men and boys above age thirteen or so were herded into a smelly cattle pen. It wasn't enough of a prison to keep anyone in who wanted to get out, but it did confine the men and make it easier for the Romans to post guards around them. The women and children were taken away to the largest barn, and the doors were barred. Leigh hated seeing Julie go. He watched her right up to the moment she vanished into the shadowed barn. She did not look back once.

The farmer, paid by Titus Macrinus, fed the prisoners with help from his four children. Half a short loaf of bread per man, a gourd dipper of water apiece, and that was all.

Emile made the cut to go with the men, even though he was small for his age. He found a spot by a fence post above the omnipresent cow dung and wedged himself there. The sun was setting among some low western hills. The sky was beautifully bronzed by the failing rays. From his perch he could see a white statue on a pedestal out behind the farmer's big, tumbledown house. From the shape it was female, about a quarter the size of an adult woman. He tried to dredge up images from his academy art class. Was it the goddess Venus? Minerva? On a farm it ought to be the harvest goddess, what was her name? Per-Pers-Persephone?

As he watched, chin on a rail worn smooth by years of cows rubbing against it, a girl about his age came out of the house. She balanced a tall urn on one hip and a small basket on the other. To the statue she went. A meter away, she stopped, curtsied, and placed the basket on the pedestal before the statue. Emile smiled. He was seeing a Roman country girl making an offering to a pagan goddess. It looked genuine. She wasn't performing for any audience. As far as Emile could tell, the girl didn't know she was being watched.

Curtsying again, the girl poured liquid from the urn on the base of the pedestal. It was shiny and thick, probably olive oil. The girl bobbed her head and went back inside. Emile could see red and brown fruit (or was it bread?) in the basket. His stomach churned. Too bad they didn't feed their prisoners as well as they did their idols.

One of the more pompous male passengers slipped and sat down hard in a pile of manure. The guards laughed and pointed.

Some of the *Carleton* men helped the fallen man stand. When Emile was finished taking in the scene, he looked again at the white statue.

The food was gone.

The basket was still there. It hadn't moved. The oil stain shone in the failing sunlight. There was no one around who could have taken the offering and escaped from Emile's view. That was odd enough, but as Emile studied this puzzle, a strange mystery drove the frown from his face.

The statue's pose had changed. Instead of its former languid posture, hands down, gazing with cold marble eyes at the ground, it was now holding its head up. The stone hands were palm up in front of its face, and it was looking directly at Emile.

CHAPTER 11

Night came with whispers. Jenny was in the front corner of the barn, leaning against the rough wall. It was made of plaster or mud, mashed into a lattice of woven sticks. Warm from the day's sunshine, it smelled, like everything else on this antique Roman farm, of cow dung.

Jenny had given up a place in the far end of the barn to some of the older women and mothers with children. There was a lot of hay scattered back there, so it was more comfortable than her spot near the door. When they saw her take a less comfortable spot for herself, some of the other girls, the American, Julie, and French Vietnamese girl, Linh, joined Jenny. Eleanor Quarrel was in the opposite corner, cradling her burned arm.

Jenny couldn't sleep. She was tired, exhausted even, as if she'd run a major race. All that climbing, rowing, and walking miles proved more demanding than she expected. That made her think she would have to vary her training in the future, to do more than running. She should take up vertical climbing, maybe weights. Her father used to run with wrist and ankle weights, but Jenny's mother would not allow her to use them. It was too easy for weights to damage a still-growing girl's joints, she said. They argued about it, but her mother won.

Running through options for future training, she slipped into half-sleep. Then she heard the whispers. They were nearby. The voices were low. Masculine. She couldn't quite make out what they were saying—

A hand clamped hard over her mouth. At the same time, she felt heavy pressure on her chest. Surprised, Jenny opened her eyes and saw an unfamiliar face up close. It was one of the soldiers. His breath smelled of olive oil and wine. Besides a hand over her mouth, he had his knee jammed hard against her so she couldn't move.

"*Quietis!*" he hissed. Jenny got that.

There were two other shadowy figures behind the man. One had Linh Prudhomme in a similar grip. The third bent down and grabbed Julie. She instantly flailed about in panic. Jenny saw the man's hand rise and fall. She heard the blow, and Julie stopped fighting.

Without another word, Jenny was dragged to her feet. The man never uncovered her mouth, but seized her right arm and twisted it hard behind her back. For a second, she considered resisting, but the hand left her face and returned to her throat holding a very sharp knife. Linh was likewise held silent by a blade. The third man picked up a limp Julie by the waist. They sidled out quietly. Jenny thought she saw Eleanor stir. She wanted to shout, to yell for help and warn Eleanor in case there were more attackers about, but the iron edge at her throat dug in and she knew she wouldn't live to make anything more than a gasp.

The girls were forced outside, around the barn toward another, smaller shed. By now Jenny had recognized their abductors as three of the legionnaires who had captured them. She also knew what was going to happen. Time warp, Bermuda

Triangle, or weird island of cultists didn't matter. She and the girls were about to be raped.

Eleanor did waken when Julie was struck. She saw the outlines of three soldiers standing over her companions and saw them dragged out. She froze when the man holding Julie stared at her. Eleanor understood what was happening, too. She waited a few seconds, then got up on her hands and knees. She crept to the open barn door and watched the legionnaires disappear around the corner with their captives.

Eleanor thought of screaming there and then. She decided against it. There were knives at Linh and Jenny's throats, and screaming might only get the girls killed. Besides, who in the barn could help her? Old Mrs. Ellis? The lady with two kids?

She remembered Julie's brother. He would do anything to save his sister. Eleanor dashed out of the barn, bent low. She was able to make it to the cow pen without being stopped by guards. That made sense; the men abducting the girls were the guards on watch between the barn and the pen.

"Leigh! Leigh Morrison!" she gasped. Someone sat up within the dark corral. It was the French guy.

"Help! The girls! They've been taken!"

Another head popped up. This time it was Hans Bachmann.

"Where's Leigh Morrison? His sister's in danger!" Eleanor all but cried.

Hans moved over two sleeping figures and roused Leigh. He, Hans, and France Martin ducked between the rails. Eleanor pointed to the low shed beyond the barn.

"They went that way!"

Crouching, the boys followed her. At the last minute, a fourth figure joined them—Emile Becquerel.

"Go back!" Eleanor said. "You're too young for this!"

"Too young for what?"

She couldn't say it. "You're too small, okay?"

"Why, are you starting a basketball game?" he shot back.

There was no more time to argue. Eleanor and the four guys dashed through the darkness.

Only twenty yards away, Julie was lost. She had felt someone touch her, so she kicked out, only to get floored with a blow that knocked her eyes back into her head. When the veil slowly cleared, she felt herself being carried, quite rudely. She started to protest and received another smack on the back of her head. This hurt again, but it also made her mad. She bent over the meaty arm around her waist and sank her teeth into it. Her captor hissed loudly and let her fall to the ground. The breath went out of Julie. She lay there, dazed.

"Miserabilis creatura!"

Iron scraped as the soldier drew a dagger from its scabbard. Driven along behind Julie and her abductor, Linh saw the man drop her and take out his knife. He stood over her, ready to plunge the blade into Julie's back.

Linh screamed, blade at her throat or no. Farther back, Leigh and the others heard the cry and broke into a full run. The light was poor. There was no starlight or moon, and no artificial light anywhere, but it was clear enough for Leigh to tackle the nearest soldier from behind. He made a perfect illegal clip and cut the man's legs out from under him. This happened to be Jenny's captor. He went down. She sprang free, and with Hans running up beside her, they fell on the second man, struggling with Linh Prudhomme.

The ruckus distracted the first soldier from killing Julie. He turned, knife in hand, to face France and Eleanor. He cut sideways at France, who barely threw himself out of the way in time. Eleanor skidded to a stop. She cast about for a weapon and found nothing but a wooden hayfork leaning against the shed. Eleanor grabbed this and jabbed at the soldier standing over Julie. He laughed shortly and snatched the tool from her grasp.

Emile quickly regretted joining the rescue. Leigh was down, wrestling a man cursing in Latin. Jenny pulled Linh free of her abductor while Hans desperately kept him busy. Eleanor and France looked certain to die, so Emile flattened himself against the shed, trying to go unseen. His foot nudged something heavy. He picked it up. It was half a brick.

Leigh's opponent was tough. He wasn't as big as Leigh, but wiry and very strong. The soldier knew how to fight, while Leigh only had football and some high school wrestling experience to draw on. The soldier got a hand on Leigh's throat and tightened his grip. Blood bellowed in the American's ears until he drove a fist twice into the man's gut as hard as he could punch.

Jenny flung the slender Linh away and leaped at the man who had held her. Hans had him on one side, now Jenny grappled on the other. The legionnaire's eyes were wide with surprise. She stamped on his foot. Powered by Olympic-hopeful legs, she broke the man's ankle. Howling, he went down.

Julie was up on her hands and knees. So far, the night had been a series of nasty blows and confusion. When she saw France and Eleanor dancing out of reach of the soldier's blade, she yelled a few choice words of English and kicked him in the rump. He promptly backhanded Julie in the nose. She reeled away.

Feinting with his knife, the legionnaire wedged a leg between France's ankles and tripped him. Down he went. Next thing he knew, a burning hot sensation flooded his back. He'd been stabbed. France tried to rise, but all strength fled his limbs.

Disappointed to see the boy still moving, the soldier raised his knife again. At that moment, he was hit in the face by half a brick. Eleanor turned to see Emile recovering from his first and only throw.

Many footfalls thudded in the lane between the barn and shed. The rest of the guards were coming, with swords drawn. Linh saw their blades gleam in the dark and knew their lives were over.

"*Sto qua vos es! Operor non permoveo!*"

Only Hans knew this meant "Stand where you are! Don't move!" but the intent of the command was clear. The soldiers quickly filled the lane, disarming and separating everyone.

Then there was light.

Overhead, there was a tremendous flash, as if a gigantic camera had gone off a hundred yards up in the sky. Everyone froze—everyone. Lying in the muck, bleeding, France saw everything highlighted in bright glare and sharp shadows. The terrible pain in his back lessened as a gentle wave of heat flowed through him.

The Republic soldiers were as stiff as statues, swords upraised, mouths open in midshout. Leigh was poised on top of his opponent, arms tangled and teeth bared. Hans was staring at the centurion commanding the guards, probably conjugating Latin verbs even while paralyzed. Linh, her clothing torn, was gazing down at the man they'd subdued. Lurking under the eaves of the shed, Emile looked younger and smaller than ever.

Julie was in the strangest posture. She was poised on one foot, impossibly balanced in the act of falling. Her nose was bleeding, but she looked ferociously angry.

Eleanor had dropped to her knees, trying to ward off any more attacks on France.

The light vanished. It was there, and then it was not.

France's pain was gone. He put a hand to the spot over his right kidney where the legionnaire had stabbed him. His shirt was cut, but the wound was gone. There wasn't even any blood.

Julie spun around, caught herself, and stopped. She put a hand to her lips. No blood.

The centurion quickly directed his troops to round them up, but he was quite calm about it. The eight teens were escorted back to their places while the three would-be rapists were given a fierce tongue-lashing by the centurion. Hans caught the word *verbera*, "a beating," and knew the offenders were going to get more than chewed out.

Shuffling back to the corral surrounded by surprisingly even-tempered guards, Leigh said, "What just happened?"

Hans said, "I don't know."

"What was that light?"

France felt his back again and didn't answer. Whatever it was, he was grateful for it.

Back in the barn, Jenny sat down heavily in her corner. Given all that had happened, she wanted to shout, to run, to kick something or someone as hard as she could. Instead, she felt an incredible calm settle over her. In moments she was asleep. Far back in her mind, her brain cried out in outrage, but her body went slack when her eyelids closed.

Julie took a little longer to submit, but she too seemed unnaturally calm after the violence they'd barely escaped. She remembered it all: the blows, the struggle, the smell of the soldier who gripped her so roughly. She remembered but for some reason didn't care. Julie saw Jenny slump into slumber and marveled at her coolness. Then she sank back into silence and darkness, wrapped in unnatural peace.

Linh could not stop trembling. As for Eleanor, Linh didn't see her. She was with them when the guards herded them into the barn. Where was she now?

Linh sat in the dark, shaking. She wondered if the others had perceived what she had. As they were stricken by the brilliant light in the sky, Linh heard voices along with the glare—voices inside the light. She couldn't tell how many or who they were, but she heard a distinct undertone of muttering. They terrified her. Who had she heard? God? Angels? Beings from outer space? She did not believe in any of these things, but she heard what she heard. Perhaps the most frightening thing of all was the fact no one else seemed to have heard anything.

The night was close around her. Linh detected no more voices, and shortly before sunrise, her fear waned enough to let her sleep.

One by one the boys subsided. Hans felt like he did the time he was given anesthetic gas at the dentist. His arms and legs felt set in concrete while his mind raced around inside his skull, frantic to get out. Only when the dentist increased the flow of oxygen did Hans pass out. Now as he thought about this experience, the same thing happened. His terror at being paralyzed faded. The last thing he saw was Leigh Morrison slumped against a corral post. He looked asleep, but there were tears trickling down his face.

Leigh told himself he had failed. That SOB grabbed Julie, and he wasn't able to stop him. If that light hadn't gone off, he, Hans, and France would be dead now, and worse would have happened to Julie and the girls. The flash saved everybody. Good thing, whatever it was . . . His burning eyes closed.

Snores and raspy breathing around France made him feel very alone. He wanted to talk to somebody about what happened, but everyone was asleep. He called out in a loud whisper to Hans, who didn't respond. The American guy looked comatose. Where was the Belgian chocolate hater? France turned stiffly—his neck felt like it was in a vise—but he didn't see Emile anywhere. Did the guards take him away?

He lay there a long time, one cheek in the dirt. Unable to move, all France could see was a bit of the pen, the barn where the women and children were kept, and some of the path up to the farmhouse. After a time, he heard faint movement nearby. Slowly, a pair of tiny white feet appeared in his narrow view. At first he thought one of the farm children was out, prowling around, but the feet (and legs above them) were remarkably pale, whiter than any flesh ought to be. They crossed in front of France, close enough for him to hear the tiny footfalls. He struggled to lift his head but only managed to grunt a little from the futile effort. Nevertheless, his visitor seemed startled by the sound and fled.

France looked on in amazement as the little prowler ran past the barn. It wasn't a person at all, by the look of it. The slim figure, the white limbs were quite clear—and quite impossible.

The goddess statue the farmer kept in a shrine in his yard was walking around, inspecting the captives. France had seen the statue earlier, after the farmer's daughter left an offering to it. Now it hurried away on slender marble feet. It glanced back once and met the gaze of his open eye. Though its movements were as fluid as any woman's, its face was an unliving mask of marble.

It took a long time after that for France to fall asleep.

Dawn stirred the farm anew. The stout farmer and his family got to work at first light, as farmers have always done. They did not pretend to be quiet, and soon the *Carleton* captives stirred from their dewy places, blinking at the sunrise.

110

The first thing France did was check his back. The cut in his shirt was still there, but his skin was unpierced. The night's adventure seemed so unreal, but there was a hole in the shirt where the soldier had stabbed him. Just as strange were the miniature footprints in the dirt around him, perfect impressions of tiny female feet.

His amazement was cut short when Leigh called out to him. France followed the American's pointing hand and saw three men, stripped of their arms and armor, tied to posts in the farmer's yard. They hung by their bindings, limp and lifeless.

The centurion strode past, barking orders.

"Ration breakfast this morning! No fires! The march will begin as soon as the prisoners are roused and in order!"

France understood every word he said.

A soldier with a lion's skin wrapped around his shoulders doubled up and replied, "Can we refill our canteens at the farmer's well?"

"Detail three men to fill them all," said the centurion.

He understood the exchange completely. Were the soldiers now speaking French? To the centurion France said mildly, "Sir, what will happen to the men who attacked the girls last night?"

Without batting an eye, the centurion snapped, "They have paid the price of indiscipline!" He moved on, bawling at his men to get them moving.

Hans sidled up. "Either my Latin has vastly improved overnight or they're speaking German this morning!"

"French, you mean."

They gave each other a startled look. Hans closed his eyes and sang softly, "'O Christmas tree, O Christmas tree, thy leaves are so unchanging . . .'" He opened his eyes. "That was German, was it not?"

France shook his head. Concentrating, he tried to recite "La Marseillaise" in his native language. Hans assured him he followed every word.

All over the farm the *Carleton* party were freely using their newfound fluency. People who hadn't spoken to each other during the entire voyage due to language barriers now addressed each other with ease and clarity.

Leigh was so disturbed by this development, he squatted in the corral writing in the dirt with a twig. France and Hans spotted him staring hard at what he had written.

"What is it?" France said.

Leigh's brow furrowed deeply. "I tried to write, 'I am eighteen years old,' in English." What was traced in the dirt read *"Ego sum duodeviginti annus vetus."*

"That's not English, is it?" he asked helplessly.

"It's Latin!" said France at the same time Hans did.

Something very strange was going on. Stranger still was the fact that most of the people from the *Carleton* accepted this profound change with little more than a shrug and a smile. The situation, though perilous, suddenly felt a lot less dangerous now that everyone understood what everyone else was saying. What mechanism brought this about, no one knew—and few seemed to care.

The women and children filed out of the barn, prodded by soldiers. There was much yawning and stretching, but the feel of things had radically changed. Legionnaires moved among the prisoners, dispensing bread, water, and small, hard apples to every open hand. Their swords were sheathed, and no one appeared distressed by their captivity. Children laughed and darted among the stationary adults. One of the farmer's children followed behind the soldiers passing out fruit, collecting apple cores to feed to their hogs.

Not all the women were relaxed. Julie was glad her nose wasn't broken, but she remembered every indignity of the previous night. When she asked about the man who abducted her, his fate was pointed out to her. Seeing a man beaten lifeless, tied to a post, made her sick inside. The *Carleton* women around her took it all in stride.

Linh, sluggish from lack of sleep, was so amazed she could understand her captors, her throat locked up, leaving her speechless. It was Jenny who made the connection no one else noticed.

"The flash of light last night, that's what did it," she said, munching an apple between swigs of well water. Julie asked how. "I dunno. All I know is everything is different since the bright light." That could not be denied.

The prisoners lined up in the road without complaint. Soldiers noisily counted them twice, coming up two short both times. Annoyed, the centurion pushed his way through the crowd, eyeing their faces. He soon discovered who was missing.

"A boy, black hair, this high." He held a hand edge against his shoulder. "The swarthy girl with the bandage on her arm. Find them!"

Eleanor was in the barn, asleep. She had covered herself in straw and not heard the call to rise. Looking dazed and young, Ms. Martinez led her out to join the others.

Emile proved harder to find. The centurion was about to declare him escaped and start a hunt when the farmer's wife descended the hill from her house calling, "He's with us! O great sir, the boy is with us!"

The centurion said, "In your house?"

113

The farmer's wife nodded. "When Aurora opened my eyes, he was at the table reading my husband's almanac."

Sometime before dawn, Emile had entered the house and helped himself to some cider. He sat by an open glassless window and read the only book the farmer possessed, a short scroll containing a list of omens, good and bad, and the best dates for planting crops.

"Who does he think he is, Tribune Titus? Get him out here!"

Appearing relaxed, Emile came down the rocky path to join the rest of the *Carleton* people.

Hans whispered to him, "Are you well?"

"Very well, thank you."

"What happened to you?"

Emile gazed skyward. "There was a flash . . . I was looking right at it. I couldn't see for a while and stumbled until I found myself in the farmer's house."

"We all know Latin!" said Leigh.

Emile smiled. "Yes. High time, too."

CHAPTER 12

On the way to Eternus Urbs, Leigh decided to escape. He had always wanted to, but on the beach or in the pine barrens, there was nowhere to go. The Latin soldiers (that's what Hans said people from a country called Latium would be called) were well armed and knew their business. After the three soldiers were executed for attempted rape, all muttered talk of escape ceased. Leigh nourished freedom in his mind. As their journey lengthened, he began searching for new possibilities for escape. It would not be a mass exodus. The curious passivity of most of the *Carleton* survivors continued. Only the eight of them involved in the brawl at the farm seemed unchanged

Half a day from the farm, they reached a great, wide road, arched in the center and well paved, a real Roman road. Signposts pointed the way to places called Voluptario, Fumidus Villa, and Eternus Urbs. Traffic increased, too. Wagons drawn by oxen were common, laden with goods for trade in town. Farmers pushed barrows of produce, and single travelers went on foot or horseback. Everyone wore the simplest clothes—shifts, kilts, and poncholike garments against the morning chill.

Julie asked where all the togas were. Didn't those old Romans wear bedsheets all the time?

"Not bedsheets," said Emile. He had taken to lingering behind the others, watching and listening. "Togas are real garments, and only true-born male citizens are allowed to wear them."

"I bet you'd look lovely in one," Julie replied.

Once a chariot rattled past. It was pulled by a matched pair of snow-white horses, the most beautiful animals Linh had ever seen. Too bad the man driving them was short, bald, and had an enormous nose, made even more prominent by the wart on the end. Homely he was, but the centurion cleared the road to let him by. Six sturdy men plodded along behind him on an odd mix of elderly horses, donkeys, and a mule.

"All hail Lucius Calvus!" the centurion said after the chariot clattered over the hill and out of sight. He laughed.

"Who's he?" asked Hans.

"One of the richest men in the city out inspecting his holdings. See his escort?" said the centurion. His name, they had discovered, was Durus Silex. "Rich as he is, he won't mount his guard properly and let's them founder along like a troupe of comedians."

On either side of the road were many prosperous farms. The land was covered with them, growing everything from olives to grapes to hectares of grain, still green and rippling like ocean waves with every puff of breeze. It was this bounty, and the fact that many people were about, that gave Leigh hope of escape. Now there were places to hide and people to blend in with. The fact that he could read and write Latin now only made escape seem more possible.

When he wasn't tied up helping carry Mrs. Ellis's litter, Leigh stayed by France Martin and Hans Bachmann. They were ready to run away, too. France was convinced they faced a life of slavery if they didn't.

Hans's concerns were more abstract. He still couldn't wrap his mind around their predicament. How did they—men, women, and children of the twenty-first century—find themselves shipwrecked in an unknown place resembling ancient Italy? How had they started speaking Latin overnight? Why did their captors not seem to notice the change? How had France and Julie Morrison recover so swiftly and completely from their injuries? Hans had no answers. Such ignorance was hard to handle.

Emile loped ahead a few paces. France tapped Leigh on the arm and gestured. Leigh nodded. The three of them walked faster until they caught up with Emile.

"Listen," said Leigh quietly. "We want to talk to you."

"About what?"

Down went his voice. "Escape."

"Really? Where to?"

"Somewhere away from Silex and his men," France replied. "I don't know what they intend for us when we reach the city, but I'm sure it isn't good. I don't want to be a slave!"

"Or die in the Arena," added Leigh.

Emile laughed. The others flinched at the bold sound.

"You've seen too many sword-and-sandal epics," Emile said, chuckling.

"What do you think they'll do with us?" demanded Leigh.

"I have no idea."

"Don't you care?" asked France.

Emile took a deep breath and let it out slowly. "We are in a mystery," he said at last. "I want to see how it comes out."

They abandoned him, falling back near the end of the line of captives. Bringing up the rear of the column were the archers. They walked with their bows strung, but their arrows were in their quivers.

Early in the afternoon they passed through a small town, Fumidus Villa. This was the biggest place they'd seen yet, with sturdy two- and three-story buildings of timber and stone. The road widened out into a square ("forum" Silex called it) that was lined on two sides with ramshackle stalls and booths made of weathered lumber and canvas. It was market day, but by this hour, sales were nearly over. Most of the stalls were empty, and the rest were selling off what they could to finish. A carpet of trampled hay, horse dung, and squashed vegetables covered the square.

"Hail, soldier! What ya got there?" called a scruffy stall-keeper. The table in front of her had a few knobby carrots and runty onions left on it.

"Newcomers for the capital," the centurion replied.

Hans noticed his choice of words: not prisoners, captives, or slaves, but newcomers.

Silex let his men break ranks and buy food from the vendors. Lacking money, the *Carleton* people stood back until the centurion told the merchants to feed them, too. What about payment, some of them loudly demanded.

"Submit your costs to the First Citizen!" Judging by the faces of the vendors, no one cared to bother the First Citizen of the Republic over a few leftover vegetables.

Leigh sized up his chances. The guards were busy eating, drinking, or flirting with girls in the square. Centurion Silex stood in the midst of the crowd, fists on hips, keeping an eye on everything, but he couldn't see what was going on at the fringes of the square. Leigh could work his way through the people, get Julie, and run for it as soon as they reached the far edge of the crowd. If the *Carleton* people made trouble, tying up the soldiers, more of them might get away.

He gave Hans and France the high sign and started through the crowd to Julie. She was with the runner, Jenny, and the quiet Linh. Leigh moved from Julie's blind side and slipped his hand in hers.

Julie flinched and swung hard, meaning to smack the impudent male taking her hand right across the face. Leigh caught her before she connected.

"Let's get out of here," he said, forming the words with his lips but barely speaking aloud. She replied by almost jerking his arm out his socket, so fast did she make for freedom.

"Slow down," he said anxiously. "Don't draw attention—"

Julie stopped short. "You're right." Hand in hand, smiling sweetly at everyone they passed, the Morrisons made their way out of the forum.

Jenny saw them go. What were they up to? Julie had guts, she knew, but she wasn't convinced her brother had much in the way of brains. Still, things happened when the Morrisons were around. Slowly, almost reluctantly, she followed them.

Linh turned around and noticed her companions leaving. Alone in the square full of soldiers, townsfolk, and the *Carleton* people, they seemed to be doing something with purpose. Arms folded, Linh started after Jenny. She hadn't gone four steps before catching the eye of Eleanor Quarrel. Eleanor had been quiet since the Big Flash, as Linh thought of it. She cocked her head when she saw Linh. Without a word, Eleanor fell in step beside her.

Hans and France let themselves drift backward to the outer edge of the crowd. Leigh and Julie joined them. Leigh was ready to slip away right then, but France held him back. He could see Jenny coming, and behind her Linh and Eleanor. When the seven teens were together, Leigh led them toward the nearest cover, a muddy, narrow lane between two houses on the south side of the forum. They had to cover twenty yards without being noticed.

"Where are we going?" Julie asked too loudly.

From the side of his mouth, Leigh hissed, "Away. Out of here!"

"But where to?" She mocked his tone and expression.

Leigh had no idea. He hadn't thought past the getting away part.

"Back to the sea," Hans murmured. "Maybe a passing ship will—"

"We can't get off the island."

They stopped, and one by one stared at Eleanor, who had made this flat announcement.

"How do you know this is an island?" asked Jenny.

"Must be."

Julie got in her face. "So why can't we get off it?"

Eleanor smiled in a peaceful, vacant way. She was so unchallenging, Julie stepped back, nonplussed.

"Come on, " Leigh urged. They still had a dozen yards to go.

They only made it about two. A loud voice behind them proclaimed, "Hello! What are you doing?"

Leigh tried to ignore the voice. He knew it was Emile. Gripping Julie's hand tightly, he quickened his step.

"Wait! Don't go!"

Silex heard the call, too, and spotted the teens stealing away. He shouted to his men, and a couple dozen legionnaires pushed through the crowd and surrounded the teens. For a moment Leigh resisted, shoving a hard-faced soldier away. The Latins closed in, roughly pushing Hans and France into Jenny, Linh, and Eleanor. One soldier made to collar Julie. She faced him, smiling her nastiest smile, and held up a fist. The tough legionnaire stopped dead in his tracks.

Emile sauntered behind them, smiling like an idiot. Did he know what he had done? Cursing under his breath, Leigh stopped pushing and stared at the worn pavement.

"What's this?" the centurion demanded. He saw one of his soldiers still had an apple in his hand and slapped it away. "Leaving, are you?"

"You've no right to keep us prisoner!" Julie shouted. "We're free people!"

"Every citizen of the Republic is free," Silex said. "You are citizens now, or soon will be, once we reach the city."

France was puzzled. Citizens?

Hans said, "We did not ask to be citizens of your Republic."

"It is your choice. Either you are citizens or you are invaders. You have seen the fate of those who enter our country uninvited." Behind him, Emile was still smiling broadly. France noticed Eleanor was likewise sporting an unnecessary grin.

Hans started back to the docile crowd of *Carleton* survivors. Jenny and Linh followed him. France pulled at Leigh's sleeve.

"Come," he said. "This is not the way."

Julie stamped her foot. "Damn it, why does this always happen? It's like we're under a microscope or something, watched every second!"

"Never mind," Leigh said. "He is right."

He trailed after the others, leaving Julie alone. She blinked through angry tears. She wasn't mad at the Latins, or at Emile for blowing the whistle.

"Why do you start things you can't finish?" she yelled at her brother. "You always do! You were gonna manage our band, and where did that go? And the Sunwei convertible—it was mine if you could fix it. You never did! Why do you wuss out all the time?"

Leigh didn't answer. He glared at Emile, protected by a line of armed guards. It was his fault. If he hadn't spoken up, they could have made it.

Back with the *Carleton* group, France said to Leigh, "Don't worry about it. There will be another time."

"Everyone's so passive," Hans remarked. He scanned the crowd. The American navy men, the Irish football team, Mr. Chen and his brothers, Trevedi, what was left of the *Carleton*'s crew—all stood in the forum, munching an apple or carrot. They were supremely unconcerned by their predicament. To Hans they seemed almost—

"Brainwashed," he said aloud. He had a hard time saying it, finding it difficult to dredge up the word to go with his clear idea. He wondered what the equivalent in Latin for "brainwash" was, but every attempt he made to think in an alternate language failed.

Silex had the seven teens who tried to escape put in leg irons. Julie loudly protested. Linh wept. Jenny and Leigh glowered, while the rest were quieted by the sight of bared steel blades. Last to be shackled was France. Emile was not chained until Leigh made a bitter comment about his freedom. The centurion promptly ordered the Belgian teen added to the chain gang.

France found himself joined to Emile by a meter of iron links. Even the Latins didn't trust a squealer.

The march resumed. Some of the legionnaires wanted to remain in Fumidus overnight, but Silex vetoed that. Time was pressing. They had to be in Eternus Urbs by tomorrow night. Orders.

Chains jingling as they shuffled forward, France wondered what the hurry was.

On they went, through the afternoon, along a wide highway busy with foot and animal-drawn traffic. Walking chained together proved as dangerous as it was humiliating. Everyone had to shuffle along in synch or risk being tripped. At one point, Hans got out of step and fell, dragging Leigh and Jenny down with him and badly bruising his knee. They all developed blisters where the shackles rubbed their ankles. With every mile, Leigh's hatred for Emile grew. Emile kept pace, apparently unconcerned.

They passed more military units marching away from the capital. Centurion Silex reported to a passing tribune their short fight with "Ys barbarians" on the beach where the *Carleton* people were found. The tribune related other border skirmishes with Ys. If this kept up, he said, the First Citizen would ask the Senate to declare war on the neighboring realm.

France found this overheard news fascinating. The Latins did not seem to find it strange to be facing foes from a completely different period in history. There were so many things about their situation that didn't add up. France tried to sort things out for a while, but soon gave up trying to make it make sense. There was too much he didn't know.

Seen from the road, the Republic was an ordered, prosperous place, primitive by twenty-first-century standards, but not without civilization. As they neared the capital, the buildings got finer and bigger. Near dusk, Silex's command passed a magnificent white temple on a hill overlooking the road. The style was purely Roman, with ornate columns, broad white steps, and robed priests passing in and out carrying offerings from local citizens. Jenny wondered aloud whose temple it was.

"It's a temple of Diana," Emile said.

From behind him, France said, "How do you know that?"

"By the friezes on the pediment."

"The who on the what?" asked Julie.

"The carvings under the roof," Eleanor replied. She hadn't said two words since being chained.

The temple was half a mile away. Everyone could see there were figures carved into the area below the roof peak, but no one could see what they represented—no one but Emile.

"Glad to hear they have freezers," said Julie. "I sure could go for a cold Coke."

"'Friezes,' not 'freezers,'" Hans said, hobbling along. "It's the wide central section of an entablature, usually decorated with bas-reliefs."

"Whatever . . ."

They saw things not so beautiful, too. At a crossroads, they passed a dead man hanging from a gibbet. He'd been there awhile. His clothes were in tatters. So was the rest of him. A wooden sign tied to his feet read *Thief-Murderer-Atheist* in crudely daubed letters.

Everyone stared. Silex let the *Carleton* people slow almost to a stop. The lesson of the hanged man was clear.

"They hang people? That's not like the Romans," Hans observed.

France swallowed. It was hard to do.

"Maybe they are out of crosses," he muttered.

124

"I understand the thief and killer part, but why do they call him an atheist?" asked Julie. Looking at the decaying dead man, her face was pale but her voice did not waver.

"'Unbeliever' is a better way to read the word," Emile said. He scuffed his feet a little faster, trying to get the others to move along. "He must have denied the gods. That's a crime. Remember what happened to Socrates?"

Jenny didn't know anything about Socrates, whoever he was, but seeing the executed man convinced her she had to escape. Linh wondered how long it would be before someone she knew ended up like that poor man.

Silex barked at the column of *Carleton* people to get moving. The sun was going down. At his urging, the legionnaires began prodding their prisoners along, hurrying them. The pace got to many, particularly the men carrying Mrs. Ellis's litter. Near dusk, one of them tripped on a high cobblestone and sprawled on the road. The front end of the litter hit the pavement, spilling Mrs. Ellis out.

Leigh, last in line of the chained teens, was horrified. He planted his feet to stop his comrades. Shouting for help, he tried to double back to help the old lady. By the time he got enough slack in the chain to reach her, she was up and standing by her fallen helper. The man's ankle was badly twisted. She was fine.

"My God, you're standing!" Leigh gasped.

"What?" Mrs. Ellis looked down at her thin legs. "So I am!"

The others crowded around. Someone asked how long it had been since Mrs. Ellis had stood on her own.

She took a few experimental steps. "Seven years." She took a couple more. "And I haven't walked unaided in ten!"

"Get moving!" the centurion boomed. The injured man—one of the Irishmen—got a lift from his teammates. Supported on either side, he was able to stand and move.

"Forward!" Silex said. "We sleep in Eternus tonight! The rest of you may sleep with Pluto if you don't get moving!" Julie wondered why he threatened them with a cartoon dog.

The stars were out when they first sighted the walls of the city. They stretched away as far as anyone could see in the growing darkness, gray and indistinct but definitely there. Directly ahead, the road led to a massive fortified gate, which was standing wide open. Torches atop the wall and a bonfire off the road highlighted the scene. Soldiers stood on guard at the gate, stopping everyone entering or leaving.

"My feet hurt," Julie declared.

"Everything hurts," said Hans. His knee had swollen after his spill and ached. It painfully disproved a theory he'd been toying with since Mrs. Ellis's amazing recovery. The injuries France and Julie got fighting off their attackers healed almost instantly. Since coming ashore, Mrs. Ellis legs had recovered. So why did his knee hurt so much? Whatever healing agent worked on France, Julie, and the old lady wasn't working on him, or on Mr. Shanahan, the man who wrenched his ankle when he fell.

Silex ordered the column to halt. His men separated themselves and stood to one side while a troop of soldiers from the gatehouse trotted out to take their place. In the interval between, it would have been easy for anyone from the *Carleton* to bolt for freedom. The soldiers were away, and the fires fractured the night, making it easier to hide in. No one moved—the eight teens chained could not, and the rest did not. The *Carleton* people stood quietly gazing at the monumental gate with curiosity, not fear.

With the new guard in place, a Latin officer, younger than Silex, rode out of the gate on a beautiful gray stallion. He gave his name as Antoninus Valerius. To Linh he looked like a statue of some Greek god, with curly golden hair and a smooth, unemotional face.

"Newcomers?" he said to the centurion.

"Yes, optimus."

"A promising lot?"

"Promising, noble sir."

Valerius stretched in his stirrups to survey the crowd.

"Why are some chained? Did they give you trouble?"

Silex shrugged. "They gave sign of wanting to run. The irons were a precaution."

"Take them off." Silex started to protest, but the noble Valerius silenced him with an upraised finger.

"We must trust the gods to open their eyes," he said loftily. At that, the centurion clenched his jaw and said nothing.

With hammers and chisels the chains were struck off. Julie swore at the blisters around her ankle. Leigh glanced to both sides of the road, judging how fast he could sprint into the safety of darkness.

Jenny caught his arm. At her glance, he saw archers atop the wall, watching them. He wouldn't get five steps without being riddled with arrows.

"Where do you come from?" Antoninus Valerius asked the *Carleton* people.

Chief Steward Bernardi, looking a bit puzzled, said, "We come from—from—many places. We arrived—by sea."

"It matters little now. You will soon become citizens of the Republic. Obey and prosper."

Valerius turned his horse around to lead them into the city. France thought of the hanged man at the crossroads.

Obey and prosper. The unspoken counterpart of that advice: Disobey and die.

Slowly, with exhausted limbs and sore feet, the survivors of the S.S. *Sir Guy Carleton* entered the Eternal City.

CHAPTER 13

France's first impression of the capital of the Republic of Latium was how dark it was. Only a few torches lit the streets. After passing through the fortified gatehouse, they crossed a wide avenue running inside the city wall. Dogs darted out of the shadows and barked at them, only to be driven off by shouting soldiers. Beyond the street were many more or less identical buildings, rising up three or four stories. As they tramped past, France had fleeting glimpses of timber and brick facades, shuttered windows and shop doors. This made sense. In many parts of Europe, the ancient pattern still existed: ground floors were for shops, upper floors were homes.

Jenny saw windows on the upper floors open. Dull orange light shone out, the glow of oil lamps or candles. People were silhouetted by the light while looking down at the strange parade in the street. Some of them called down comments:

"Soldier! Soldier, save one for me!"

"Ha, is the army taking old folks and babies now?"

"More barbarians! Aren't there enough barbarians in Eternus already?"

"I like them when they're new! Limbs of iron and heads of mush!"

And more like that. The leering made her skin crawl. What did they mean, heads of mush?

But oh! It felt good to have those chains off! Jenny longed to run. She hadn't run since the day before the ship ran aground, which was, what, six days ago? Seven? It was hard to remember. It felt like they'd been marooned in this weird place forever.

A young male voice yelled something crude at Julie. She replied in the same vein. At that, a clay pot full of waste hurtled down, smashing a few feet away from her. Some of it got on the legionnaires, who complained loudly to Valerius.

He pointed to a door on his right. "Third floor, that house."

Yelling battle cries, five soldiers broke down the door and swarmed inside. There was a lot of shouting and a few screams. The column of soldiers and *Carleton* survivors were past the building when they heard a scream louder than the others. A young man with a mop of dark hair, wearing some sort of robe, catapulted out the same window as the chamber pot. He was soon in the same condition as the pot when it hit the pavement. Cheering their victory, the soldiers emerged from the house and ran to rejoin their company. All had bruised and battered faces. One of them spat a few bloody teeth onto the street. But they had won. The fool who threw a chamber pot at them got what was coming to him.

"Why can't you stay out of trouble?" Leigh hissed at his sister's elbow.

"What did I do?" Julie protested.

Was there any point telling her? Leigh sighed and moved on.

They went this way and that through the dark streets, following Antoninus Valerius on his horse. So far the city looked much the same—meandering streets, house blocks, a few market squares. They also saw an occasional temple. Most of these were modest buildings, columned and roofed like little Parthenons, set in their own small squares.

The first few temples they saw were marked by stands of burning torches blazing by the front steps. One sanctuary stood out. It was much larger, more like the temple of Diana they saw in the country, and it stood in a wide plaza, surrounded by a hectare of open ground. The strangest thing about it was it glowed. A soft bluish light surrounded the building. It cast no shadows, but it was bright enough to read a PDD by. There were statues at the corners of the roof and at the peak. After being in the dark so long, seeing a well-lit building was unsettling. It made Linh yearn for the lights of Paris. She slowed then stopped, staring at the distant marble building. Other followed suit.

Valerius bowed his head in passing. So did the soldiers. A few even removed their helmets in respect.

"What's that, the emperor's palace?" Leigh wondered.

Without conferring, everyone looked not to Hans, but to Emile. He smiled and said, "That is the temple of Mercury Illustro, Mercury the Illuminator."

"Never heard of him," said Hans. "How do you know what it is?"

"I don't. Just joking."

Eleanor linked her arm in Linh's and got her moving before the soldiers decided to prod her.

Not long after passing the lit temple, they arrived at the firelit legion camp. They crossed over a bridge (water flowing underneath) and stopped at the neatly finished wooden stockade surrounding the camp. High watchtowers bristling with torches overtopped the wall. Some official-looking men met Valerius at the gate. They consulted privately for a moment, and then the noble Valerius issued crisp orders.

The *Carleton* people were divided again, not by sex this time, but by age. The oldest people, led by Mrs. Ellis and Chief Steward Bernardi, followed a Latin man bearing a blazing brand. Another clerkish-looking fellow led away the middle-aged adults, and a third took charge of those in their twenties and thirties. Kiran Trevedi, the American navy men, and the Irish footballers departed without a word of protest. Mothers and fathers left their children, who waited by themselves and did not cry.

Leigh stayed tense all through the process. He'd seen old movies about the Holocaust, where children and parents were separated like this. It always meant bad things were going to happen. He was ready to join any brawl that started when parents protested, but none did. The entire procedure was less exciting than taking the London Underground. Nobody pushed or shoved, yelled or wept. Leigh found himself standing there, keyed up with no one to fight.

The teens and younger children were a small group, only sixteen of the one hundred fifty survivors. A Latin woman, about thirty, appeared to guide them. She had a plain, pale face. Her dark hair was pulled back and tied in a simple ponytail.

"Children," she said. "I am Sylvia Alumna. Please follow me."

"Where are we going?" said Jenny.

"To bed," the Latin woman said. "It is late."

To bed in a military camp? What did that mean? Julie looked around for the kind of men who had bothered her before. There were soldiers about, but officers, too, so maybe it was okay.

The Sylvia woman led them to a barnlike barracks, a long single-roomed building with a dirt floor and rows of cots. Some of the cots were already occupied by kid-sized humps covered in scraps of dark blanket. Sylvia Alumna put the girls on one side of the hall and the boys on the other. She pointed out chamber pots and pitchers of fresh water if anyone was thirsty.

"Good night," she said. "May Somnus guide you to your rest."

"Somnus?" muttered Leigh.

"The god of sleep," said Hans.

She left. The young children crawled onto their cots, covered up with blankets, and went to sleep.

Leigh couldn't believe it. He checked the door. No guards. He could see all the way to the torchlit stockade gate. It was wide open.

"We can leave anytime we want!" he declared in a loud whisper to his friends.

"And go where?" France said. "We're in the middle of an armed camp, in the capital city of these people. Where can we go?"

Leigh's shoulders sagged. "Are you all giving up?"

"I'm not," said Jenny. "But I am going to sleep."

Hans groaned a bit when he lay down. His knee was throbbing, but lying down helped.

"Sleep sounds good to me."

"We'll fight 'em tomorrow," said Julie, yawning.

No one wanted to escape with him? Leigh sat down heavily on his cot. It was just a rectangle of canvas stretched over a wooden frame, but he was so tired, it felt like a zero-G bed in an orbital spa.

"Where the hell are we?" he said, holding his head in his hands. His face was sore from his misadventures.

France lay down and sighed heavily. "Right now, I don't care." Hans was already gripped by Somnus.

Leigh raised his head. The girls' side of the hall showed nothing but lumpy shapes under blankets, snoozing. The only other person awake was Emile. He sat on his cot on the other side of Hans, gazing curiously at the rafters overhead.

"Hey, chocolate boy, aren't you tired?"

"Yes."

"Go to sleep, then."

"This style of architecture is not authentic," Emile said, sliding his feet onto the cot. "More medieval than Roman."

"Who cares?" Leigh certainly didn't. He lay down on his side, and though he was stiff with exhaustion, he kept watching Emile until his eyes collapsed shut. The Belgian boy sat on his cot staring at the ceiling for a long time, long after everyone else had succumbed to sleep.

France had odd dreams. He saw a tall figure glowing faintly blue like the temple they saw, walking slowly along the row of cots, eyeing each of them in turn. Someone else followed behind the tall figure, hidden by shadow.

It paused at the foot of France's cot.

"The patterns here are indistinct," murmured the tall being. The phantom trailing behind said something France didn't make out. "No, let them alone. They have been chosen for other purposes."

The shadowed figure asked a question. The glowing figure leaned over France, who saw the stranger was very tall, abnormally so. He felt the blue aura on his face, like static electricity. It made his skin prickle like the touch of a hundred tiny needles.

"He's awake!" declared the voice quite close to France.

The teen opened his eyes and bolted upright, heart hammering. The barracks was completely dark and empty. Even Emile was sleeping, facedown on his flimsy cot. Breathing fast, France got up and looked around. There was no one like his dream around, but he did detect an odd smell—sharp and bleachy. He had been to his father's manufacturing plant enough times to recognize ozone, which was made when ordinary air was exposed to high-voltage electricity.

Shaking, he went to the nearest chamber pot. It was on the floor below a glassless window. He stood there looking out. Someone was there, looking back at him. The light was poor, but he could see enough to know it was Sylvia Alumna. In the air above her was a slowly turning ball of pale blue fire the size of a basketball . . .

"He's awake."

France stumbled backward from the window. Was it a dream? Or had he interrupted some kind of nocturnal inspection?

There was so much not right here, but the great flash in the night, the blue glowing ball, and the lighted temple smacked of technology. There were strange forces at work here, things not part of ancient Rome or the modern world France felt so far from.

Cold fingers touched his neck. France yelped and drew away, only to find Linh standing behind him, pallid as a ghost.

"Damn, don't do that!" he gasped.

"Did you see it? The light?" she whispered. France nodded. "What was it?"

"I don't know. Some kind of surveillance device." Police all over Europe used silent, electrically powered drones to keep watch for terrorists and other criminals. France decided the blue ball of light was a drone of some kind that had flown in the window to examine them while they slept. The figure he thought he saw was just a dream, imposed on the real object hovering over his bed.

He explained his theory to Linh. Instead of being frightened by the idea they were being watched, she actually smiled.

"Thank goodness!" she said. "Surveillance drones I can understand. I was starting to believe we were in the hands of sorcerers!"

She trembled, chilled in short sleeves and bare feet. France took the blanket from his cot and draped it over her shoulders.

"What will you use?" she whispered. "You'll be cold!"

He shrugged and lay down with his back to her.

"Good night."

She didn't answer, and for a moment nothing happened. Then France felt Linh settle on the edge of his cot. She raised her feet and lay down beside him, drawing the blanket over both of them.

He wanted to say thank you, but the words stuck in his throat. Linh's breathing slowed, became regular, and she went to sleep. Looking up at the rafters, France stayed awake until the last traces of the blue glow outside faded away.

CHAPTER 14

All was noise and confusion. Sylvia Alumna appeared in the center of the barracks, beating a brass cymbal and calling, "Rise, rise! Sol has risen, and so must you!"

Men in short skirted tunics were in the hall, pushing wheeled carts along the aisle between the cots. The children and teens roused slowly, grumbling and rubbing their eyes against intrusive daylight. A few, like Julie Morrison, covered their heads with their blankets to keep out the light and noise. It didn't help. Men from the carts snatched the blankets away.

Linh pried her eyes open. She wasn't across the hall with the girls, but curled up on a narrow cot with someone else. Brushing long hair from her face, she saw François Martin, still dozing, about two inches from her face.

Linh jumped up, almost losing her balance. Sitting up on the next cot, Hans Bachmann said calmly, "Hello. Get cold last night?"

Linh put hands to her flaming cheeks.

"Y-yes," she stammered, and fled to other side of the room.

France stirred. He looked around for Linh and, not finding her, sat up scrubbing his face. Bristles of beard scratched his hands. Normally, France took the usual depilatories for facial hair, but those had gone down with the ship. At this rate he'd have a beard in a month or two.

The cart-pushers turned out to be slaves whose job it was to feed everyone. With the manner of college lecture, Emile explained that in some eras of ancient Rome, slaves had to wear headbands or collars that marked them as slaves. The cart-pushers all wore brass collars around their necks.

In the carts were clay cauldrons of steaming white stuff they ladled into wooden bowls and shoved at the children. Jenny got a bowl and a wooden spoon. She tried the food. White beans, stewed with reddish shreds of meat—probably bacon. It was scalding, but didn't taste too bad.

Leigh sniffed his bowl. He thought it was oatmeal until he tasted it. Peas porridge hot, he mused.

Behind the food carts came other slaves bearing armfuls of cloth. This proved to be Republic style clothing—sleeveless shifts for the girls, tunics and short kilts for the boys. When the bowls of porridge were empty, the teens and children were forced to stand by their cots, disrobe, and don the new garments. For the first time in days, the broad group of *Carleton* survivors resisted. Julie spoke for the girls when she flatly refused to give up her modern outfit for a shapeless shift, beaded thong belt, sandals, and no underwear.

Sylvia Alumna faced Julie. "You will change out of those barbarian rags at once," she said calmly. "Or I shall summon the guard to do it for you."

Outside the barracks there were hundreds, maybe thousands, of tough legionnaires. No one doubted for a minute Sylvia Alumna would do exactly what she promised—no one but Julie Morrison.

She glared right back at the older woman.

"Listen up, sweetheart," she said. "I'm not dressing in that crap. This ain't Mardi Gras, and I'm not pledging your stupid sorority!"

Leigh started to intervene. A grizzled slave put out an arm to stop him.

Sylvia turned to one of the slaves and told him to fetch the centurion of the watch. Leigh tried to stop him, but he was held fast by two strong slaves.

No one moved. No one spoke. A few of the young children started undressing. France heard sobbing from that end of the hall.

A perfectly massive Latin soldier returned with the slave. His crest was sideways, indicating he was a centurion. His broad shoulders looked like they would burst through his armor, and his arms were covered with tufts of rusty red hair.

"Where's the trouble?" he said. His voice sounded like a piece of heavy furniture falling down stairs.

"That one." Sylvia Alumna pointed at Julie. Without another warning, the centurion seized her by the wrist and twisted her arm behind her back. Leigh shouted for him to stop. Two more slaves grabbed him and threw him to the floor.

Julie yelped in pain, adding some sharp comments about the centurion's ancestors. Quite casually, he slapped her, and with the same hand tore the New York DeZiner blouse off her with one powerful yank.

As one, the other teens moved as if to help their comrade. The slaves paired off against them. Three circled Jenny, as she was a head taller than any of them.

With no effort or emotion, the centurion stripped Julie. She collapsed to the floor, angry and ashamed. The soldier tossed the Latin clothing on her saying, "There. Get dressed."

He strode out. Sylvia Alumna looked at the frightened faces around her and said, "Does anyone else require help?"

France turned his back on the room and undressed. The male outfit at least had an undergarment, a kind of diaperlike cloth wrapped around the waist and between the thighs. He pulled on the kilt and tunic, then squatted to fit the sandals on his feet. By the time he stood up, most everyone was dressed. Leigh had tears shining on his face. France glanced at Julie. She was tying the sash around her waist. Her left arm was scarlet from being wrenched. She knotted the belt with a savage tug and stood, arms folded, staring at the floor.

The slaves gathered up the modern clothing. Hans fingered the hem of his skirt. It was some kind of thick homespun, too coarse for linen and too light for wool. It struck him as he looked at his new clothes and sandals how well it all fit. A quick check of the others showed that their outfits all fit, too. He would expect somebody to have gotten sandals too small or shift too large, especially in a group as mixed in size as theirs, but everyone was neatly dressed.

All their accessories were taken—PDDs and Info-Coaches (which didn't work anyway), watches, rings, even earrings.

"You will follow me," Sylvia said. "We are going to the Forum Diluculo."

"Are we to be slaves?" Jenny demanded.

"Be quiet and no harm will come to you." She turned and walked out. The slaves stood back, waiting for the teens and children to go.

Leigh tried to put an arm around his sister's waist. She pushed him away with a snarl.

140

France found himself walking between Hans and Linh. She was distant, embarrassed no doubt. Hans limped on his bad knee and talked steadily in a low, confidential tone.

"We mustn't forget this experience is real," he said. "Strange or ridiculous as it might seem, it is real and very dangerous."

"We're going to be slaves," France said darkly.

"Maybe not."

"What else would they want us for?"

"I'm not sure," Hans said. "We've been treated too well to end up as slaves."

"You think this is good treatment?" asked Linh.

"In the context of ancient Roman culture, yes. There's more in store for us than simple slavery."

That scared Linh more than thoughts of cruel servitude. Were they to be killed or sacrificed in some horrible way? She had vague memories of her middle-school history class reading about how in some ancient societies sacrificial victims were treated gently up to the moment they had their hearts cut out . . .

They left the military camp and crossed a green, parklike area in brilliant sunshine. The sun was warm. Beyond the park, buildings resumed, but they were larger and more individualistic. There were names chiseled into marble pylons out front of these mansions: CALLIDVS, OPVLENS, GNARVS, PRISCVS, PERICVLOSVS. At one point, Emile wandered off from the group to finger the gold inlaid letters of the name PRISCVS, only to be guided back into line by one of the escorting slaves.

The mansions faced a grand square. This was Forum Diluculo, one of the main squares in Eternus Urbs. Though the hour was early—only an hour or so past dawn—the square was rapidly filling with the people.

141

Jenny was alert, but quite calm. She was used to wearing light clothing while running, though the lack of underclothes was kind of disturbing. The crowd of people around them thickened. It was a more diverse crowd, too. Many people were dressed like them, in simple homespun, but there were others more richly dressed in well-colored gowns or bright white togas. She saw farmers and merchants, white-haired old folks and handsome young people. The air was alive with chatter.

"A denarius is too much for a dozen chickens—!"

"Wine is good today; try the red!"

"Bread, bread, bread—"

"I heard she left her husband for that charioteer in the circus—!"

"—Not a speck more! Half a denarius is all I will pay!"

Things were so lively and natural, Jenny almost forgot how impossible it all was. It was the twenty-first century, not 200 B.C. She glanced to either side at Eleanor and Linh, who were also taking in the market square with wonder. Traders and shoppers jostled past them without a second glance. In their bland Roman clothing, they already fit in, at least outwardly.

In the southwest corner of the forum stood an elaborate stone platform. About three feet high, it was about fifteen feet on each side and faced with false half-columns. A wide set of steps led up to an open, empty stage.

Seeing Sylvia Alumna was leading them there, Leigh knew they were walking into a slave auction. He would never be a slave, never serve a master and be beaten, abused. He craned his neck searching for Julie. Still subdued from her rough treatment at the barracks, she was a few steps behind, next to the weird Belgian kid, Emile.

A middle-aged man in a finely made toga climbed onto the platform, followed by a man carrying a long brass horn. At a signal, a man with the horn blew a long, wavering note that quieted the crowd—at least that part of the crowd nearest the stage.

The horn blower put aside his instrument and unrolled a short scroll. In a loud but clear voice he shouted, "Citizens! Pray give silence! By order of the Senate and First Citizen of the Republic of Latium, a party of newcomers will be offered for claims. The usual laws of Year Twenty-six of the First Citizen shall apply in all cases! Heed the words of the honorable quaestor, Publius Marcus!"

The herald said "quaestor," but the *Carleton* people understood him to mean an official secretary or clerk.

A fair degree of calm came over the forum crowd. Leigh could see pairs of soldiers here and there, none close by. He doubted he could escape. If he bolted, citizens of the Republic around him would seize him before he got away.

Sylvia Alumna gestured to the first of the young *Carleton* survivors, François Martin. Haltingly, France climbed the stone steps. Publius Marcus waved him forward impatiently. France walked slowly forward, stopping between Marcus and the herald.

"Here we have a young man of sixteen years," Marcus declaimed in a booming, theatrical voice. (How does he know my age? France wondered.) "Educated, literate, and intelligent, yet strong and healthy. Who wishes to claim him?"

France stood there feeling like a horse at a livestock auction. The people closest to the stage were obviously sizing him up. He wondered what the going rate for a slave was.

Two men in the crowd some yards apart disputed over him. As they were shouting at each other and not at the platform,

France couldn't quite follow what they were saying, but they didn't seem to be bidding on him. It sounded more like they were arguing who had the greater need for a young man of his sort.

Publius Marcus held up both hands, halting the argument. "I award this youth to Antoninus Arius Falco, builder!"

No mention was made of money. Falco, a broad-shouldered man with just a fringe of gray hair and shaggy eyebrows, stomped up the steps to claim France.

In clipped words he said, "Come, boy. You will learn the builder's trade."

"I know nothing about building," France protested.

"You have some wits, gods willing. You will learn. Come."

When France found he couldn't make his feet move, Falco and the herald took him by the arms and propelled him to the steps. Before France could say good-bye or anything else to his companions, he was marched off into the crowd.

Summoned by the quaestor, Hans limped on stage.

"Don't let his lameness fool you!" Marcus said. "His injury will heal! This boy of seventeen is very well educated and has a wide knowledge of the world."

Up in front of the curious crowd, Hans shifted from his good leg to his bad and back again. Like France, he didn't understand how anyone here knew his age or his abilities.

In short order, the man who lost out on France claimed him. His name was Gaius Aemilius Piso, and he was a public scrivener—a maker and copier of books and documents.

"Have I no say in what becomes of me?" Hans managed to say. Publius Marcus acted as if he hadn't heard him speak at all. Piso waited at the bottom of the steps for him. He hung a wooden docket around Hans's neck.

"Can you read that?" he said. He was a tall man, stooped at the shoulders though he wasn't very old.

Hans lifted the strip of wood and read aloud: "Piso's Books and Documents. Fine Calligraphy, Best & Blackest Ink. By the Chiron Fountain, in the Street of the Paper-Makers."

"That's my address, in case you get lost." Piso hitched up his patched toga and loped away, leaving Hans to catch up.

No one forced him to follow Piso. Hans watched the bent figure of Piso wind through the forum crowd. Hans called out, "Am I a slave now?" Piso kept going without answering.

In the meantime, Jenny Hopkins had gone up and was claimed by priestesses of the Temple of Ceres. They were three austere-looking women in dark, earthy gowns, with scarves on their heads. Again, no money was mentioned. The priestesses simply claimed Jenny as a new acolyte, and she was expected to go with them. Leader of the trio was Scipina, who looked to be in her early thirties. She had a dark complexion and black hair, but she did not appear to be of African ancestry, like Jenny. Scipina looked more East Indian.

"What if I don't go with you?" Jenny said.

"Then you will be considered a barbarian and driven out of the city," Scipina replied. In the Republic, if a person was not a citizen, he was a barbarian. As a barbarian, he had no protection, no rights, and could not be paid for work. He couldn't even be a slave; slaves had certain rights under the laws of the Republic. Barbarians had none.

Now Jenny understood. The *Carleton* survivors were to be absorbed into the Republic. If they resisted, they would be cast out to suffer whatever fate awaited them—starvation, murder, rape, or all three.

Jenny stepped into the triangle of priestesses. She was taller than any of them by a full head.

"Forward, child of the goddess," Scipina said. "Do not speak until we are once again in the sacred precinct of the temple."

On and on the process went. Those that remained learned this platform was called the Locus Vindicatum, the Place of Claims, where newcomers to the Republic were turned over to any citizen willing to take them in. Linh Prudhomme was taken by a large family in need of a governess for their children. A bearded physician named Zosimus chose Emile Becquerel. Eleanor Quarrel, still strangely subdued, was taken in by a druggist living in the far northern district of the city. The younger children were parceled out to adoptive parents, though strangely, no care was taken to keep siblings together. Even odder, none of the children separated from their brother or sister made any fuss about it.

Leigh and Julie Morrison were held back to the end. At last, Leigh was called to the platform. Given his age and size, Leigh was promptly inducted into the army of the Republic. And who should be waiting for him at the foot of the steps but the same red-haired centurion who had so brutally forced Julie to undress. Leigh loudly protested he didn't want to go into the legions and was solidly whacked with the centurion's baton.

Seeing this, Julie didn't wait to be called but stalked up on stage. Arms folded, she scowled at the crowd below. Some of them laughed at her belligerence.

Publius Marcus eyed her. "Just sixteen, citizens, but with the proud heart of Juno. Who will claim this one?"

Men in the audience made some crude suggestions. Julie was too slight for manual labor, too spoiled for housework, and not intellectual enough for brain work. At last, a woman called out, "She may have Juno's heart, but the rest of her can serve Venus."

Marcus shaded his eyes to see who spoke. "Do you claim her, Luxuria?"

The jeers faded. Most eyes turned to the woman Marcus called Luxuria. She was a fleshy, pale woman in her forties who wore an obvious wig of curly golden hair piled high on her head.

"I'll take her."

Men in the crowd cheered. Leigh, still smarting from the centurion's blow, asked the soldier by his side why they did.

"Don't you know? Luxuria runs one of the best brothels in the city," he said.

Leigh jolted as if hit with a taser. "Julia!" he cried, "don't go with her!"

Young men in the crowd between Leigh and his sister heard her name and repeated it, chanting, "Julia! Julia! Julia!" Julie couldn't hear Leigh over the uproar. She flounced down the steps to Luxuria, who waited for her.

"What do you do?" Julie said bluntly.

Luxuria took the girl's chin in her hand. "I sell dreams," she said. "So will you."

Julie thought about smacking the woman's hand away, but something in Luxuria's expression stopped her. Far off in the crowd, Leigh's anguished cries were drowned out by the noise of the forum.

CHAPTER 15

The house of Falco proved to be an airy, sunlit place, with high ceilings, wide open windows, smelling pleasantly of freshly cut wood. Half a dozen men and one woman were at work when Falco and France arrived. The woman was Mrs. Falco, called "Bacca," though that seemed to be her nickname, not her real name. She was a plump woman with her graying hair drawn back in a tight bun. Her face was friendly, and she smiled when France was brought in.

"Who's this?" said Bacca.

"New boy," Falco replied. "What's your name, by the way?"

France knew his name, but when it came time to say it, it came out "Gallus."

Falco grunted approval. With Bacca following, he led France through the front room of the house outdoors to a courtyard. There, workmen were sharpening tools, sweeping up wood shavings, or hammering away on what looked like a pile of window shutters. Falco greeted his men with single syllables while Bacca introduced them. They were all older than France by a good many years—most were in their thirties—and one, Quercus, was at least sixty. France was sort of amused that one man's name was Nero. He didn't resemble the dissipated emperor of history, being lean and hard muscled from years of carpentry.

Lunch at the house of Falco was intimate. The workmen set up a trestle table on the shady side of the courtyard and brought a couple of benches out of the house. Bacca set out wicker platters of fruit, olives, and fat, flat loaves of bread. A tall clay pitcher held some amber liquid the men drank with great relish. France sipped some. It was apple cider, well fermented. He looked around for water. Not seeing any, he asked.

"Of course, a lad like you should drink water, not fiery stuff like these old men. They need it to keep their hearts going all afternoon!" said Bacca.

"Drink enough and it puts me to sleep," Quercus said.

"Breathing puts you to sleep," Nero declared. The men laughed, all except Falco. He grunted twice.

When the master was finished, the meal ended. The men drifted back to work. Bacca cleared the table. France got up, but Falco asked him to sit down again.

"You know reading?" France said he did. "Writing?" Of course, though France had no experience with Latium methods. He remembered something from school about Romans writing on wooden tablets covered in wax.

"Numbers?"

"I am good with numbers," France said.

"Good."

Falco went into the house and returned with a couple of tightly wound scrolls. He put these before France, who unrolled the top one carefully. It was a carefully drawn plan of a large house. Falco asked France to read the measurements written inside the room plans.

"'Fourteen feet, eight digits,'" he read. Something about that bothered France. Prompted to go on, he read other lines and numbers. As Falco rolled up the first plan, satisfied, it struck France what was wrong with what he had just seen.

The plans used Arabic numbers! Roman numerals were letters, of course: I, V, X, C, and so on. Falco's plans were plainly labeled with familiar Arabic numbers: 14, 8, 76. It was a small discrepancy, but it had a big meaning.

Ever since the *Carleton* had lost communication and then gone aground, no one had any idea what was happening to them. All the crazy theories France's fellow travelers advanced about time travel or the Bermuda Triangle were rubbish. They weren't back in time. There was no Republic of Latium in ancient times to start with, and no one in the Roman Empire used Arabic numerals. France didn't know as much history as Hans, but he knew Hindu-Arabic numbers didn't reach Europe until the Middle Ages, centuries after the Roman Empire fell. They had not gone back in time. It was still 2055, and the *Carleton* people were being held against their will in some kind of weird, all-pervasive theme park. But where were they, and how could they get home?

Falco smacked him lightly on the side of the head. "Wake up," he said. France had gotten lost in his speculations. His new master—but not his owner, he realized—wanted him to copy a set of house plans but increase the dimensions by a factor of four. Equipped with ancient drafting tools—a reed pen, a pot of oily black ink, an unmarked hardwood ruler, and a piece of old felt to blot excess ink, France set to work.

A couple miles away, Jenny sat nervously on a cold marble bench. The priestesses of Ceres had left her there, in the courtyard of the temple without any instruction. It was beautiful there, with well-tended plants and shrubs, and a high wall of honey-colored sandstone encircling the sacred precinct of the temple.

The temple itself, set back from the street on a path paved with chips of white quartz, was not as imposing as Jenny had imagined. She thought she was going to a severe, Parthenon-like place, as imposing as the facade of the British Museum, but she was wrong. The temple of Ceres was small but elegant, round instead of rectangular. There were columns all around of the simplest kind (Doric? Ionic? Jenny tried to remember her junior-year art history class), entwined with vines. A low white dome topped the temple. Along the top of the colonnade were fancy stone pots filled with lush, growing plants. Jenny wondered how the priestesses watered them way up there.

Suddenly she felt a curious tug, as if someone invisible had given her gown a gentle pull. She looked around, but no one was in sight. Then she heard a low, female voice call out, "Genera," and Jenny knew that was her Latin name. She got up, unsure where to go. Something tugged at her again, only this time it felt more like her insides were being pulled, not just her clothes. Alarmed, Jenny waved her hands to ward off the unseen summons.

"Genera, come."

The voice called her again. It seemed to come from within the temple. Jenny followed the path, ascended the few steps, and crossed the shaded patio to the open doors of the temple. She passed through an antechamber crowded with offerings— bundles of lilies and iris, baskets of fruit, even sheaves of cattails tied together like miniature sheaves of wheat. The antechamber was cool and dim, but beyond the sun shone down through an atrium in the temple dome. Someone was waiting for her there. Jenny entered into the presence of the goddess.

Under the dome was a fine, slightly larger than life-sized statue of a woman. A shaft of sunlight fell directly on the image of Ceres, who leaned lightly on a long staff topped by a garland of leaves. Her hair was done up in a long braid, which was then wrapped around her forehead like a crown. The statue was carved from some kind of smooth, pinkish stone, polished to a soft sheen. She was dressed in real clothing like a peasant woman, though the garments were made of fine, shimmering cloth.

It was a beautiful work of art, but it was only a statue, and whatever awe Jenny felt quickly gave way to annoyance. She didn't believe in goddesses, especially stone ones that pretended to speak.

"I did speak," said a warm, mature woman's voice.

"It's a nice trick," Jenny replied loudly, looking around for the concealed priestess who was doing the talking. "But this is wasted on me."

"You do not believe?"

"In gods and goddesses? Not bloody likely."

Instantly a piercing pain lanced through her chest. Jenny's heart felt as if she was impaled on a steel stake. She gasped and fell to her knees, hands clasped to her heart.

"It always takes force to convince unbelievers. Beauty and mystery are not enough. It takes pain, does it not?"

The pain was real enough. Jenny trembled from head to toe. Sweat ran in streams from her nose and chin.

"Stop . . . !" she wheezed.

"A little longer, and you will believe," said the voice.

Jenny fell on her side, hands clutching at her ravaged heart. Her vision shrank to a narrow tunnel. All she could see were the feet at the base of Ceres's statue.

"Enough."

The pain ended so suddenly, Jenny was unable to draw a breath.

"Stand, believer."

From crushing pain, Jenny was filled with absolute well-being. Her vision cleared, and the terrible cramps in her chest were replaced with healing warmth. She practically leaped to her feet. The rush to her head was like winning a dozen gold medals and setting a dozen new world records.

"You are strong," said the voice. "Go forth and use that strength in my service."

Jenny gazed up at the benevolent face of the statue. "I-I will."

Priestesses appeared behind her. They tried to take her by the arms, but Jenny would not let them. She backed away from the image of Ceres, never taking her eyes off it.

"You are accepted by the goddess," said Scipina. "Come. I will instruct you in your duties."

They passed outside. The formerly empty courtyard around the temple was now well populated with drably dressed workers, all women, busily pruning, watering, or cultivating the garden surrounding the temple. Scipina directed one of the gardeners to surrender her tool to Jenny. A lean, dark-haired woman of about forty handed over a pair of iron shears. Jenny stared. It wasn't the tool that startled her. She quickly smothered her surprise. Taking the shears, she went where Scipina directed and began clipping off dried-up blossoms from an enormous bed of iris.

Jenny knew the woman who gave her the shears. She was the ship's signals officer, Ms. Señales. She was supposed to be dead—Jenny saw her go down with the other officers when the *Carleton* sank, but there she was, alive and serving the great nature goddess. Though she and Jenny were only a handshake apart when the tool was passed, there was no recognition in Ms. Señales's eyes. It was clear she had no idea who Jenny Hopkins was.

"I know you," she said. "From the ship?"

"You are mistaken, dear sister. We have not met before," said Ms. Señales.

Jenny seized her hand. "Are you sure?"

Scipina broke her grip. "It is forbidden to touch an elder of the temple." To Ms. Señales she said, "Go and make yourself pure again."

Jenny watched the *Carleton*'s signals officer go. She had a thousand questions bubbling in her head, but to the stern Scipina she simply said, "I'm sorry. I don't know all the rules yet."

"We will forbear," said the priestess. "Because you are new. Next time you transgress, there will be correction." Jenny put a hand to her heart, remembering the pain.

She clipped dead flowers for a long time. The pain Jenny had endured was considerable, but it took more than punishment to change her mind. None of these weirdoes knew how hard she trained—the muscle aches, the pinched nerves, running on bad knees, or how she placed second at the 2052 Champions Club Cup with an untreated broken wrist.

Something else: the "goddess" left a clue behind about the source of her power. When Jenny got up, freed from the terrible pain, she distinctly smelled the sharp tang of ozone. Ozone, she knew, was made when high voltage electricity passed through ordinary air. Ceres, however dangerous, was plugged into a wall socket somewhere.

As the sun set on the day, the *Carleton's* people were scattered across Eternus Urbs. Hans Bachmann was face to face with an enigma of his own. His master, the scrivener Piso, had all the equipment Hans expected a Roman scribe would have: racks of drying parchment, pots of ink made from soot and olive oil, and long tables where patient workers hunched, copying one long manuscript onto fresh scrolls. What Hans did not expect to find was a hand-powered printing press with cast lead type.

"Magister, what is this?" Hans asked, stunned by the sight.

"You are a bumpkin," Piso replied. "I thought you were educated! Do you not know the stilus apparatus, the writing machine?"

"I know what it is, magister! I never thought to see one here! It is . . ." He started to say "It is an anachronism!" but he didn't know how to say it. Nor could he find a way to say the printing press was invented a thousand years after the Roman Empire fell, so how could there be one in the Latin Republic?

"We're very modern in Eternus Urbs," Piso said. "The barbarians of Ys or Ardennus may not have writing machines, but we certainly do."

Hans examined the press closely. It resembled the ones he had seen in Mainz, in the Museum of Printing. It had a heavy frame of wood and a big hand-cut wooden screw held together with wooden pegs. The bed on which pages were printed was a slab of marble. Lying in a frame on the bed were lines of backward letters cast in lead. Hans tried to read the backward text.

"Here, dolt," said Piso, handing him a printed broadsheet. It was a big sheet of paper, thirty inches square. In bold Latin font it proclaimed:

BARBARIANS ON THE FRONTIER!

THE WOLVES OF YS AMBUSH REPUBLIC
TRAVELERS!
CONSUL SEPTIMUS GLORIORUS VOWS
REPRISALS
XVIII LEGION RECALLED FROM THE NORTH TO
FACE THE BARBARIAN THREAT
THE FIRST CITIZEN'S WATCHWORD IS
VIGILANCE!

In smaller type, the broadsheet described debate in the Senate about how best to punish Ys for its insults to the Republic. Hans soon grew bored reading it. Even in this weird retro republic, government proclamations were unbearably dull.

Piso had an order to print two thousand of these sheets. All over the city there were simple kiosks where government information sheets were posted. Apparently, Piso had been busy printing these sheets lately. Ys was being very troublesome, which was good for Piso's business.

"We met some Ys soldiers," Hans began, but Piso walked away to bawl out one of his employees for dropping a small jar of ink.

Hans thought he might get to operate the press, but no such luck. Piso set him to scanning finished sheets hanging on clotheslines in the sunny courtyard in the center of his house. It was bright there, and hot while the sun was out. Not a breath of wind stirred inside the four walls. Hans inspected sheet after sheet for errors or misprints. When he finished a batch of fifty or so broadsheets, a pair of skinny boys came in, took them down, and hung up fresh ones. Only 1,950 to go, Hans thought wearily.

When he did find a poorly printed letter, he had to write it in by hand with a slim, brushy-tipped pen. At first Hans tried to match the rigid Roman font with his brush strokes, but after thirty or forty corrections, he simply wrote in the correct letter and let it go at that. If Piso noticed, he didn't complain.

After sundown, most of Piso's workers went home. Being a *desolo*, an "abandoned one," Hans would eat and sleep in Piso's house.

He ate with the family. Piso's wife, Avia, was a slim, dark-haired woman who barely spoke in her husband's presence (a situation he seemed to prefer). Piso had two sons, Castorius and Pollux, who were twins. Castorius was in the army, in the city's X Cohort. Pollux worked for his father but had his own home next door.

Piso also had a daughter, Lidicera. She looked a lot like her mother, with smooth black hair down to her waist, sharp black eyes, and advanced ideas of her effect on men. She served Hans during dinner, leaning over him to pour wine mixed with water in his cup, passing him a platter of olives and hard-boiled eggs. She was pretty hot, and she knew it. Hans instinctively knew if he showed her any attention, Piso would throw him out on the street—and maybe have him beaten for daring to covet the boss's daughter.

Of all the people Hans had met in this strange Roman fantasy world, Lidicera was the only one who asked him where he came from and what he did before he reached the Republic. He tried to tell her (and her mother and father, seated nearby) about Germany and Europe in the twenty-first century. He couldn't. Though his memory of his own past life was clear, when he got to a term for which there was no word in Latin, he simply could not speak. He tried to say "personal data device, airplane, European Union," or any modern place-name in Germany and found himself unable to render any of these things in Latin.

He felt foolish, brow furrowed and stammering as he tried to describe the *Carleton* and his voyage.

"Ships are unsafe," Piso said flatly. "I'd never get on one." Hans asked why.

"They sink, don't they?"

"I can't imagine living anywhere but the Republic," Avia said. "All those barbarians . . ."

"Were there girls with you on your voyage?" asked Lidicera.

"Yes, quite a few." Hans wondered where Jenny, Julie, Eleanor, and Linh were right now.

She leaned forward, resting her chin on her hands. "Were they pretty?"

Hans glanced her way and saw everything she wanted him to see. He quickly shifted his gaze to his employer, who was gnawing a roasted chicken leg with frightening efficiency.

"I suppose so," Hans said. "One girl was—" He thought about the shipwreck. "They were all brave and intelligent."

"Is that so important?"

"I think so."

Lidicera smiled a lot. Apparently, she found him amusing. Fortunately for Hans, when her father finished dinner, the meal was over for everyone. Avia lit a lamp and led Hans to his place to sleep. It was in the attic, among stored bundles of printing paper and tall jars of parchment rolls. A pallet of straw and a very dusty blanket were his bed.

"Good night," Avia said. "Somnus take you soon."

He was tired. His knee ached, too, though he thought it was getting better. Avia left with the lamp, leaving Hans in total darkness. When his eyes grew accustomed to the dark, he saw slender white beams of light filtering in through chinks in the terra-cotta tiles. Exploring, he found a hatch in the roof. It was heavy, but he got it open. Cool air rushed in.

The light was from the moon. He hadn't seen it in so long, he'd almost forgotten to expect it. Because it was so full and round, Hans wondered how he had missed it for so many nights.

He could see down to the street. People came and went, some on horseback but most on foot. A trio of young men staggered past, singing a drunken song about Luxuria's House of Pleasure. Must be a brothel, Hans thought.

Someone touched his arm lightly from behind. Hans almost leaped through the hatch.

Lidicera laughed, covering her teeth with her hand to muffle the sound.

"Nervous, aren't you?"

"You shouldn't be here," he said, alarmed. Visions of the dead soldier who tried to molest Julie Morrison and the others filled his head. If Piso appeared, Lidicera was the just the type to cry rape.

"It's my house. I go where I please. What were you looking at?"

He moved away as far as the hatch frame would allow. "The moon."

"I like her, too."

"'Her?'"

"Diana, the goddess." Lidicera held out her tan arms to the white globe in the sky. "'Pale goddess, queen of virgins, keep me safe,'" she recited.

She looked at Hans. "I used to say that every night."

"Oh? What do you say now?"

"Now I pray to Venus."

A muffled voice downstairs called Lidicera. Hans suggested she go.

"Yes, yes. It's only your first night here." Lidicera faded into the shadows. Her voiced drifted back. "I hope you're with us a long time, Ioannus." That was Johann, rendered in Latin. When Lidicera said it, it sounded like "Yonus."

Angry words drifted up through the floor when Lidicera met her mother. Hans closed the hatch and went to his meager bed. It took a surprisingly long time for him to fall asleep.

CHAPTER 16

Julie listened hard to the darkness. It was alive with little noises: bumps, creaks, groans, and faintly muffled voices. She had been in Luxuria's house three days, but every nightfall lent the place an entirely different, frightening flavor.

By day it was a spacious, four-story building in the Fourth Ward, a block from the large but tacky temple of Venus. They had come right through the square in front of the temple, so Julie got a good look at it (she thought it was Luxuria's house at first, given the way her new mistress kept referring to it as "our house"). The temple was built entirely of alternating courses of rose marble and red granite, which made it look like a fancy candy shop. There were a dozen or more great statues in the square, mostly muscular males barely dressed. Luxuria explained these were images of Venus's most famous lovers: Mars, Vulcan, Adonis, Anchises, and so on. Venus got around. Julie knew Mars was a planet, and Vulcan was the home of Mr. Spock, but the other names were ancient gibberish. One beefcake in a loincloth looked pretty much like another.

Compared with Venus's pink palace, the house of Luxuria was tasteful, even plain. The ground floor was whitewashed, and the upper floors half-timbered over brick. There was a garden

161

between the front door and the street, surrounded by a seven-foot-high wall. Large double gates protected the entrance to the garden. A guard minded the gates. He was a giant of a man, nearly seven feet tall. Simply dressed, the giant didn't wear one of those big knives the macho Republic types liked so much. Julie guessed when you were as big as this guy, you didn't need weapons.

He was called Ramesses. Julie laughed when she heard the name. Luxuria asked her to explain. Ramesses was the name of an ancient king. Why was that funny? Julie couldn't bring herself to explain she knew the name from ads for condoms.

Luxuria's garden was delightful. Neat as a hospital, it was crowded with flowers and herbs serviced by a cloud of golden bees. Julie was not into flowers herself, but her mom was, so she knew many of the varieties by sight. Luxuria noted her interest.

"You know flowers?"

"A little," said Julie. "Do you want me to tend the garden?"

Luxuria replied, "I do all the gardening myself."

A slave boy, seven or eight years old, opened the door for them. Inside, the entry hall was shaded and cool. A mechanical fan, wafted by an elderly slave tugging on a rope, stirred the air. Four women lounging on couches stood up as Luxuria came in. A female slave took her mistress's cloak and silently disappeared with it.

"Maia, Hypatia, you're free, are you?" Two of the women, good-looking in a loose, lush way, smiled and agreed. "Hera, how's your cough?"

A slightly older woman, maybe thirty, coughed a bit in reply. Luxuria frowned.

"Go to Dr. Dioscorides at once. No one wants a bedmate wheezing and coughing all over them." The woman called Hera bowed and hurried out.

The last woman had Asian features, which surprised Julie a little. She had seen quite a few African people sprinkled among the Latins, but no other Asian people so far. This woman was short and plump, and smirked a lot. Unlike the others, she did not seem at all intimidated by Luxuria.

"Roxana. Was the proconsul here again this afternoon?" Luxuria asked.

"Yes, domina."

"Were you good to him this time?"

Roxana made a mocking gesture of surprise. "Of course, domina! I treated him like a god."

"Which god? Not Uranus, I hope."

Roxana bowed her head. She said, "No, domina." Julie could hear the sarcasm dripping from her voice.

The older woman slave brought Luxuria a book. Julie peeked over her shoulder and saw it was a ledger filled with columns of names and figures. Luxuria checked the total at the bottom of the last page and sniffed.

"Not good," she said, closing the ledger softly. "Revenue is definitely down."

"Competition?" Julie said.

Luxuria handed the book back to the slave. "Sameness. In my business variety means success. I will be improving our variety soon."

It took Julie too long to realize what Luxuria meant. As the older woman beckoned her to follow her into the heart of the building, Julie's knees went rubbery.

"I can't do this," she said.

Luxuria paused in the doorway. A few steps away, Roxana sat down on a couch, plainly watching and listening.

"Anyone can do it," Luxuria said calmly. "Anyone."

"Not me!"

"Why not? Are you promised to serve a goddess as a virgin? You do not look the part."

Julie struggled for a way to say what she wanted to say that didn't sound too offensive, and gave up.

"This is a dirty business! It's demeaning! I won't be part of it!"

"She's a princess, that's it," Roxana observed. "Bred to marry some prince of her parents' choosing."

"Hold your tongue!" Luxuria said. "Come, girl. None of us know what the gods have in store for us. What you do here may not be what you fear."

She held out an arm. Slowly Julie walked past her through the curtained door.

From her couch Roxana recited, "'Truly, Eros, thou art a dunce, and dost thou know the garment from the Man; every harlot was a virgin once, nor canst thou change the Olympians' plan.'"

Luxuria let the curtain fall behind them. Julie muttered a pungent word.

"Someday I shall have Roxana's throat cut," Luxuria said quite casually. "But you, my girl, had better beware of her. She has powerful patrons who enjoy her favors. A word from her in the right ear, and you might end up in the river Styx."

"Are you afraid of her?" Julie asked.

Luxuria passed her in the gloomy corridor.

"No. I have friends, too."

She led Julie through a maze of halls and doors. The house was pretty quiet that time of day. They passed a kitchen, where trays of refreshments were being prepared. Julie saw pieces of glistening brown meat on skewers, bowls of figs and strawberries, and what looked like long breadsticks being dipped in melted butter. Her stomach growled, but Luxuria kept walking.

They emerged in a shaded courtyard. All these Latin houses seemed to be hollow in the center. In the center of the yard was a marble fountain. Water streamed out of a statue of a winged teenage boy standing on one side of the fountain. Julie rolled her eyes at the "art."

Several wooden tubs lay by the fountain, heaped with dirty laundry. Luxuria pointed to the tubs.

"Your first job is to get these clean," she said. Julie was so astonished, Luxuria had to repeat herself, a task she plainly did not relish.

"You mean, I don't have to—?" Julie cast a glance at the floors above.

"What, you? A reluctant virgin? There are some who put on an act like that, but not in my house. For now, you do laundry. Later, you may assist in the kitchen."

Julie felt like kissing her. Hand washing laundry was no fun, but it was better than the alternative.

So she washed. The water was cold, and there was no soap, so Julie had to get down on her knees and scrub with her hands. She washed sheets, towels, and odd underclothes that were kind of like old-fashioned slips she'd seen women wear in old movies. Her first batches were not clean enough, so she had to scrub them again. She did this until nightfall, and the next day, and the next. Her hands turned red and her knees ached, but any time

Julie felt like complaining, she looked at Roxana, Maia, Hypatia, and the other women and decided her problems were not so bad.

Only at night did she feel afraid. Sometimes she had to deliver wine or hors d'oeuvres to one of the rooms. She did as she was told, but she always kept her mouth shut. Julie saw things, things a sixteen-year-old girl seldom saw (or wanted to see). No one bothered her though. The male customers treated her like furniture, and the women did as their natures demanded.

Roxana was sarcastic and cruel, but a woman called Amalthea turned out to be quite kind. Amalthea was only eighteen, but she had been working for Luxuria more than a year. Maia was a widow who had lost her farm when her husband was killed in a barbarian raid. With no other means of supporting herself, she came to Eternus and ended up working for Luxuria.

The woman who called herself Hypatia, on the other hand, was smart and tough. Somehow, she didn't mind the work and used her clients to gain favors and influence. She invested her money according to tips she got in bed. Out of the boss lady's hearing, she would say she intended to run her own house someday. Her friend Hera was a simple woman whose goal in life was to get along and be liked by as many people as possible. There were other women in the house, but they did not live there, so Julie didn't get to know them.

At night, she kept to her room unless called. She sat on her narrow bed wishing she had a real door she could lock instead of a flimsy curtain. She listened, and heard all the little sounds of the brothel at night. It was not as raucous as she imagined it would be. Bursts of laughter filtered through the walls now and then, or singing. (Luxuria had a hired singer, Clio, who entertained some nights. She was not one of Luxuria's ladies and kept a scarred bodyguard around at all times to remind amorous patrons of her virtue.) As the night drew on, the sounds got fainter, harder to identify. Sighs. Gasps. Sometimes weeping.

Where was Leigh? Where was the German guy, Hans? What had happened to them all? Sitting alone in the dark, Julie could not imagine their fate.

Julie was always the first one roused by the housekeeper. Because she was the newest member of the household, she had to accompany the housekeeper, a stone-faced woman named Abdica, to the forum for the day's food. Julie was surprised to discover the Latins kept almost no food on hand. They didn't have refrigerators, or canned goods, or vacuum-sealed, pasteurized anything. Fresh or not so fresh, food had to be bought every day and woe to Abdica if they ran out of anything before the next market. Luxuria had her man Ramesses slap the housekeeper—or any of the women—if they broke any of her rules. By the time Julie was there a week, she got backhanded, just once, for not getting Hypatia's undergarments clean enough.

"What do you expect?" she said when Luxuria made her take the offending garments. They were dingy gray, not white as demanded.

"I don't have any . . ." She wanted to say "bleach," but she couldn't think of the word. She stammered out, *"Niveus— candidus—albus—,"* but none of these were right. For her defiance Luxuria had Ramesses slap her down. Julie fell to the floor, stars going off in her head from the blow. Dazed, she let loose a string of choice invective. Ramesses drew back his hand for a second blow for his own sake, but Luxuria stopped him.

"You're no child of gentle birth," she said. "You curse like a riverboat man."

"Think so? You should hear my friend Melodia. Now she can cuss."

In the forum one morning, Julie spotted Linh. She was wearing a rather nice gown, pale red, with a matching scarf draped over her head. Two little kids had her by the hands, and two others followed behind her, a boy about thirteen and a girl about fourteen. The boy had a wicked leer, while the older girl looked distinctly pained. So did Linh.

Julie dared leave Abdica's side to speak to her. She called her name, and it came out "Linnea! Linnea!"

"Julia? Is it you?"

They clasped hands. Up close, Linh looked exhausted. Her dark eyes were ringed with shadows, and her nails, once clean and elegantly shaped, were chipped and dirty. Linh explained she had been taken to be a governess at the home of a Republic official, Antoninus Livius the Younger. Livius's four children were supposed to be in her care, but they were each in their own way such terrors that poor Linh felt like their hostage, not their governess.

The younger children, Gaius and Drusilla, were spoiled brats who expected to have everything they wanted because their father was a minor member of the government. The older boy, Drusus, was a lecherous creep. The oldest child, Helen, thought she was too old to have a governess, especially a girl only a couple years older than herself.

Linh explained all this in hushed tones while Gaius and Drusilla darted around them, poking and pulling each other's hair. Drusus kept sticking his face too close to Julie's or Linh's, trying to listen in. Helen hung back, twisting her elaborately curled hair around one finger and trying to radiate all the boredom she could generate.

"Are you all right?" Linh asked. "I mean, have they made you—?"

"No, no," Julie replied. "I make like Cinderella most of the time: wash clothes, scrub floors, run errands."

"You work at a house of pleasure?" asked Drusus. His lip was covered with fine black hair, and his thick eyebrows met atop his nose. "I want to go! Can you get me in?"

"In about ten years," Julie said dryly.

"It would be worth it if you'll be there," he said. He brushed a lock of hair away from Julie's ear. She swatted his hand.

"I won't be."

"Then I should come sooner. How's next week?"

"Oh, come right on!" Julie said with mock enthusiasm. Drusus grinned until she added, "If you want a fast kick in the family jewels!"

It took Drusus a moment to figure out what she meant. He reddened. Grabbing Julie by the elbow, he made a very crude threat. Linh called to Helen to restrain her brother. Twisting her curl, Helen looked away.

Julie smiled sweetly. "There's a very large man at Luxuria's who follows us girls, making sure no one molests us. His name is Ramesses, and he's killed fourteen men with his bare hands." She held up her hands as if wringing an imaginary neck. "Want to make it fifteen?"

The color left Drusus's face. He let go.

"Never mind, little Venus. Linnea looks after me very well!" He wrapped an arm around the taller girl's waist. She shuddered and brushed him off.

Abdica called Julie sharply.

"Gotta go. Where are you staying?"

Linh said, "The house of Livius, on Messenger Street."

Just then, Gaius dived under Linh's gown and wriggled between her feet to escape the wrath of his sister Drusilla. Linh gasped and stepped back quickly, bringing her knees tightly together.

"Behave yourself!" she said, voice quavering.

"Can we talk again?" asked Julie.

Before Linh could answer, Abdica stomped through the forum crowd and seized Julie by the braid in her hair. Julie yowled. She didn't fight back. If she did, Luxuria would have Ramesses beat her.

"Bye, Linnea! We gotta talk again!"

"Have you seen any of the others?" Linh called as Julie skipped backward, painfully drawn by her own hair.

"No! Ow, damn it, stop—!"

She disappeared into the crowd. After solemnly warning the Livius children to behave, Linh walked on. Helen had flute lessons with a music master in the park by the temple of Mercury. After that, Drusus had rhetoric and mathematics with a tutor at the Academy of Philosophers in the Silent Forum. Gaius and Drusilla were along simply because their mother wanted them out of her hair for the morning.

With much cajoling, she got the Livius children to the park. Officially it was called the Field of Mercury, and it was used by teachers, philosophers, and other learned types as an open-air classroom. Linh delivered Helen to her teacher, Master Mediatus, and looked the other way when Drusus snuck off on his own. He was probably going off to peep in the girl's bathhouse or harass other people's sisters in the park.

She sat down on a marble bench. Gaius and Drusilla chased each other in and out of the shrubbery. As long as no blood was spilled, Linh didn't care. This was the first time she'd been able to sit down since waking up this morning.

It wasn't long before a familiar face walked by, reading a scroll.

"Elianora!"

Eleanor Quarrel looked up from her reading. She regarded Linh blankly.

"Do I know you, citizen?"

Linh blinked in surprise. "It's me, Linnea. From the—from the ship."

She let the scroll crawl shut. "What ship, citizen?"

Linh bit her lip. Most of the *Carleton* people had lost all memory of their former lives, but the teens who had witnessed the great flash of light that night at the farm seemed immune to memory loss. Now here was her friend Eleanor, acting like she had no idea who Linh was or how they'd gotten here.

"Don't you know who I am?"

"A girl of good family, I can tell by your manners and speech. Where did we meet before?"

Linh drew in a breath. "On a ship. You had to sail without your mother. We played games together on the voyage."

Mention of Eleanor's mother caused a ripple of recognition. "My mother is . . . dead," Eleanor said slowly. "She died in the provinces of . . . plague."

Linh leaned out and took her by the hand. Drawing the unresisting Eleanor to her, she said in a low voice, "Do you remember the boy in black? Aemilius?" That was how Emile's name came out in Latin.

Eleanor slowly sat down. "I remember . . . a boy who wore black. He bothered me, then he—he—"

"He saved you when the ship was sinking!"

Her eyelids fluttered. "Yes."

"Have you seen him? Or anyone else we used to know?" Linh asked. From the mulberry bushes, a loud squall erupted. Gaius or Drusilla had finally hurt themselves.

"I work in the pharmacy of Dr. Dioscorides," Eleanor said. "I've seen no one."

Linh glanced at the scroll as she rose. It was a list of recipes for medicines, with things such as rose petals, six drachms; oil of olives, two digits, handwritten in columns.

"I have to go," Linh said, pressing the fallen scroll on her friend. "I hope to see you again." At least she knew where Eleanor was living, with a druggist named Dioscorides.

She dashed off to find the children. Drusus came loping across the green park, pursued by a pair of glaring scholars. There was no telling what he did to offend them.

Alone on the bench, Eleanor said aloud to no one, "That was one of my friends."

Beside her a handsome young man about twenty years old appeared out of thin air. He wore a short kilt and loose tunic that displayed a lot of his lean, muscular chest. A circlet of green laurel leaves crowned his head.

"Yes, that one," he said. "I've been watching her and the others."

"They do not seem at home here."

The beautiful young man frowned. "No, they don't. I wonder why?"

"Something protected them," said Eleanor vaguely.

Sharply her companion replied, "What protected them? Or who?"

"I don't know, but they do not seem at home here . . ."

He took hold of her wrist tightly. The scroll fell to the grass.

"Who am I?" he demanded.

"Apollo, god of light, bringer of music, and lord of the Future."

He released her. "Very good. Whom do you serve, Elianora?"

"Dr. Dioscorides."

"That is true for now, but I have plans for you . . ."

Linh gathered the children of Antoninus Livius around her. Helen's lesson was over. It was time for Drusus's schooling. She cast a look back at Eleanor. She was still sitting on the marble bench, gazing at the monumental skyline of Eternus Urbs. Though alone, her lips moved now and then as though she was talking to somebody.

"I want you to see the girl Linnea again," Apollo said, "and anyone else like her who is not at home here."

"Why should I see them, God of Light?"

"I want to know what they think and do."

"I will tell you all, lord."

"You may remember, too. I wish to know more about you."

Even as he said it, memories came flooding back to her. Eleanor remembered the condo in Cape Town with her mother, going to the beach, eating curry at the market, her mother's face. She remembered, but everything seemed distant and without meaning, like scenes from an old movie.

"Good. Recall everything. I would understand you newcomers and your ways."

Apollo stood. His feet trod the air as he hovered a good five inches off the ground.

"Go now. I shall be watching you."

He abruptly turned away, blurring into nonexistence. Shivering, Eleanor wrapped her arms around herself. Goosebumps covered her arms. The God of Light is with me, she thought over and over. Apollo is with me.

CHAPTER 17

The Army of the Republic was a lot like a football team.

Leigh Morrison discovered this quickly, and it helped him a lot coping with the strangeness of the situation. He and other recruits were yelled at, made to run in groups, and fight in close formation. The only thing missing was a ball. Of course, none of Leigh's former coaches wore armor or beat slackers with a wooden rod.

"Quick time, quick time!" the centurion roared. A block of one hundred men, all recruits clad in dirty tunics and flimsy sandals, had to run as hard as they could without trampling on the man in front of them—or get trampled by the recruit behind. The red-haired centurion whacked every man on the outside edge of the formation as he passed him. Leigh got his share of "encouragement." The drillmaster's name was Gordius, but everyone called him Rufus Panthera, the Red Lion.

"Worthless filth!" he bellowed. "None of you will last a day against the barbarians! Sword-fodder, that's what you are! Cordwood! No, cordwood is useful, you can burn it. You dungheads are corpses in waiting!"

That was typical of the abuse Rufus dealt out from sunup to sundown. Leigh's group was training to be infantry of the legion, the toughest job in the army. Only the biggest and strongest recruits were taken for the infantry. Lesser men became archers, cavalry, or skirmishers. The officers took one look at Leigh and passed him on to the infantry. It was a compliment, in a way. He soon regretted it.

Nothing he did was right. He was slow, Rufus yelled. He was clumsy. He was weak, no better than a woman. Why didn't he put on a dress and go home? Leigh gritted his teeth and avoided looking the centurion in the eye. Guys who did that lost teeth— or eyes.

Slowly the group of one hundred men shrank. After a few days, they were ninety. More drills in the hot sun, more route marches through swamps and hills, and the century lessened to eighty-one. Leigh wondered what happened to the men who were gone. Usually they vanished overnight, their bunks empty in the morning. No explanation was offered, and wise recruits did not ask questions.

He avoided making friends. Leigh was convinced he could get away at some point, and he did not want friendships getting in the way. It wasn't hard being alone. Like football tryouts, there was a lot of competition among the recruits. Some of them played the tough guy, trying to outman everyone else. Others were morose or miserable, homesick, or just plain terrified. Though Rufus and the other centurions casually beat them, real punishments were far worse. A man from the next century group was flogged nearly to death for insubordination. Desertion was punishable by decimation. Leigh heard about how entire units were punished by having every tenth man put to death. No one in Leigh's group ran away. If anybody tried, the other recruits would have dragged him back.

Leigh had to admit Roman methods were effective. He was in good shape, but after a couple weeks training, he felt stronger and tougher than he ever had in his life. They began to wear heavy leather armor and spar with wooden weapons. Rufus yelled a little less and hit them less often.

At the end of six weeks of training, Leigh's group was drawn up on the Field of Mars, outside the permanent camp. A ranking officer, introduced as the proconsul, gave a short, dull speech about honor and duty to the Republic. A battle standard was consecrated to the god of war and given to the group. Henceforth they were skirmishers of the XI Legion.

Rufus barked, "Levius Moro!"

That was Leigh. He doubled to the front of the line and stopped dead in front of the centurion and proconsul. Long before, Leigh learned the Romans didn't salute. That practice didn't start until the Middle Ages.

"Is this the man?" said the proconsul. He was an older man, with white sideburns and eyebrows, and a trace of white whiskers on his chin. From his heavy muscles and scarred hands, Leigh reckoned he'd been quite a fighter in his youth.

"Yes, dominus," said Rufus.

The proconsul nodded, and Rufus thrust the standard into Leigh's hands. It was a pole about six feet high with a brass plaque on top shaped like an open scroll. The numbers XI were molded into the metal. Atop the plaque was a crouching animal. It looked like a dog, but Leigh figured it was meant to be a wolf, symbol of the XI Legion.

"For your steady work, your obedience, and your strength, Centurion Gordius has nominated you to be aquilifer of this century," said the proconsul.

Leigh shot a quick sideways glance at Rufus. Like his JV football coach, Rufus yelled a lot but recognized Leigh's good attitude and hard work. The aquilifer was next in rank to the centurion. He carried the standard and protected it in battle. Now Leigh was corporal to Rufus's sergeant.

"You have the makings of a real soldier, Levius," Rufus said gruffly.

"Thank you, centurion! And thank you, Proconsul!"

He went back to the ranks, carrying the standard. It wasn't light. Idly, Leigh wondered what kind of damage he could do if he swatted somebody with it. The standard wasn't only a physical burden. A legion's standards were sacred. The men were expected to die to protect it, and as aquilifer, Leigh was supposed to be the first man to fall defending that pole.

The proconsul and Rufus exchanged a few words, then the older man departed. Rufus called Leigh forward again. Apart from the other recruits, the centurion addressed Leigh in the most normal tone of voice the American teen had ever heard him use.

"You have a new task, Aquilifer. Pick a maniple of men from the recruits for duty in the city tonight."

Sweat trickled under the rim of Leigh's leather helmet. He wasn't allowed to wipe it away while listening to a superior.

"I am to command a maniple?" That was one hundred twenty soldiers.

"No, imbecile. I will command, but you will lead a patrol in the streets." In the Republic, soldiers also acted as police. Leigh was getting his first assignment to the city night watch.

"Any advice on who I should pick, centurion?"

"The idiots behind you will do. Wear full leather kit, swords, but no shields."

Hmm, swords. Leigh asked if they were allowed to use them.

"What do you think, philosopher? Use your head for something besides a target! For brawlers and drunks, use the flat of the blade. Thieves you may kill if they resist. Women and slaves tie up and bring back to camp so they can be claimed later."

Leigh vowed he would do his best. Inside, he tingled at the thought he might be able to escape the legion. Tonight would be the first time since arriving in Eternus that he would not be watched and guarded.

Rufus spat in the dust. "Remember, the laws of the legion still apply." Leigh must have flinched because the centurion added, "Having made aquilifer, don't soil my name by deserting. I'll hunt you down myself and offer your carcass on the altar of Mars."

Never was a threat more sincere. Clutching the standard, Leigh asked for permission to go. Rufus waved him off. Leigh did as he was told and chose all the men left in his training group.

Because they had duty all night, Leigh's maniple had the afternoon off from drill. They still had to police their barracks, clean and prepare their equipment, and so on, but compared to drilling under the tender direction of Rufus Panthera, the afternoon was like a day at the beach.

Before the sun set, they marched out. Leigh didn't have to carry the weighty standard in the city. To signify his rank, he was given the special uniform of an aquilifer, a lion's skin. The lion's open jaw fit over his helmet, and the dangling front paws were tied around his neck. Honor or not, the pelt was hot and heavy. Still, Leigh felt rather proud leading seventy-eight men out of camp. Rufus rode ahead of them on a stubby-legged pony. He looked ridiculous on it, but no one dared say so.

At the Field of Mercury, the maniple broke into separate patrols. Leigh had twenty men under his direct command. They were to patrol the ward around the Temple of Mercury, an area of twelve square blocks.

"There are temples, taverns, and shops in the area. Watch out for drunks and cutpurses," Rufus told him. "There are also two brothels. Unless you are called, stay out of them. If I find any man in my century in a brothel with a woman, I'll cut his balls off." Leigh believed him without question.

"Is the house of Luxuria in our ward?" Leigh asked, trying to sound detached. It is, Rufus declared. He gave Leigh a hard look.

"Remember what I said. I don't want my new aquilifer singing soprano."

"Neither do I, centurion!"

The streets of Eternus were dark. Overhanging buildings blotted what starlight or moonlight there was, making the streets as murky as a Mumbai blackout. In Leigh's maniple they were allowed four torches, which were spaced two up front, one in the center, and one carried by a man in the last rank. Rufus told them not to tiptoe around. They were to clank along, talking loudly, to make it clear to anyone in the street that the army was out and on duty.

Not much happened at first. They caught a poor man who had robbed a tanner's shop. The soldiers roughed him up until Leigh made them stop, and then he was sent to the city prefect's building, escorted by two of Leigh's men. Some kids threw eggs at them from a rooftop. Leigh ignored that. They helped a man right a one-horse cart that had turned over while trying to make a sharp left corner. The driver seemed very surprised Leigh's maniple helped him. He was so grateful, he gave the men several squat clay bottles of wine.

"I don't think we can accept," Leigh said doubtfully, holding a bottle in each hand.

"Nonsense!" insisted the driver. "Just be sure to give one to your centurion." He winked. "Hide them from your officers. They can buy their own."

Cheered by the gifts, Leigh's men continued their rounds. From a quiet shop street they marched into a well-lit boulevard. Torches and braziers burned at intervals all along the block. Revelers drifted from one side of the street to another. This was the street one of the local recruits called "Bucket of Blood Lane." It was lined with wine shops and gambling dens.

"All right," said Leigh, squaring his shoulders. "Maniple, close order by fours! Forward!"

They marched down the wide street in locked step, iron nails striking sparks when their sandals struck the cobblestones. People idling in the street moved out of their way, but they stayed to eye the approaching soldiers.

It was Leigh's intention to march the length of the street and go on. They didn't get the chance. A third of the way along, the door of a saloon burst open and a knot of cursing, struggling men rolled out into the street.

"Maniple, halt!"

Well-practiced, the Republic soldiers stopped as one. Leigh said in a loud, hopefully commanding voice, "You there! Break it up!"

The fight went on. One man got kicked in the face. He spit teeth on the street and punched his attacker savagely in the gut.

"Break it up!"

"That won't do it, son of Mars," someone called from the sidelines. "You're going to have to get your hands dirty."

Everyone was watching. The Latins respected bold, forceful action, so Leigh ordered the front four ranks, sixteen men, to break up the brawl. They waded in, kicking the combatants and whacking a few on the head with their sheathed swords. Sheathed or not, a Latin blade could crack a man's skull open. Some of the brawlers ended up lying faceup in the street, not moving.

"Somebody claim them, or I'll have to take them to the city prefect," Leigh shouted. A few people shuffled forward to drag the unconscious men away.

"Aquilifer, should we go in the wine shop to investigate the fight?" one of Leigh's men asked.

He agreed. Backed by another three ranks of men, Leigh strode into the smoky, ill-lit shop. The rest of the maniple he ordered to stand fast in the street.

All talk ceased. A lot of hard faces stared at the soldiers over cups of dark red wine. Under his lion skin, Leigh sweated.

"Who started the fight?" he demanded. The only answer was a cough from the back of the room.

"Brawling is against the prefect's orders," Leigh went on. He didn't know if this was true or not, but it sounded good. "Someone talk to me, or I'll clear the place and order it closed."

A man in a long white apron—the owner—hurried forward.

"Noble warrior," he whined, "don't shut me down! I'm a poor man, a humble man—"

"And a peddler of filthy wine," said a thick voice behind them.

"Shut your hole! I know you, Arius, you started the fight! Talking religion in my shop! I won't have it!" Arius made an anatomically impossible suggestion to the groveling owner.

"Catamite! Get out of my shop and don't come back!" he shrilled.

In reply, a short, three-legged stool hurtled past Leigh's head. It hit the shop owner square in the face. Blood spurted from his nose. Down he went, spraying it all over Leigh's white leather breastplate.

"All right men!" said one of the soldiers behind Leigh. "Clear 'em out!"

Before Leigh could say anything, the room erupted. His twelve men attacked anyone within reach. Stools and clay cups flew, thudding off walls and skulls all around them. With his men committed, Leigh had no choice but to defend himself. He had a baton, mostly as a symbol of his rank. With his back to his own squad, he batted aside a stool and laid his stick hard on the neck of a Latin charging at him. The guy crumpled at Leigh's feet.

He felt a curious rush at his success. For weeks since coming to this crazy, backward place, people had been beating on him. It felt good—yes, good—to give back a little of what he'd been getting.

Unfortunately, there were more people in the shop than he had first thought. They kept coming out of the shadows, more of them, and some weren't armed with table legs or fists. Leigh saw the iron glint of knife blades among them.

"Knives!" he shouted. "Men, swords!"

The scabbards came off, clattering on the floor. The sight of forged metal took the fight out of most of their enemies. They bolted for the door. A thin guy with a long scar on his face traded fast cuts with Leigh, but his knife was outranged, and he quickly gave up and fled. Leigh let him go. In moments, the shop was empty. A dozen men lay around them, bleeding and unconscious. Two of Leigh's men had scalp wounds from projectiles. Watching the motionless men on the floor carefully, Leigh ordered his men to back out.

Outside, the street was empty except for the rest of Leigh's maniple. Leigh pulled the scarf from around his neck and mopped his face. Glancing at it, he saw it was streaked with red.

His second-in-command, a slightly older guy named Aurelius, stepped out of line.

"Aquilifer! Are you well?"

"Well enough. You could've come in to help, you know."

Aurelius shrugged. "Our orders were to stay outside and keep order," he said.

"And what if we got massacred in there?"

He smiled. "Then I would have arrested the killers and taken them to the city prefect."

It was Leigh's turn to smile. "I guess I can't expect more than that."

The gamblers, drunks, and other idlers had fled when the sound of the fight reached the street. With no one to arrest, Leigh ordered his men to line up as before. As he took his place at their head, he glimpsed an apparition in white a block away, hovering near the mouth of an alley.

"Who's there?" he called. Night wind stirred pale clothing, but the figure did not move or reply.

Leigh straightened his cloak and checked the sword on his hip. "Stay here," he told Aurelius.

"Don't go, sir. It may be a trick."

He'd thought of that. Why would anyone bother to ambush a lowly trainee, a newly minted aquilifer? He repeated his order for the maniple to stay put.

Leigh walked down the center of the empty street. All the shutters were closed in all the windows facing the street. Here

183

and there, lamplight gleamed through cracks under doors or between shutters.

The ghostly figure did not move. Leigh half-convinced himself it wasn't a person at all, only a scrap of cloth billowing in the breeze. He changed his mind when he saw it shrink back into the alley.

He looked back once at Aurelius and his men. He waved everything was okay.

"Who's there? Do you need help?" he called. Ten yards away, he saw slender hands and feet showing outside the smoke-gray cloak. He slowed, letting his hand rest on the pommel of his short Roman sword.

"The fight's over," Leigh said calmly. "Do you need to get somewhere? My men and I will escort you."

"Are you Levius Moro?" said the stranger in soft tones. The Latin handle still sounded strange to Leigh, but he knew that was his name here.

"That's me. Who are you?"

She stepped out into the better light. He knew her instantly—Eleanor Quarrel, Elianora in the Republic.

"Elianora?"

"I have a message for you, Levius Moro. From your sister, Julia."

He rushed forward, taking Eleanor by the hands. "Where is she? Is she all right?"

Eleanor leaned away from him, but didn't try to pull free.

"She is well, but afraid. Soon the mistress of the house of Luxuria will consecrate her to the service of Venus—"

"They're going to make her a prostitute?"

Eleanor nodded.

He let go of her hands. "Where is this house?"

"Two streets to the west and a block forward."

That was in their assigned patrol area, but not on their present line of march. Still, Leigh wasn't going to go about his business while dirty old men did awful things to his sister. He thought hard.

"Wait," he told Eleanor. He turned to his men and called through cupped hands, "Maniple, this way, quick!"

The newly trained soldiers trotted to him. He told Aurelius he was going to escort the young woman home. Aurelius would continue the patrol. Leigh would catch up with them by the Field of Mercury after seeing the frightened girl home.

Aurelius didn't hide his skepticism. "Do you know this girl, sir?"

"We . . . traveled here together from . . . the provinces." Leigh knew his explanation was weak, but he was counting on the discipline of his troops to get them out of the way.

"Rufus won't like it if he finds out, sir."

"Continue your patrol," he said. Aurelius vowed he would.

"I hope to see the aquilifer in the Field of Mercury," he said.

The maniple marched away. Leigh drew close to Eleanor.

"Do you remember?" he whispered. "The *Carleton,* the shipwreck?"

Her eyes darted from side to side. "Hurry. Already your sister may be lost to the service of Venus!"

She knew what to say to get Leigh going. Taking her hand, he let Eleanor lead him away down the dark alley to the house of Luxuria.

CHAPTER 18

A single lamp glowed by the garden gate. By it stood Ramesses, the giant guard Luxuria employed to keep order in her house. As Eleanor and Leigh approached, the big man held out his hand to stop them.

Leigh tensed. He'd never used a sword to kill someone, but at that moment, he was considering his chances of taking down this giant.

"No women allowed," Ramesses said in an appropriately deep voice. "Only those working here, or hired singers and dancers."

Eleanor opened her mouth, but Leigh shushed her.

"It's all right," he said. "I can manage."

"But—"

"Do you remember our friend, Gallus?" Leigh knew in his head somehow that was France Martin. He hoped Eleanor remembered him. She nodded mutely.

Putting on a casual tone, Leigh said, "Find Gallus, and tell him where I am, will you?" Latin soldiers were expected to be macho around girls, so he patted her on the cheek, adding, "That's a good girl."

Dismayed, Eleanor stood and stared as Ramesses led Leigh to the door.

"Sword," said the giant. Leigh held on to the pommel. "You must give up your sword and any knives, legionnaire. No one enters the House of Luxuria armed."

Grimacing, Leigh surrendered his blade. "I better get it back!"

"You ask Ramesses. I'll have your sword."

Heart thumping, Leigh went inside. He smelled incense at once and heard the lilt of a harp. A woman's voice sang sweetly in a low, throaty voice:

Wine, wine is not the answer, stranger.
Sleep is not your friend,
Seek peace in the arms of a lover, stranger
It only costs a dream.

A dream and five denarii, Leigh thought. He'd heard enough barracks gossip to know what the going rate was in an Eternus brothel.

From a dark hall, Leigh emerged in a moderately big room with a low ceiling. The walls painted with frescoes—elaborately painted scenes from mythology. Naughty scenes they were, too, of frisky gods, nymphs, and ugly guys with hairy legs and hooves. Leigh did not look at them too closely. He could feel his ears getting hot just glancing at them, and he didn't want to give himself away as too much of a nerd.

Around the room were couches. Men—the clients—reclined on these couches, eating, drinking, and laughing while the courtesans of their choice sat with them. The singer, a plump woman with an obvious, curly black wig, was in the far corner. Her harpist was a downright dangerous-looking man with a leather eye patch. He played remarkably well with thick, lethal-looking fingers.

An attractive woman somewhere between forty and fifty appeared in front of Leigh. She would have looked better without the clownish makeup she wore, but he knew enough not to say so. All the women in the room were heavily painted, even the singer.

"Welcome, young hero!" said the woman with a warm smile. "An aquilifer! We haven't had a man of your stature here in some time."

"I heard that, Luxuria!" said a lean, gray-haired man on a couch behind her.

"You're not a young warrior anymore, Lucius," she replied. "Your fights are in the Senate, not the battlefield. But you were a lion in battle, I know."

Senator Lucius laughed and would have carried on the argument, but his companion kissed him ardently, and he forgot what he was arguing about.

Luxuria slipped her arm around Leigh's. "Your first time here, is it not? I never forget a face, especially not a handsome one like yours. Let me show you around."

She did not introduce him to the other men, or the women already entertaining them. They walked arm in arm into the next room, which was less decorated but better lit. A table against one wall was tastefully heaped with refreshments. Four women of different builds and coloring loitered near the table. When Leigh saw who was standing in the corner holding a tall pitcher of wine, he almost choked. It was Julie.

She was dressed in a simpler version of the gown Luxuria wore, a sleeveless sheath gathered tightly at the waist with a wide fabric sash. Her face was powdered and red rouge was dabbed on her cheeks. Julie's hair was drawn back in a severe bun, a style calculated to show off her neck and shoulders.

"Let me introduce you," Luxuria said. She drew Leigh up in front of a tall blond woman in her midtwenties. "This is Eurydice."

Eurydice lowered her eyes. It was an act, but she did it well.

"What may we call you, young hero?" Luxuria asked.

"Levius Moro."

A loud crash from the corner signaled Julie's recognition. She had dropped her pitcher. Blood-red wine spilled on the tile floor. Julie dropped to her knees and sopped up the spill with a white cloth. Leigh pulled free of Luxuria and went to help her.

"What are you doing here!" Julie hissed.

"Trying to get you out," Leigh muttered.

"You're going to get us both killed!"

"So, you want to stay here? Is that it?"

Luxuria loomed over them. "Gallant Levius, leave the girl to her work."

He stood. The other courtesans stood about idly watching Julie struggle with the spill. No one helped her.

"In addition to Eurydice, I would like you to meet Callisto, Livia, and Daphne."

The other women were older than Eurydice, and all put on an air of languid ease that passed for sexy in the Republic. Leigh had wondered what it would be like going to a brothel. Right now, aside from being worried sick about Julie, he was mostly unimpressed. Luxuria's women were all attractive—the one called Livia was quite beautiful—but their painted faces and air of phony sophistication left him cold. The girls he met in London clubs on weekends at college were a lot more interesting.

"Ladies, I'm honored," he said, trying to sound formal. It came out lame. Julie rolled her eyes.

"What is your pleasure, young Levius?" Luxuria said.

Leigh tried to look interested, but he was too concerned about Julie. The thought of strange men coming in here, picking her out like some download, and paying for the privilege made sweat break out on his face. Luxuria saw his nervousness. She misinterpreted it.

Smiling, she said, "Take your time, young hero. I can tell you're not accustomed to this."

"No, ma'am, I'm not."

She circulated away to greet new arrivals. Eurydice poured a cup of wine for Leigh and pressed it into his hands. He swallowed hard, said thank you, and took a sip. It was strong, and very sweet, like a medicated cough drop.

When he paid her no more attention, Eurydice drifted away. Julie finished cleaning up and left the room, carrying wine-soaked rags in her skirt. Leigh started to follow her, but a dour-looking middle-aged woman wearing a slave's headband blocked the door Julie passed through.

Leigh retreated to a corner and studied the room. He couldn't stay here all night. The maniple would miss him, and if Rufus Panthera found out where he was, he'd damage Leigh in vital places. Really, he might have Leigh skinned for dereliction of duty. The army of the Republic was not a forgiving place.

Julie returned in a fresh gown. Leigh darted over and took her hand.

"I'm tracking down the others," he said. "Once I find Gallus and Ioannus, I'll come back for you," he hissed.

"When?" she demanded in a fierce whisper. "Do you know what's going on here? Luxuria's showing me off to her regular customers! If one of them makes an offer, I'll be rented to the highest bidder!"

"Don't say that!"

"It's true—!"

Luxuria suddenly returned. She was not smiling.

"Young hero of the Republic," she said in a firm, controlled voice, "if you want this girl, it can be arranged, but you must speak to me about it, not her."

For a second Leigh was revolted, being mistaken for a customer, and then he realized this was a golden opportunity.

"How much?" he said bluntly. Julie snatched her arm free and glared at him.

"Defender of the nation! If you are this bold in battle, our country will always be great." Luxuria smiled, but her lips were tight together. She lowered her voice. "For a new girl, there is a premium."

Leigh said, "Of course."

Very quietly she said, "Twenty denarii."

Julie almost choked. She'd been around long enough to know that was several times what the most desired women in the house went for.

It meant nothing to Leigh. Saving Julie was all he cared about. He quickly said, "Done."

Luxuria smiled broadly. "If you would follow me—"

"No," said Leigh. "It can't be tonight. I have my duties. I must get back to my men right away."

For the first time, Luxuria seemed surprised. "If not now, when?"

"Two nights from now," Leigh said, glancing at Julie to be sure she was listening. "But I want to be the first—you understand? If not, there is no deal."

Luxuria considered. "Two nights from tonight? Very well, gallant warrior. But no longer. As you can see"—she held up Julie's face by two fingers under her chin—"such a prize will not long go unplucked."

I've never wanted to hit a woman before, Leigh fumed. Outwardly, he tried to be worldly.

"Should I leave a deposit?"

Luxuria laughed. "I am not a sandalmaker! Your word as a soldier of the Republic is good enough, brave Levius!"

Leigh thrust his undrunk cup of wine on Julie and hurried out. In this watchless society, it was hard to judge the passage of time accurately. If he was late getting back to the maniple, he'd never be able to come back for Julie. Ramesses the guard gave him back his sword without a word.

By the time he reached the Field of Mercury, he saw the rear ranks of his unit marching away. He ran after them and caught up. Aurelius was leading them. Leigh drew his sword and waved it behind the marching men.

"Move on, lazy bastards," he shouted. The legionnaires in training saw their aquilifer and parted ranks for him. Aurelius called for the men to halt.

"Aquilifer, I thought you had deserted!"

"No such foolishness. I can't tell time around here!" Leigh replied, panting.

Aurelius frowned. "'Tell time'? Has the aquilifer been drinking?"

It occurred to Leigh his breath must smell of the strong, syrupy wine he tasted at Luxuria's. He grinned.

"A bit of refreshment from a grateful girl to a hero of the Republic," he said.

Aurelius raised an eyebrow. "Was that your only refreshment?"

"Never mind! Let's not keep the Red Lion waiting!"

At a quick step, the maniple resumed its march. The streets around them were empty and still.

Two streets away, Hans heard the tramp of soldiers' feet and flattened himself in a doorway so he wouldn't be seen. As he had feared, it had not taken long for him to get into trouble with Piso.

It wasn't his fault. He worked honestly and diligently for Piso, graduating from proofreading to composition in just a few weeks. Everything Piso printed was in the same eighteen-point Latin font, naturally. Turning handwritten text into printed words only deepened the mysteries of the Republic for Hans. Though there was a senate, various public officials, army officers, and so on, the real power lay with the Princeps, the First Citizen of the Republic. Hans knew the early Roman emperors used the princeps title to imply they were merely the leading citizen in a republic instead of an absolute monarch. No one was fooled by that for very long.

The First Citizen of the Republic of Latium was a shadowy figure with total authority, yet he didn't seem to interfere with the daily running of the country. He didn't even have a name, at least not one anyone used. Hans carefully asked Piso once who the First Citizen was. He replied, "Our eternal guide and model." His name was so august, it was not mentioned—and the eternal part made Hans suspect the office was a figurehead, an empty chair no one dared fill.

All this became moot when Lidicera made her move on Hans. Considering how amorous she was, she waited a long time, almost three weeks, before cornering Hans in the print shop when her mother and father were out. First, she was in the doorway; next, standing too close; then, she was nuzzling his neck and suggesting things that made Hans blush. He stood up, knocking over his stool, and backed away, with Lidicera in close pursuit. She cornered him and was in the process of biting his lower lip when old Piso walked in.

That was all it took. Though he must have known what his daughter was like, Piso blew up, threatening to denounce Hans to the city prefect as a barbarian spy. As there was no due process in Latium, this could mean arrest and torture for Hans. He denied any wicked intentions, and in the end, Piso relented enough just to kick him out of the shop. While this drama was going on, Lidicera stood by, leaning on the composing table, putting together dirty words in backward metal type.

Being kicked out was worse than it sounded. Hans literally had nothing—no food, no shelter, no place to go, and nothing to do. He soon saw firsthand how rootless people were harassed in the city. A beggar he met was beaten up by the street patrol and carted off to the city prefect, a merciless man named Margentus. The beggar would be held in jail for thirty days, and at the end of that time, if no one came forward to help (and if he didn't cough up some cash), he'd be sold into slavery.

Hans spent his days in the city parks, trying not to be noticed by anyone. He began to feel real hunger. Desperate thoughts filled his head. He wondered what he would do first: become a thief, a beggar, or get caught by the city guard.

Now, in a dark street two blocks from the Field of Mercury, he hid at the sound of the maniple's night patrol. When their footfalls faded, he dared put his head out to see if the coast was clear. It wasn't. Standing a few meters away, silhouetted against the starry sky, was a draped figure.

"W-who's there?" Hans stammered.

"A friend."

The voice was feminine and familiar. He squinted at the featureless outline.

"Genera?" That was Jenny Hopkins's Latin name he somehow knew.

The figure came closer. Pale hands appeared, easing back the drapery covering her head.

"Elianora?" Hans almost laughed with relief. "Elianora, is that you?"

It was her. Her manner was strange, detached, but it was good to see a familiar face!

"Levius Moro and his sister, Julia, need your help," she said, coming closer still. She explained how Julie had ended up in a brothel and how Leigh needed help getting her out.

"I will help!" Hans vowed, and then he looked away, stricken. "But I am starving. Do you have anything to eat, Elianora?"

She said nothing, but took his hand. Hans let himself be led like a child for many streets until he reached a fine, upper-class building on the far side of the Field of Mercury. It was built of the usual brick, but the doors and windows were faced with marble. In the lintel over the door was chiseled the word MEDICVS.

"This is the home of my master, Dr. Dioscorides," Eleanor whispered. "He sleeps above. Do not waken him."

She unlocked the door with a huge iron key. They went into the doctor's dark consulting room, which smelled strongly of strange spices and medicines. Eleanor lit a candle. She used a strike anywhere match—more technology the ancient Romans did not possess.

Two walls were lined with benches for patients. A lone chair across the room served as the doctor's examination table. Beyond that were shelves and cabinets crammed with all sorts of weird organic items used in Latin medicine: dried herbs, pressed flowers, stones, jars of murky liquids, and mummified parts of animals. Overhead, a stuffed baby alligator hung from the ceiling on string.

Amid the homely medicines and Spartan benches, one item was out of place. A gleaming white statue of a god, a quarter life-size, sat on a black stone pedestal opposite the door. In the poor light, it seemed to glow on its own.

Hans eyed the statue. "Aesculapius?" he asked, naming the Roman god of medicine.

"Apollo," she replied, gazing at the image with a faint smile.

He thought nothing more about it. Apollo was the god of healing, so it wasn't odd to find a votive statue in a doctor's office.

Weary, he sat down in the doctor's chair. Hans must have dozed a little, for the next thing he knew, Eleanor was gently shaking him awake.

"Food," she said. "Eat."

With dirty fingers, he tore apart the half-loaf of round bread she had brought, liberally doused with the oily fish sauce the Latins used like ketchup on everything. Hans didn't care. At this point, he would have happily eaten a strip of shoe leather.

"Can you take me to Levius?" he said through a mouthful of food. Sitting primly facing him, Eleanor agreed she could. But they had another task to do first.

"We must speak to Gallus," she said. "I know where he is."

"And Genera," Hans added. Eleanor shook her head.

"She is sworn to goddess Ceres. The penalties for deserting a temple are grave."

"So is working in a brothel."

Though he was exhausted from days of hunger and sleeping in ditches or doorways, Hans urged Eleanor to take him to France Martin.

"There is another like you—Linnea. You may enlist her instead of the acolyte Genera."

"I want them both," Hans insisted. "At least we can put the situation to them, and they can make their own choice."

Something went plop in the dark corner of the room. Hans leaped to his feet. Eleanor took the candle into the pyramid of darkness and showed him what made the noise. It was a clepsydra, or water clock, which marked time using water dripping from one bowl into another.

Flexing his fingers, Hans said, "Let's get going." Eleanor promised to follow as soon as she put out the light.

Hans slipped outside. When he was gone, Eleanor stood close to the statue of Apollo and whispered, "Lord, did you hear?"

"Yes, I heard."

"What am I to do?"

"Let the young newcomers do as they will."

"Is that best, lord? Will you stop them from fleeing the city?"

The god was silent. Eleanor whispered his name, but the statue said nothing.

Who knows what gods think? Their ways are mysterious, or they would not be gods.

Before leaving, Eleanor went to the doctor's closed cupboard. She took one of his keen knives and tucked it inside her gown. To extinguish the candle, she pushed the palm of one hand into the flame. It went out. Her skin blistered, but she felt no pain.

CHAPTER 19

Linh slept with her door blocked. As a servant, she wasn't allowed a lock or latch, so every night she blocked the door to her room with her only piece of furniture besides her bed. The four-legged stool was sturdy, but it wouldn't keep out a determined intruder. All Linh could hope for was that anyone breaking in would make so much noise, the Livius household would rally to her defense.

She blocked the door mainly to keep out Drusus. He was too cowardly to assault her, but Linh didn't want to wake up some time and find him snuggled up with her. So she blocked the door every night.

Her thoughts were harsh when she heard scratching on her door. She said, "Go away, Drusus!" twice, but the tapping continued. She threw back her thin blanket and stalked to the door, stubbing her toe along the way. Biting her lip and cursing silently, Linh put her lips close to the door and hissed, "Go to bed, Drusus! I'll tell your father if you don't!"

"—not Drusus," she heard a muffled voice say through the panel. It sounded like a girl. Linh hazarded a peep. There were two figures outside. She started to slam the door, but a strong hand gripped the panel and pushed her back.

"Linnea! Don't make a fuss—it's me, Ioannus!"

Hans, here? Linh relented. In swept Hans Bachmann and Eleanor Quarrel, looking flushed and frantic. Both talked at once, and in no time, Linh learned about Julie Morrison's terrible predicament. Would she come along and help Julie escape?

"Before you answer," Eleanor said, "know that this is deathly serious business. Julia can be flogged for abandoning her mistress. Levius could be executed for desertion."

"Yes, and I'll be sold into slavery for being a vagrant," Hans added hastily. "It's plain we have to get out of Eternus Urbs forever, and the Republic, too, if possible."

"Where will we go?" Linh wondered aloud. No one had an answer.

Standing apart in the near darkness, Eleanor said quietly, "To the north and west lies Ys, the realm of the barbarians. Southeast is the wasteland of Heka."

Hans turned to look at her. "You've learned a lot. That's good. What's this Heka like?"

"A desert of sand and sun, hostile to all life."

"Can't be that bad," Linh said. "We're on an island, after all. How different from Latium can it be?"

"We know what the people of Ys are like," said Hans. He'd had enough of muscular idiots with swords. "If we get out of Eternus, I say we head south. If Heka has a bad reputation, maybe the Latins won't follow us there. In any event, if we get to the sea, we may spot a passing ship."

Linh threw a light wrap around her shoulders and followed Hans and Eleanor out. Wordlessly, Eleanor led them through the black and empty streets to the house of Falco, the builder. Along the way, it struck Hans how knowledgeable Eleanor had become during their short time in Eternus. She knew about Latium's neighbors, and she knew where to find Linh and France—come to think of it, she was lying in wait for him, too, and he was homeless, adrift in the streets! How did Eleanor know so much?

He stopped so short, Linh walked into his back.

"Elianora," he said, "I have a question. More than one, really."

A few feet away, the girl paused, a shadow among shadows. Distantly she replied, "What?"

Hans put it to her bluntly. "How did you know the things you know?"

"The god has aided me, to see justice done."

Linh and Hans exchanged worried looks.

"The 'gods' aren't real," Linh said.

"Oh, but they are." Eleanor moved on. Her last words drifted back. "They watch us, even now."

Linh shuddered a little and instinctively peered back over her shoulder. Aside from an expanse of brick wall and a few closed shutters, there was nothing behind them.

Hans took her by the arm, and they hurried after Eleanor. They went quite a ways through the residential wards of Eternus, out of the District of Mercury to the artisans' quarter, the District of Vulcan. When they topped a good-sized hill, they were able to look down on a large portion of Eternus. It was like a black reef in the sea, set with many warm, tiny lights. Here and there, a great temple shone in the night, glowing with its own power. Hans was reminded of casinos he'd seen at Nice and Monaco, classical piles bathed in garish light all through the night. Even so, Eternus was a mighty sight. None of them had ever seen so much of it at one time before.

"How many people live here, do you think?" Linh asked.

"Half a million?" guessed Hans.

"Three hundred forty-nine thousand, six hundred sixty-two," Eleanor recited. For some reason, the precision of her

200

answer made Hans laugh. Linh joined in, a little titter she hid behind her hand.

"That's only a guess," Eleanor said, deadpan. Hans and Linh laughed harder.

They found the house of Falco. It was shut tight. Hans considered boosting Linh over the wall surrounding the rear courtyard, but she spotted shards of sharp glass imbedded in the top of the wall. They were debating how to get in when they heard the watch coming. Hans hid in a deep doorway while Linh and Eleanor pretended to be strolling down the street. The watch—eight men from the XXIII Legion—passed by, marching in close order. They eyed the girls, but Linh looked away so haughtily, they laughed and marched on. Hans emerged when they were gone.

"There's no easy way in," he said.

Just then, a door in the courtyard wall opened. A man emerged with a large jar under his arm. He poured the contents in the gutter and started back. Linh darted out quiet as a bird. The man let the door shut, and she slipped the hem of her shawl under the latch as it closed. When they heard the inside door close, she waved her companions over.

"I have the latch!" she whispered. Carefully they pulled up on her shawl. The latch slipped off its hook. The door was open!

They crossed the cluttered courtyard in single file, Hans and Linh tiptoeing, and Eleanor gliding with uncanny silence. There were timber frames under construction, piles of bricks, and wooden steps being cut out and pegged together. They avoided all this. Eleanor led them to a covered porch on the south side of the yard.

She pointed to the second door. Hans tried the latch. It yielded. One by one, they slipped inside.

There was no safe way to wake France, so Hans clamped a hand over his mouth while Linh knelt in a sliver of light cast by an open atrium. France flinched hard, but instantly relaxed when he saw Linh spliced by shadows beside him.

Hans lifted his hand.

"What the hell are you doing?" France said, too loud. Eleanor, by the door, put a finger to her lips.

"How many of you are here?"

"Ioannes, Linnea, Elianora."

France sat up. He wasn't wearing anything but a sort of breechcloth. Linh turned away, redder than usual.

Hans outlined their problem. France listened gravely without revealing anything he thought or felt.

"I'm doing well here," he said when Hans finished. "I've discovered I like woodworking and house building."

Hans stared. Linh, facing away, said, "So you're happy to stay here and see Julia end up a prostitute?"

"I didn't say that."

"So, will you join us?" asked Hans.

France drew up his knees and locked his arms around them.

"Have you thought more about why we're here—and where 'here' is?" He let the question hang in the air and went on. "I have some ideas."

"What about Julia—?"

"Julia can wait a moment. I want to say aloud some of the things I've been thinking." France lowered his chin to his arms. "First, we never left our time. It's still the twenty-first century and still planet Earth we're on. Agreed?" Hans and Linh said yes. Eleanor said nothing.

"This place is exactly where we think it is—the North Atlantic ocean, somewhere between Europe and North America."

"But there's nothing there," said Linh. "A few islands, like Ireland and Iceland, but no place like this!"

"And yet here we are," said France. "In this parody of ancient Rome. With Arabic numerals and electrically charged arrowheads."

Hans's voice rose. "They have printing presses and moveable type!"

"And matches," said Linh.

"We're not back in time. This place is some kind of secret enclave, hidden from the outside world. How, I don't know. But I am sure whoever runs this place caused the wreck of the *Carleton.*"

"Why would they do that?" asked Linh.

"Fresh blood," Hans said, catching on. "'Newcomers,' they called us. They captured us alive and brought us to the city to be assimilated—"

"They've done this before!" Linh cried. Eleanor, by the door, whispered, "Shh!"

"Many times, probably," said France. "Think of all the planes and ships that have disappeared in the Atlantic. Hundreds of ships and planes, thousands of people! We're dealing with amazing technology, very powerful. They can brainwash people into believing they live in an ancient Roman republic. They made us speak Latin, all in a flash."

Eleanor cleared her throat. The others glanced at her. She turned away to peek out the door, diligently watching for trouble.

"Most amazing of all, they healed me instantly when I was badly wounded." France's hand went to the spot over his kidney where the soldier had stabbed him. There wasn't even a scar, but he knew exactly where the blade had gone in.

"Who has such power?" Linh said.

France stood up. "That, I don't know."

"All very interesting," Hans said. "But what about Julia and Levius? If he tries to help his sister alone, they'll kill him, and maybe her, too."

"Who knows how to find Levius?" They looked to Eleanor, who nodded slightly. "Ask him to meet us on the Field of Mercury tomorrow night, by the Temple of Mercury."

"What if he can't get away?" Linh said.

"Then he'd better get used to the idea of his sister serving Venus in the house of Luxuria."

Eleanor said, "I will get him there. At what hour?"

France glanced up through the atrium. "As soon after sundown as he can manage. We'll need all the darkness we can get to cover our escape."

"Are we all going?" Hans said. "If so, I want Genera to go, too."

"What about Aemilius?"

None of them had thought about Emile Becquerel. "I think he succumbed to the brainwashing like all the others," France said.

Hans and France were not allowed to approach the Temple of Ceres, being male, so Linh offered to find Jenny and tell her what was happening. If she had been brainwashed, too, then they would have to leave her behind.

Hans and Eleanor said good-bye and crept out. Before Linh could follow them, France caught her by the hand.

He focused hard and tried to say "Take care!" in French, but what came out was *"Commodo exsisto curiosus!"*

When she did not pull away, he took the chance and touched his cheek to hers. He felt a flare of warmth there, and Linh slipped away. Then France was alone in the empty darkness of his room.

CHAPTER 20

Jenny stood in line to greet the sun. As the newest and least of the priestesses, her place was behind all the others. Through a veil of sheer linen, she saw the rose crescent of sunlight spread across the eastern horizon, go amber, and then suffuse the sky with clear white light.

"Ave! Ave!" chanted the older priestesses. The lesser servants of the goddess, not allowed to speak, shook tinkly instruments called sistrums in time with their elders' song. This went on until the sun was fully risen.

Enough already, Jenny thought. No punishing pain followed her disrespectful thought. She wasn't surprised. She had learned that the infallible, all-powerful goddess was none of those things. Ceres could punish you for acting or speaking sacrilegiously, but she couldn't read minds. This suggested something very concrete and mundane was at work. Cameras? Microphones? Somehow, the goddess's senses were no better than Jenny's, though her wrath was more painful.

After greeting the sun, the temple was ritually cleaned, which meant a real scrub down with primitive brooms, mops, but no useful cleaners, not even soap. The garden detail went to work pruning and weeding, watering and debugging the temple grounds. It all reminded Jenny of being in some fanatical organic nursery, with a thick layer of pagan superstition on top.

She was surprised to have a visitor in the midst of her duties weeding the flower beds. No one ever came to see the priestesses except important officials or wealthy patrons seeking the goddess's help. When the second senior hierophantess Urgula called Jenny away from her work, her first thought was she'd done something wrong. Urgula, a humorless woman in her midfifties with iron-gray hair, never had a kind word about Jenny's work.

"Someone to see you, Genera," she said. She was quite calm about it.

"Who is it?"

"Her."

Urgula pointed to a columned gazebolike structure standing thirty yards from the temple. It was a shrine of Proserpina, the daughter of Ceres kidnapped and taken to the underworld by dirty old Pluto, god of the dead.

"I didn't ask anyone here," Jenny said quickly.

"It's all right. She has the grace of the gods with her. Go and speak to her, then return to your duties."

Jenny was amazed. Who was this visitor that grumpy Urgula showed so much respect for? She hitched up her annoyingly long skirt and crossed the still dewy grass to the shrine. The person waiting there was a woman of modest height, wrapped in a homespun gown. Her head was modestly covered. Only at arm's length did she recognize Eleanor Quarrel, from the *Carleton*.

"Good god!" Jenny said. "How did you get here?"

"Good god indeed," Eleanor replied. "Do you remember Gallus, Ioannes, and the fair Linnea?"

In her mind, these names were translated into France, Hans, and Linh. Jenny vowed she remembered them well.

"They need you."

She explained, in cool words and simple gestures, the plight of Julie Morrison and how the group of teens planned to help her escape.

"You'll all have to go if that happens," Jenny said, dropping into a whisper. She asked when the rescue plot was to take place.

"Tonight."

Jenny rocked back against a cold stone column. "So soon?"

Eleanor said, "Julia's mistress is determined to initiate her into the mysteries of Venus." Under the euphemisms, Jenny got the message. Julie's days as Cinderella were ending. It was time to go to the ball.

"I'm with you!" Jenny hissed. "This place is driving me crazy! Rules, rules, rules, a lot of ancient claptrap designed to keep the young ones working for the old ones!" She paused, waiting for the lance of pain to strike. Nothing happened. She went on, "After sunset we're confined to our dorm, but I can get out. The windows are high, but not too high for me!"

Standing next to the statue of Proserpina, Eleanor looked as stone-faced as the goddess. "Be by the Temple of Mercury as soon after dark as you can. We will be waiting."

Eleanor turned to go. Jenny said, "What about that weird kid Aemilius?"

"No one has seen him. Gallus says he must have lost his memory, like the others."

She walked quickly away, feet kicking up the hem of her long gown. Despite her message, Jenny had the odd feeling Eleanor was angry for some reason. Did she not approve of their escape? Why would that be so?

The day passed in a dull blur. She had never longed for sunset so much in her life. Her preoccupation was so high, she did all her chores more quickly and thoroughly than she ever had, which won her praise from Scipina herself. Jenny tried to look humble, but inside she was thinking, I'll soon be rid of you!

They sang hymns to the goddess after dinner and went to their quarters for the night. Jenny was tired and dropped solidly onto her bare straw mattress. It would have been easy to fall asleep until dawn, but thoughts raced about in her head and kept her awake.

The room around her was filled with even breathing and soft sighs. Jenny sat up, pulled on her sandals, and sat perched on the edge of the bed, waiting for one of the watchdogs—Urgula, for example—to sense her being awake. No one stirred. Jenny picked up the chamberpot at the foot of her bed. If stopped, she could claim she was taking it out to empty or else break it over her interrogator's head. Either way, she was going.

She had only the vaguest notion of where the Temple of Mercury was. The dim streets outside the sacred enclave of Ceres were busy as Latins hurried about finishing their last business of the day. Because she was garbed as a priestess, no one bothered Jenny. The laws about molesting clerics were severe. She heard a story once about a drunken merchant who laid hands on a priestess of Diana. He was tied to a pillar and shot full of silver arrows by the other women of the temple.

A mile away, Leigh Morrison was polishing his equipment. He had an inspection the next day before the proconsul, and Rufus Panthera meant every man in his cohort to pass perfectly. For all his hard work, he had earned a night off, and he bluntly told Rufus he intended to visit the House of Luxuria. The grim centurion approved, but he reminded Leigh that Luxuria's fees were high. There was another house, Berenice's, that many of the legion patronized. They knew how to treat a soldier there, he said.

Leigh pretended to take the advice to heart. He had a few denarii saved up, and he won some more by introducing his comrades in the cohort to Vegas-style craps. He was still short of the twenty denarii he promised to pay Luxuria. All he could do was pad his purse with copper coins and hope it would fool Luxuria long enough to get Julie out.

Rufus Panthera inspected Leigh's maniple and passed them. He offered a rare smile.

"You louts are finally turning into soldiers," he said. "That's good. One day you may be worthy of the legions."

The men cheered themselves, and those with leave dispersed. Leigh lingered. When the barracks was empty, he slipped his newly honed and polished short sword, his gladius, under his tunic and threw a wool cloak over his shoulders to help hide it. He nodded to the guards at the camp gate, who knew about his destination and offered to take his place.

You wish, he thought. The idea of any of these macho creeps getting near Julie made his blood boil.

A block outside camp, he was picked up by Eleanor. She was standing so still inside a street shrine, Leigh mistook her for a votive statue. There were little shrines like this all over Eternus, mostly devoted to foreign gods like Isis or Serapis. They were tolerated, but only the great national gods had real temples.

Eleanor emerged from the tiny roof enclosure so quietly, Leigh drew back, his hand going for the hilt of his sword. She saw this and froze.

"You are armed!"

"Damn right I am. This is going to work."

"Will you shed blood?"

He stepped around her and kept going. Hobbled a bit by her long gown, Eleanor tried to keep up.

Dusk became night just about the moment they reached the Field of Mercury. They found France and Linh standing beneath a chestnut tree—rather closely, Leigh noticed—and as they drew near, Hans came out of the lengthening shadows on the lawn between the street and a row of ceremonial cedars. They came together in a small circle. No one said anything until Hans murmured, "Genera?"

"I spoke to her," Eleanor replied. "She's coming."

"We'll wait," said France.

"Not too long," Leigh said.

In the Field of Mercury, as the stars came out, darkness closed in on them. Eleanor became a statue again. Linh shivered, even though the night was mild. France stood closer to her, and then took her hand. Leigh stood with arms folded, looking very martial in his kilt and military cloak. Only Hans moved. He walked in a slow circle around the others, studying the surrounding darkness as if he could pierce it with his eyes alone.

They heard a soft, rapid thumping. Drawing together, they watched Jenny emerge from Maia Way, the large street that made up the east border of the park. Her sandals dangled from her hands as she ran, barefoot.

She arrived, breathing hard. "Dammit," she said, "to be this winded after running a little more than a mile! I am out of shape!" Linh remarked she hadn't even broken a sweat.

Leigh interrupted any further homecoming. "We gotta go."

It would be suspicious for them to go to Luxuria's together, so they broke up into two groups. Leigh, France, and Hans went together, posing as guys on a night out. They talked loudly and laughed, being as obvious as possible. Linh, Jenny, and Eleanor trailed by a full block, as quiet as they could be. Only once were they bothered, by a pair of workmen reeking of wine. As soon as they saw Jenny's priestess garb, they turned pale and made themselves scarce.

In the street outside Luxuria's, the boys saw three men waiting to enter the house. The giant guard, Ramesses, checked them for weapons. He was thorough, and found a dagger on one man and brass knuckles on another.

Leigh put out his arm to halt his friends.

"We can't go straight in," he said. "I have a sword."

"Give it to the giant and go in," said Hans.

"No. I might need it."

"What, then?"

Leigh beckoned them to follow him. He circled around Luxuria's usual entrance. The garden wall was a little more than head-high, but the enclosure was so small Ramesses couldn't fail to see them climb over. Leigh slipped into a very narrow alley along the north side of the house. He had to moved sideways to fit. France and Hans, less muscular, found the tight gap easier going.

Leigh stopped when he judged he was halfway into the alley. Two faceless walls loomed above him. Luxuria's had a ledge about two and a half meters up, and there were windows facing the alley on the second floor.

"Can you get up there?" he whispered to France. The latter shrugged.

"I'll try."

Hans and Leigh boosted France up to the ledge. He got a leg up, and then rolled onto a wide ledge. The second story of Luxuria's house was set back a little. France sat up, letting his feet dangle into the darkness. He leaned forward and looked down. It was so dark, he couldn't see his friends right below him.

"It's wide enough to walk on!" he said.

A voice floated up. "Can you get in a window?"

France stood up and crept along the slate ledge, heart hammering. The nearest window was covered with a louvered shutter. He pried the slats apart with his fingers and peered inside. Recoiling, he remembered they were sneaking into a brothel. What he'd seen convinced him this was not a room they should try to enter.

He sidled down the ledge, trying the next window. The room beyond the shutter was as black as Pluto's heart. France strained to hear if anything was going on inside. He heard nothing. Growing bolder, he gave the shutter a hard tug. It was firmly latched.

Below, Leigh gnawed his lip. Time was passing, and the longer they were gone, the more likely they were to be caught by somebody—Rufus, Jenny's priestesses, France's builder . . . He was about to risk calling out when France's ghostly face appeared above them, several yards back toward the street.

"Here!" he hissed.

Hans and Leigh got under him. France said, "Give me your sword, Levius!" Leigh didn't want to surrender the weapon until France reminded him he couldn't get it past Ramesses. There's a window up here, leading to an empty room, France told him. Send Hans up with the sword. They'd hide in the room. When Leigh found Julie, he could bring her upstairs to the same empty room and they would all escape.

Leigh agreed. He hung his gladius around Hans's neck, then braced himself while Hans climbed him like a ladder. France grabbed his friend by the tunic and hauled him up to the ledge.

"I'm going in the front door," Leigh called out hoarsely. "Wait for me."

France and Hans slid along to the empty room. Hans used the sword to pry the shutter open. It made a single loud squeak, and the latch pin fell to the floor inside with a tinkle. Both of them held absolutely still, waiting for light and discovery to lash out at them. When all remained quiet, France and Hans climbed in the window. The empty room turned out to be a lavatory. Groping around, they found a pedestal sink and commode, carved from cold, hard marble.

"Must be a shock," Hans murmured, thinking of what it must be like to sit on frigid marble.

"Check the door," France said a little louder. Hans found it opposite the window. There was no latch on it. Standards of privacy were different in the Republic.

France rolled a heavy urn against the door. If anyone tried to come in, they would have to make enough effort that they would surely be heard.

From the street, Jenny, Linh, and Eleanor watched a slow but steady stream of patrons arrive at Luxuria's door. Some arrived on foot. Affluent Eternus men came in sedan chairs borne on the arms of burly porters. Before long, a dashing figure on horseback clattered up to the garden gate. He was a silver-haired man in fancy armor, with a long scarlet cape that covered his horse's hindquarters. He was followed closely by two other riders carrying strange-looking objects on their shoulders—bundles of rods about a yard long, in which was stuck a long-handled axe. The axe head stuck straight out.

"An important man," Linh said, shrinking into the shadows. "Those men with him are lictors, special honor guards."

"Honor guards at a brothel?" said Jenny.

"It is Consul Marius," Eleanor said. "A very good friend of Luxuria." Linh and Jenny didn't ask how Eleanor knew this.

213

Consul Marius leaped lightly down from his horse, tossed the reins to one of the lictors, and went through the garden gate, laughing. From her spot, Jenny saw the giant doorman did not search one of the chief officers of the Republic for weapons.

She shifted against the sunken door. Where were Leigh and the others? Could he get Julie out with Marius on the scene? Maybe it would help. Maybe everyone inside would be so busy bowing and scraping and kissing the consul's hand, they wouldn't notice the Morrisons slipping out . . .

Leigh presented himself at the gate after Consul Marius passed inside. The lictors took up posts in the street, guarding the entrance. Leigh eyed them, but put on a lecherous leer and strode boldly into the garden.

"Wait," said Ramesses in his deep voice. He patted Leigh down with hands the size of tennis rackets. His purse, stuffed with coins, got only a brief squeeze.

"Pass, my lord," said Ramesses, standing back and sweeping ahead of Leigh with his enormous arm. Trying to look haughty, Leigh swaggered into the house.

Quite a party was going on. Clio was singing at the top of her lungs, with pipers backing her up, and a boy playing a tambor, a sort of flat, round drum. Luxuria's ladies were in their finest gowns—and some were already out of them—while Luxuria's patrons drank and cheered. Leigh stood unnoticed in the entry hall for a while until the woman herself appeared.

"Young hero! You return, and on an auspicious night!" she declared. From her rosy complexion and louder than normal tone, Leigh decided Luxuria had been sampling her own wine.

He hefted his purse. "Do you remember our bargain? I brought the money."

She smiled unpleasantly. "Noble warrior of the legion! How was I to know you would bring me such a sum for the treasure you desire? Alas! The flower is being picked even now."

Leigh started forward, hands clenched. Luxuria drew back, surprised.

"Oh, the ardor of youth! I envy you!"

"Where is Julia?" he said, struggling to keep his voice under control.

"Giving herself to Venus, as we speak."

He bolted past her into the main room, where the revelers had drawn back to make room for Consul Marius. Leigh blundered through several standing couples, getting colorful, nasty comments for his clumsiness. Not seeing Julie in the room, he made for the corridor to the private rooms.

Luxuria caught his arm from behind.

"Behave yourself, hero of the Republic. What is, shall be," she said calmly.

He broke her grip with an ugly word. Luxuria paled. Her mouth set in a short, hard line. Without another word, she turned and walked briskly through the crowded room, not touching anyone.

Leigh had no doubt she was summoning her servants, starting with Ramesses, to have him thrown out. He hurried down the corridor. Luxuria's private rooms did not have doors, merely curtains. He stopped at each one, saying, "Julia! Julia, are you there? It's Levius!"

When he was ignored, he swept back the curtain to see if she was inside. He interrupted four rooms. At the fifth, he was about to call his sister again when he heard loud, unfriendly voices from the party in the main room. Consul Marius would not be happy if his recreation was spoiled.

"Julia!"

He was answered by a groan. Not a guttural groan of effort, but a muffled sound of pain. Steeling himself, Leigh flung back the curtain.

Julie was backed into a corner, a three-legged stool in her hands. Her customer, a rather portly fellow with a shiny bald head, lay face down at her feet. He groaned again. No wonder—there was an egg-sized lump on his head. Julie was scowling at him, stool held high, ready to strike again.

She saw him in the doorway. The light wasn't good, so she snapped, "Keep back if you don't want a cracked skull!"

"Julia!"

She squinted at him. "Levius?"

She leaped over the sprawled man, dropping the stout wooden stool on him as she went. It hit the back of his neck. He twitched and moaned.

Julie flung her arms around Leigh's neck. Her heavy makeup smeared against his cheek.

"Get me out of here, will you? That guy wanted to—I can't even say it!"

Indistinct forms appeared at the other end of the hall. Leigh pushed Julie away and said, "Not now! We have to get out of here!"

He led her, not toward the crowd in the banquet room, but to the stairs at the far end of the hall. Julie protested that wasn't the way out. Leigh glanced back and saw Luxuria's servants armed with clubs. Filling the doorway behind them was the giant Ramesses.

He jerked her hard by the wrist. Stumbling, they reached the steps and started up. He heard someone call out, "They're trapped. Can we have them both when we catch them, Luxuria?" She must have said yes, for Leigh and Julie's pursuers gave a cheer and surged down the hall.

The upstairs rooms had doors. Leigh silently counted until he found the bathroom door. A quick pound with his fist and his name, and the door opened inward. Julie saw France and Hans.

"Ave, guys! Thanks for coming to get me!"

Leigh pushed her in. Once inside, he directed France and Hans to bar the door. They rolled a marble urn against it, and then set about tearing apart the sink and commode. The slabs of stone were not cemented in place. They piled the smooth, hard blocks against the door. Just then, someone slammed against the outside panel. Everyone flinched and drew back.

"Sword," said Leigh. Hans gave him the gladius.

"Out the window!" France urged. He, Julie, and Hans took turns climbing out on the ledge. Luxuria's sporting patrons were loudly hammering on the door with fists and feet, but laughing all the time. They were drunk. In that state, it would take them a week to break through. Leigh tossed a few parade-ground insults at them, which made them mad. They pounded harder.

"Come on!" said Hans, poking his head in the window.

Leigh sheathed his sword and went to the window. France was already in the alley with Julie. Hans tottered along the stone ledge a few steps, then lowered himself to the street.

Wood splintered behind Leigh. The idiots had stopped using their hands and found something harder to break the door down. Maybe their heads, he thought.

He jumped. It was foolish to leap an entire story, but he was wired on anger and fear. The shock of landing sent a jolt of pain flashing through his legs. Leigh wobbled and sat down with all the stars of heaven in his eyes.

He smelled perfume. Julie and France tried to drag him to his feet.

"Why did you jump, you moron? You could've broken both legs!" It was nice to know Julie was okay.

Shouts from the street echoed in front of Luxuria's. If the lictors joined the hunt, they were finished. Leigh struggled to his feet.

"Get going," he gasped. They had planned to flee the city by the north gate and Via Ortus Road.

France, Julie, and Hans hurried on. Leigh trailed behind, sword in hand, to discourage pursuit. They were just about to the next main thoroughfare when they heard loud screams coming from the house of Luxuria—or a least, from the street. Female screams. France stopped short.

"Linnea!"

"That's not her," Hans replied. "Too loud, too low."

"Keep going!" Leigh said. They vanished into the shadowed lanes off the Via Gauisus.

Leigh didn't quite make it before he heard a challenge close behind. He spun and saw Ramesses coming up fast behind him. His long legs covered ground at a frightening rate, even though he wasn't running.

"Stop! Lady Luxuria demands it!" he rumbled.

Leigh squared off, sword ready. Seeing the blade, Ramesses slowed.

"No need for that," he said slowly. "I won't hurt you if you bring the girl back."

"She's not coming back," Leigh said. "And I will hurt you if you try to stop us!"

Ramesses wasn't armed. He never needed to be. His posture was wary, but confident. He swung an open hand sideways at Leigh. He jumped back out of the way, swatting at the giant's hand with his gladius. Ramesses snatched his hand out of harm's way.

"Put that down," he said sharply. "If you cut me, I'll kill you."

"Then stay back!" Every second he held off the giant, the farther away Julie and the others could get.

They sidled around each other, first left, then right. Ramesses didn't try to punch Leigh with his great fists, but swept his huge hands sideways, like he was trying to swat an annoying fly. After one missed swing, Leigh scored the back of Ramesses's hand with the point of his blade. Blood welled out of a deep cut on the big man's hand.

Ramesses stood back examining his wound. Leigh watched him warily, panting hard. The giant didn't seem angry, but in the next instant he lashed out, snagging Leigh by the collar of his cloak. His first reaction was to try to pry Ramesses's hand loose, but it was like trying to open a steel clamp.

"You cut me," Ramesses said coldly. He pulled Leigh toward him. Leigh resisted, but his army sandals skidded on the pavement. Desperate, he thrust his sword straight out in front of him. Using his own massive arms, Ramesses' pulled Leigh in. The gladius caught him right below the breastbone.

Ramesses grunted. From pulling, he tried to shove Leigh away, but the teen leaned on his sword hilt, driving it in further.

"Hurts," said the giant, surprised.

His knees folded. He backhanded Leigh, who spun away. Wincing, Ramesses drew the blade from his chest. It fell with a clatter on the pavement. Amazingly, he staggered to his feet, his oversized robe darkening with a spreading stain of blood. He turned and, with great dignity, walked toward the house of Luxuria. He made it eight steps before collapsing in the street.

Trembling all over, Leigh picked up his sword and backed away. The blade was covered in blood. He didn't sheath it, but held it out at arm's length as he started after his sister and friends.

CHAPTER 21

Lurking in the street on the other side of the brothel, Jenny, Linh, and Eleanor stood watch. The boys disappeared around the corner, and for a long time, there was nothing to look at but the lictors standing firmly outside Luxuria's garden gate.

Linh, whose ears were keen, heard a muffled uproar coming from inside the house. She touched Jenny to alert her and glanced back at Eleanor, standing motionless in the doorway. Jenny stepped out of the deeper shadows and stared at Luxuria's, staring and staring until a crowd of men and women burst out the door into the garden. She could hear them, but not see them, because of the garden wall. At first, it sounded more like a wild party spilling outside than an angry mob. The lictors faced the gate as Luxuria's clients and ladies came in the street, half-dressed, half-undressed, and loud with wine. Consul Marius did not appear, but the lofty doorman loped through the noisy revelers, then traipsed off in the opposite direction from Jenny and her friends.

Luxuria emerged from the gate. In a loud voice, she commanded the crowd to chase down the intruders, who had stolen one of her girls. Garden stakes and tools were passed out to the men, who waved them in the air like outraged peasants in an old horror movie.

"Genera!" Linh said, fearing for her friends.

Jenny advanced into clear view in the street. Fists clenched at her sides, she did something she hadn't done since she was eight years old—she screamed as loud as she could.

That got the attention of the mob. Spying a young priestess in the street, they streamed toward her. Satisfied she'd caused a diversion, Jenny sprinted away. Passing Linh and Eleanor, she said, "Better run!"

Run they did, but they couldn't keep up with an Olympic hopeful. They would have been caught in two blocks if their pursuers hadn't been hampered by loose belts and excess wine.

It was Jenny's scream Leigh and company had heard. Many blocks from Luxuria's, France, Hans, and Julie paused to catch their breath. While they were panting in an alley between a cobbler and a tinsmith's shop, Leigh arrived. He leaned one arm against the corner wall and was sick on the pavement.

Julie said, "Not used to running, are you?"

He looked at her with aching eyes. Holding up his bloody sword, Leigh replied, "I just killed a man."

France and Hans joined them. Hans asked who Leigh fought.

"The giant. What was his name? Ramesses . . ."

Julie paled under her makeup. "You killed him?" she said in a small voice. Leigh wiped his mouth with the back of his hand and nodded.

Hans took the gladius from him.

"Come," he said gently. "We've got to get out of the city."

They tried to navigate the darkened streets, but they couldn't see much of the sky for the buildings. Nearer the heart of Eternus, they ran into nightlife: workmen carousing between wine shops, a beggar or two, a doctor on an emergency call. Fortunately, they didn't encounter the night watch.

In the Forum Facilis, they saw enough sky for Hans to get his bearings. They wanted to get out on the north side of the city, and then head south to confuse pursuit. Hans spied the North Star. They hurried on.

"I hope Linh and the others can find their way," France muttered.

"Do you?" said Julie slyly.

"We all do," her brother said. He jerked Julie forward to cut off further teasing.

This part of the city was hilly. The houses were bigger and farther apart, and they had to avoid patrols of private guards hired by the rich to protect their homes. As they neared the great temples of Mars, Mercury, and Jupiter, the skyline gave off an eerie blue glow. Each building was distinct, designed to reflect the character and glory of the god it was dedicated to. The Temple of Mars resembled a rocket, with a single pointed spire supported by stone buttresses like fins. (It was really meant to be a great spear thrust heavenward, Hans said.) The effect was strangely un-Roman. Mercury's temple had soaring wings of stone attached to the eaves, making the building look like it was about to take flight. The mighty house of Jupiter, king of the gods, reminded Leigh of nothing so much as a colossal bank building in New York City—massive columns, heavy roof, all squatting on a high set of marble steps. In turn, each of them glanced at the shining structures, blinked, and hurried on.

Skirting the brighter streets, they came to a long white wall, with no gate or markings. It was only twice head high, not like the great city wall. With France leading, they followed it. On and on it went. It never seemed to end, and they couldn't find any way through it.

"What is this, Celebrity Row?" Julie said. She kicked the wall.

The sky was dark on the other side of the wall, but the temple glow blotted out the stars. Last in line, Leigh glanced back to see if they were being followed.

"Hey," he said. "There's a door!"

Five yards behind them was an opening, barred by an iron gate. They had all passed this point. There was no gate there before.

"Weird," said Hans. He doubled back and tried the gate. It swung in with a slight squeal.

"I don't like this," Julie declared.

"Neither do I," said Leigh.

"What choice do we have?" asked Hans, standing in the open gate.

"Lots of choices! There, there, or there!" Julie pointed to areas away from the strange wall.

France passed her, passed Leigh, and slipped by Hans into the dark opening. Julie protested, but when Leigh followed him, she grumbled and did likewise.

Passing through the gate made Julie's head swim. It was pitch-black, and though she felt her feet come down on solid ground, for a moment it felt as if she was falling through a void. Something—a tree branch—brushed against her face and she realized they had entered an *ortus*, a "garden" or "park," on the estate of a wealthy Latin. She couldn't see the boys. Carefully, she called them. No one answered. A hand snaked out of the darkness behind her and clamped over her mouth. She screamed against the hand and tried to bite it.

"Be still!" Leigh whispered fiercely in her ear. "You make enough noise to be heard in Cherbourg!"

She lashed him with choice words she'd learned at Luxuria's, but she did it quietly.

Hans drifted into view. "This way . . ."

They walked between manicured hedges. The path changed from sand to paving stones. Ahead, light blazed. Torches on ornamental stands ringed a circular patio. Beyond the firelight, a great house rose up, lined with severe Doric columns. Though vast, it didn't look like a temple. There were no robed priests around. No one was around.

"What is this place?" Leigh muttered.

"Looks like a villa—a very fine, expensive villa." Hans looked back. They were atop a prominent hill. A large swath of Eternus was spread out beneath them. It was a fine view, the sort of place a king might live, or an emperor.

The idea chilled him to the bone. He said urgently, "I think we ought to get out of here right away!"

Leigh and Julie were all for that, but France had gone ahead. He walked right into the circle of firelight, unafraid.

"Come back!" Julie called. "You'll get caught—we'll all get caught!"

Unheeding, France walked through the circle of fire with slow deliberation. Leigh darted after him until he came to the torches. He froze outside the ring, unwilling to expose himself.

Hans took Julie's hand and led her around the patio. They watched, amazed, as France climbed the short set of marble steps leading up to the great columned portico. At any moment, they expected swarms of soldiers to erupt from the building and seize their friend.

France reached the porch unharmed. He looked this way and that. He beckoned his friends to join him.

"This is crazy," Leigh said, stepping into the light like someone dipping a toe into a scalding bath. Julie and Hans went up the steps beyond the firelight. All was still.

Breathing hard, Leigh eventually joined them. "What the hell are you doing?" he demanded.

"I know where we are," France said. He craned his neck to study the roof high above them.

"Where?" asked Hans.

"The palace of the First Citizen."

Julie used a rough word she learned at Luxuria's. Leigh asked France why he thought so.

"Who else would live on the highest hill in Eternus, in such a grand but anonymous palace?"

Leigh suddenly wished he was back at the brothel fighting off lictors and rowdy guests. France was undeterred. He set off down the covered porch without waiting for the others. Hans and Julie followed him, with Leigh guarding their backs.

The first doorway they came to was open. It was a single bronze panel, polished to look like gold. France could see light within. Hans grabbed him before he could go in.

"What are you doing?"

"We were led here," France replied. "Don't you see? That endless blank wall? We are supposed to be here. We're expected."

He walked in. Hans whispered loudly, "Who's expecting us?"

The air inside was warm and smelled of oil lamps and flowers. France went ahead with care, noting the beautiful mosaic floor, the tapestries on the walls, and the warm, gentle light filtering through the forest of columns. His sandaled feet scuffed the hand-cut tiles.

Leigh chewed his lip. If this was the home of the First Citizen, where were the servants? More important, where were the guards?

The corridor ended on a T-shaped intersection. A fountain burbled and splashed at the junction of three passages. Instead of the usual god or goddess statue, the fountain featured a very abstract figure carved from black stone, upswept from the fountain's basin and ending in a stylized curl, like an ocean wave in an old Japanese woodblock print.

Hans noticed this right away and said, "That's a Nango!"

"Nango?" asked Julie.

"The Japanese artist, Daisuke Nango! I've seen his work in museums in Munich and Frankfurt!"

"Did he live in Roman times?" said Leigh.

Hans frowned. "He died in 2034."

Julie caught water in her hands and tried to wash off the heavy makeup Luxuria made her wear. Using the hem of her gown, she scrubbed her cheeks and forehead until they felt raw.

"This way," murmured France.

He went left again. They passed through a darkly shadowed section of corridor before entering the end of a large rectangular room. The ceiling was very high. Water splashed in an unseen pool. Large flowers and small trees grew lavishly in dirt-filled trenches in the mosaic floor.

In the midst of this indoor garden was a couch, a low table, and a bright, flickering oil lamp. Reclining against the end of the couch was a man. The four teens froze.

The man looked up from the scroll he was reading. He appeared to be about sixty, with silver hair in a bowl cut. Thin,

226

he was not so old his body had begun to sag. The man regarded them with clear, dark eyes.

"Ah," he said. "I wasn't expecting visitors."

France stepped forward. "Weren't you?"

The old man let the scroll curl up on the table. "I have few visitors these days, but welcome, welcome. You seem to be in some distress."

"What makes you say that?" asked Julie.

"You're dirty feet speak of running. And that blade has plainly seen use." He pointed to Leigh, who had taken the bloody gladius back and still carried it.

"Are you the First Citizen?" Hans said.

"Hardly! My name is Antoninus."

"This is the First Citizen's house." France did not say it like a question.

Antoninus stood. "It is. How did you know?"

"This hilltop commands the city. Who else would live here but the Princeps?"

The man smiled. "Smart fellow."

Leigh burst out, "We've got to get out of here! Half the city will be after us by daylight!" Antoninus asked what they had done. Hans and Julie took turns explaining her escape from Luxuria's. Julie's language was rather blunt. Leigh blushed furiously.

"You are brave to help your sister and friend," Antoninus said. "Lucky, too. I hope your luck continues."

He nodded farewell and walked away into the greenery. France hurried after him.

"What do you do here?" he demanded. Antoninus ignored him until France grabbed him by the arm. The old man stared at France's hand until the latter removed it.

227

"I observe and report what I see to the First Citizen," Antoninus said.

"You're his secretary?"

"'Quaestor' is the proper title."

"We want to see him," France said.

"Impossible. No one sees the First Citizen."

"Is that because he doesn't exist?"

Antoninus frowned. "Oh, he exists. He has always existed."

He walked on. France and the others trailed behind. Antoninus quickened his pace.

"Levius, maybe we need a hostage," France said.

"Yeah, maybe so!"

"The First Citizen's right-hand man would make a good one," Julie offered. Hans agreed.

"How desperate you've become in such a short time!" Antoninus said. "Would you really kidnap me?"

"Why not?" France said.

"Would you harm me if I resisted? Would you kill me?"

"If it's you or us," said Leigh.

They were walking briskly now. France noticed they weren't getting anywhere. The couch, the lamp, and the scroll were still plainly visible behind them.

"What do you know about illusions?" he said, catching Hans's eye.

"Strange time for a question! Well, Plato said—"

"Never mind Plato. What do you say?"

Antoninus stopped and looked away, thinking of some forgotten vista. He said, "'Youths green and happy in first love, so thankful for illusion; And men caught out in what the world calls Guilt, in first confusion . . .'"

Julie said something about nuts in charge, but Hans recognized the quotation. It was from a nineteenth-century English poem by Arthur Clough, hardly a Roman.

"Who are you? What is this place?" France demanded.

"The Republic of Latium, of course."

"You know this isn't ancient Rome!" said Hans. "This is the year 2055!"

"What do such numbers mean? Here, time and place are what we make it." Antoninus leaned forward to cup a snow-white iris in his hand. The flower and vase had not been there a moment ago.

"But who makes it?" asked Julie. "You? Those plaster gods stuck all over town?"

At that, the old man looked annoyed. "The gods—have you been talking to them?"

"We're not crazy!"

"No, you're not, but here the gods do speak to mortal ears despite my best efforts to block them out," said Antoninus.

He let go of the flower and clasped his hands behind his back. The iris, vase, and short marble column on which they stood silently vanished. Leigh groaned and closed his eyes.

"We were close once, our little band. When we began, everything was equal, and we shared this place without jealousy or fear. Over time—over a very long time—we grew apart and became rivals. Then we became enemies."

"Which are you, John, Paul, George, or Ringo?" said Julie, folding her arms.

Antoninus ignored her. "Those 'gods' were once my colleagues. Now they spy on me through statues and witless worshippers . . ."

France understood at once. Antoninus was the First Citizen! He yelled as much and declared, "Let's get him!"

Leigh and France tried. They rushed Antoninus from either side, meaning to trap him between them. Instead, they ran right into each other so hard, France sprawled on the mosaic tiles.

"Where'd he go?" Julie cried.

"There!"

Hans pointed dramatically. Antoninus was back on his couch, scroll in hand.

Julie uttered a single coarse word. The boys slowly converged on the elder man, quietly reading his document.

"Ah," he said. "I wasn't expecting visitors."

"You already said that," Julie said.

"Have I? I do tend to repeat myself. The burden of age, you understand."

"None of this is right," France said. "People don't just vanish and reappear!"

"Some of us do," said Antoninus with a smile. "As you shall see."

The scroll rolled up into two soft cylinders and hit the floor.

"He's gone!"

They converged on the spot where Antoninus had been.

"I don't get this at all," Hans said, running his hands through the spot where the old man had been. "Is it drugs? Are we dreaming?"

"Maybe we can still find the First Citizen," Leigh said. "If we have him, they'll have to let us go."

France was grim. "The only way we deal with all this is to accept it. This whole place is like some crazy reenactor's paradise—if we dig into it far enough, we'll find out who's really in charge."

"You stay and play D&D if you want to," said Julie. "I'm leaving." Leigh and Hans agreed with her.

A shaft of light fell from the atrium overhead, brightening the room. At first, France thought it was more "magic" from the Latins, but Julie saw what it was.

"It's daylight," she said. "The sun's come up."

Impossible. They couldn't have been here all night! It wasn't even midnight when they freed Julie from Luxuria's. Their fight and flight may have taken an hour or two, but not all night.

"Let's get out of here," Leigh said. They hurried back the way they came. On the way, Hans picked up the scroll Antoninus had left behind. He spread the rolls apart.

"It's blank," he said, puzzled.

The lightening halls filled Leigh with dread. He had overstayed his night out. Rufus Panthera would be furious. When the fracas at the brothel and the death of Ramesses came out, the centurion would have his head on a pike, for sure.

Racing behind Leigh, France started worrying about Linh. Had she, Jenny, and Eleanor gotten away? They were supposed to meet at the city's north gate and escape together. The army, Luxuria's protectors, even the consul's lictors were probably after France and friends. Had anyone intercepted the girls? Their chances of getting there now seemed to be vanishing faster than night in Eternus Urbs.

Leigh reached the outside door first. Julie and France piled into him when he stopped abruptly, filling the door.

"What the hell?" Julie said. Then she saw what halted her brother.

The courtyard outside was filled with legionnaires—rank upon rank of infantry in helmets and shields, bowmen with electric arrows nocked, and half a dozen mounted officers. In command was no one less than Consul Marius himself.

Hans, bringing up the rear, suggested they flee in the other direction. Staring over Leigh's shoulder, France said no.

"Why not?" Hans said. He looked past Julie and saw why his friends were paralyzed.

Kneeling in a line were Jenny, Linh, Eleanor, and a fourth figure none of them recognized at first. Julie said under her breath, "It's the weird guy from the boat!"

It was Emile, no longer in black. He wore the simple homespun shift and headband of a Latin slave.

"Throw down your arms!" Consul Marius exclaimed. "Either you give them up or your fellow criminals will be executed on the spot!"

CHAPTER 22

There wasn't anything to do. Leigh flung his sword to the ground. It rang on the pavement and skittered away, to be picked up by one of the consul's guards.

A dozen soldiers trotted forward and took the defeated teens in hand, two men to each of them. They were separated and driven forward to the waiting Marius.

"Infamous criminals!" he declared. "Did you think you could get away with your crime?"

"I only wanted to save my sister," Leigh replied. A centurion cuffed him hard on the back of the head.

The consul frowned. "Sister? I speak of your attempt to assassinate the First Citizen of the Republic!"

Now France was alarmed. "My lord, we meant no such thing! We came here seeking the protection of the Princeps for taking the girl Julia from a life of forced prostitution!"

"And failing to secure his help, you resolved to kill him," Marius said. "Take them away!"

With swift and brutal efficiency they were chained hand and foot and dragged away to prison. They weren't taken to the army camp this time, but to a squat stone building on the southern side of the city, near a great stadium where public games were staged. Hans saw the arena and mumbled aloud that he always knew they would end up dying in some place like that.

Everyone was confined to a cell alone, but they were all on the same hall in the lower level of the prison. It was dark down there, no windows, and the stone walls and floor were always filmed with frigid dew. The prisoners were fed once a day (morning or night, no one could tell). France asked the jailer questions every time he brought food, but the gaunt, scarred man never answered.

Six times they were fed, so possibly six days went by. Leigh had horrible dreams even while he was awake. He saw himself marching to a chopping block to have his head cut off. His executioner was the giant Ramesses. The big man still had a huge bloodstain on his belly where Leigh impaled him. Leigh was forced to kneel with his head on the chipped slab of wood. Up went the axe—

Linh saw things, too. In the dark, dimly glowing figures walked past her door. She pressed her face to the barred slot and tried to make out who or what they were. Gradually she realized they were her friends being led one by one to the place of execution. On the fifth night, she saw herself drift by, shuffling unseen feet. Linh called out to herself, and the phantom looked straight at her with empty sockets where her eyes should have been.

Jenny paced. Her cell was exactly six steps by five and a half. That half step difference drove her crazy. It wasn't right! One-two-three-four-five-six, okay; one-two-three-four-five and a half—ridiculous! Couldn't these people do anything right?

Hans didn't eat. He drank his slimy, copper-tasting water, but he refused the tiny portion of boiled beans or stale bread. Eating it would only make him suffer agonies of hunger. If he was going to die, he didn't want to go cringing and moaning. The jailer said nothing, but took away the uneaten food each time.

Julie cried for a whole day, and then she ran out of tears. Dirty, backward SOBs, who did they think they were? This wasn't ancient Rome. Did they think they could get away with executing people in this day and age? Man, the UN needed to know about this place. The FBI, too.

In her cell, Eleanor sat very still. She prayed to Apollo to rescue her. The god did not appear.

France Martin used a stone chip to scratch a description of his plight onto the floor. He spent most of his first day doing this, ate his prison fare, and then went to sleep. When he awoke, all the writing was gone. It was dark in his cell, but he had clearly felt the deep scratches he had made in the floor stones earlier. Now the floor was smooth again.

Objective reality does not work here, not all the time, he decided. He made a list of all the impossible things he'd seen or encountered. The loss of the *Carleton* and the officers headed the list. This island, this strange ancient Roman fantasy world came next. The flash of light in the night, their learning Latin spontaneously, talking god statues, and everything else that followed made no sense unless everyone involved was controlled, brainwashed to believe what was happening was normal reality.

How could this happen? France had no idea. Who was behind it all? There were all kinds of candidates—cults, secret societies, intelligence agencies, rogue government bureaus— who knew? What mattered was that they get out of here and warn the world.

Footsteps in the corridor put an end to his reasoning. It sounded like more than just the jailer. France heard other doors being opened and, for an instant, imagined they were being set free. He could not hear what was being said, but after a short speech the doors thumped shut again.

His turn came. The jailer opened the door and stepped in, carrying an oil lamp. An armed guard entered next, and a Republic official in a spotlessly clean white toga.

"Newcomer Gallus?"

France slowly stood up. By lamplight he could see for sure his writing had vanished from the floor.

The thin gray-haired official unrolled a scroll and read from it. "By the order of the Senate and People of the Republic of Latium, you have been found guilty of blasphemy against the gods, treason against the state, and designs for murder against the First Citizen of the Republic." He rolled the parchment into a cylinder. "Do you have anything to say?"

The treason charge he understood, but why blasphemy? That's what he asked.

"You did aid and encourage a sworn priestess of Ceres to desert her temple, her goddess, and her sworn superiors, did you not?"

"There are no goddesses," France said. "And no Republic. You're living a fantasy."

The official shuddered. "Condemned out of your own mouth! Very well, the sentence stands as written."

"What is the sentence?"

"Death at the hands of the public executioner."

Something inside France trembled hard. He put out a hand to keep from falling.

"Tell me, how do you kill prisoners here?"

"The penalty for blasphemy is inhumation."

Inhu-what? Exhumation meant digging something up; so inhumation must mean being buried . . . alive.

He made no attempt to disguise his alarm. France sank against the back wall of his cell. In a small voice he said, "Are we all to be killed that way?"

"The soldier Levius, having betrayed his oath to the army, will be beheaded. The slave Aemilius will be sent to the mines to work until he dies. The newcomer Ioannes will be sold into slavery and sent to the mines—"

"I get it. What about the girl Linnea?"

The Latin clerk consulted his scroll.

"Inhumation."

France slid down the wall. "Is there any hope?"

The official tucked the tightly wound scroll under his arm.

"The laws of the Republic are fair and just," he declared. "The pillars of the nation must be upheld. The honor and discipline of the army, the gods, and our divinely inspired leader must be preserved."

With that, he turned on his heel and strode out. The jailer and guard followed, leaving France alone in the dark.

He cried. He hadn't done that since his mother left his father, three years ago. France thought he wouldn't cry ever again after that. Tears changed nothing and he felt weak for shedding them, but sitting in that lightless, chilly, damp cell there was nothing else to do.

Buried alive. He hoped at least they would put them all together, Linh and the others. Surely, they would—the Latins were too practical to dig so many individual graves.

The lump in his throat swelled until he thought he would choke then and there. Forcing himself to be calm, France drifted off in despairing slumber. Tiny terrors lit his dreams, like fireflies in a tomb.

He thought he heard the clank of the door bolt. France was in the rear corner of the cell, knees drawn up to his chin, his head resting against the hard wall. When he detected the bolt moving, he flinched awake, unsure what he heard was real. Cracking an eye, he couldn't see any telltale lamplight under the door. Maybe he imagined it.

Then he heard, quite distinctly, the scrape of sandal on stone floor. All the fear and anger bottled up inside him drove France to his feet and across the black cell in single flash of fury. He tackled whoever had come in, smashing them to the hard floor. His opponent gasped on impact.

France grabbed a handful of cloth and made a fist with the other hand, ready to smash the face of whatever Latin lackey had come in.

"Stop," said a mild voice.

France froze. "Who is it?"

"Aemilius."

He held his position. Emile, who had betrayed them on the march to Eternus? He had disappeared the day the *Carleton* people were parceled out. France assumed he had been brainwashed like the others.

"Can I get up?"

"What are you doing here?"

"I came to let you out."

France tightened his grip on the younger boy's garment. "Why? How?"

"Does it matter?"

He gave Emile a hard shake. "Yes! It does matter!"

Coughing, Emile said, "Do you want to be buried alive?"

France got off him and stood. Emile gripped his arm and hauled himself to his feet.

"My master sent me," he whispered. "All right?"

"Who is your master?"

"He is Mercury, son of Jupiter, messenger of the gods—"

Without thinking, France slapped Emile hard. The Belgian boy sobbed in the darkness.

"I know about your 'gods,'" France said coldly. "I'll not be run around like puppets on a stage!"

"Don't you want to live?" France didn't answer such an obvious question. "I am your way out of here, or do you want to die with dirt in your mouth?"

"What's in it for you?"

Quietly Emile said, "I am restoring balance to this place."

"Why do you care?"

"I prefer it to home."

"Do you remember?" France said. "The *Carleton*, Cherbourg, the shipwreck?"

"Of course I do."

"Then why did you act so—so—"

"Like a zombie?" France could sense Emile's grin in the dark. "To throw them off guard. If I showed too much memory, they would have come down on me, hard."

"Who are 'they?'"

"The powers that run this place."

He moved away. France reached out and caught him. "What is this place?"

"Have you ever heard of Hy-Brasil?"

The name stirred a long-faded memory, a history lesson from middle school. Not confident, France told Emile to ̧

"There are stories of a fogbound island west of Ireland called Brasil, or Hy-Brasil. It's not the country Brazil in South America;

that was named later. Hy-Brasil was a phantom island inhabited by a magician in a stone castle guarded by giant black rabbits."

"*Fimus*," France hissed. This was how *merde* was rendered in Latin. "There are no magicians or superbunnies here."

"No, but navigators in the fifteenth century reported spotting Hy-Brasil west of Ireland. It was lost when ships from Europe became common in the Atlantic."

France clucked his tongue. "You might as well say we're on Atlantis!"

"Some people have called this place exactly that."

He pushed past Emile and made for the door. Time was too short to waste on stupid fairy tales.

Emile hurried after him. In a loud whisper he said, "But suppose there was such a place! Suppose the people who lived there could make their island invisible to the outside world?"

France turned abruptly back. "Why?"

Emile bumped into him. "To live as they pleased. To keep their secret arts and technology to themselves. To avoid the outside world, its wars and its agonies."

France didn't even waste profanity on Emile's theory. He stepped boldly into the hall. At the far end of the corridor, a smoky pine knot burned in a wall bracket. No sign of the jailer. He tried the cell next to his and found Leigh curled up inside on the cold stone floor, asleep. He kicked Leigh's feet then stepped back out of the way of the American's flailing limbs.

"Quiet," said France. "We're going."

Leigh sprang to his feet. "Where are the others?"

"We still have to let them out."

They freed the others one by one, Leigh taking one side of the corridor, France the other. Emile hovered behind France, his hands tucked into his armpits. Whenever France glanced at him, Emile was grinning stupidly.

"What's the matter with you?"

"This is exciting." Even without his black ensemble, he was still weird.

Soon, five of them were in the passage, hugging and whispering. Jenny, Linh, and Eleanor were not there.

"Where are they?" said Hans.

"They were taken away before I got here."

France shoved the smaller boy against the wall. "Where are they?"

"I don't know! Outside the city—the Hill of Skulls, I guess."

That didn't sound like a resort. Julie asked if that was where executions took place. Emile nodded.

"We've got to find them!" France declared.

Leigh said, "Which way out?"

He pointed to the torch-lit end of the hall. Julie and Leigh leading, they made for the flame.

Around the corner, they almost tripped over the jailer, sitting upright on a bench against the wall. Leigh cocked a fist and Julie tensed to pounce, but the bony jailer sat motionless, staring into space. Puzzled, Julie waved a hand before his eyes. He didn't even blink.

"What's he been smoking?" she muttered.

"He's interrupted," whispered Emile. "Make haste! The effect does not last."

At the end of the intersecting corridor, a set of stone steps led up. Julie and Leigh took the lead again. France lingered, studying the paralyzed jailer.

"I've seen this before," he said. "At the farm. The night the soldiers tried to carry off the girls."

"Yes," said Emile. "It's called 'interruption . . .'"

"How do you know what it's called?"

"My master knows these things."

France grabbed the back of Emile's slave robe. "Who is this master?"

Emile squirmed. "I told you!" France was about to repeat the question more forcefully when the jailer's arm slipped off his lap and dangled at his side.

"You see? It's wearing off! Hurry!"

France and Emile were the last to leave. On the steps, they passed the Latin official who had read the death sentence to them. Behind him were two guards. They were interrupted, too.

Leigh relieved one guard of his sword. Hans took the other. Emile swore they didn't need weapons, but they kept them just the same.

In the corridor above, Leigh decided to open all the cell doors they passed. To his surprise, the cells he opened were empty. On the other side, Hans unbolted doors, too. Stranger still, the doors on his side of the hall didn't even close off rooms. Behind them were blank walls of solid stone.

"Now there's an escape-proof cell," Julie remarked.

Everyone they met in the prison building was paralyzed. Even the guard dogs chained to a stake in the courtyard stood stiff as statues. Hans wanted to examine the interrupted animals and people, but the others dragged him away.

"But how is it done?" he protested. No one else cared, as long as they got away.

At the door of the prison, Leigh stopped, holding a hand to warn the others to halt. It was early morning by the slant of the shadows in the street. A rustic wagon stood at the prison door, drawn by a pair of scruffy-looking horses.

"Wheels," said Leigh.

"Thoughtful of you to provide them," France said to Emile. Grinning, the latter accepted the ironic compliment.

Moving with careful nonchalance, the escapees emerged from the prison in groups of two, leaving Emile to come out last, alone. They climbed in the wagon. Hans took the reins. He knew how to drive a team. Growing up, he had handled horses at the Bavarian Summer Folkfest.

Emile stood by the back of the wagon, hands still oddly stuck in his armpits. Leigh offered a hand up.

"No."

"Aren't you coming?" asked Julie.

"No."

"Why? Do you like being a slave in this costume hellhole?"

"It's complicated. I am—"

"You're not the Aemilius who arrived on the ship with us, are you?" said France. The grin faded from Emile's face.

"No, I'm not."

Latins walked by. Vendors rolled pushcarts. Now and then someone wealthier clattered past on horseback. So far no one paid them any mind, but it felt like any moment their escape would be discovered.

"Who are you, then?" Leigh asked, perplexed.

There was no time for explanations. France told Leigh to get Emile in the wagon. Leigh jumped down and took him in hand. Emile dug in his heels.

"You can't force me. What has been done can be undone in an instant—"

Leigh put the guard's sword to Emile's back. "Get in the wagon, man. We're going to save the girls, and I think you know the way."

The sword tip in his back did not dim Emile's crazy smile, but sweat glistened on his pale forehead as he climbed aboard.

"You should escape now. Suppose the girls are already dead?"

"Shut up," France snarled. At his nod, Hans snapped the reins.

A horse wagon was no Zonda supercar, but they were away. They were an odd group—a slave, a soldier, Julie in a tattered courtesan's gown, and a pair of artisans—rolling through the streets of Eternus in a farm wagon. Leigh sat in the wagon box with his sword on his lap. They attracted a few stares and rude remarks (mostly due to Hans's inexpert driving), but no one tried to stop them.

"What happens when the Consul's people come to the jail and find us gone? Won't they hunt us down?" Leigh wondered.

"They will forget you ever existed," Emile replied.

France said, "More interruption?" The Belgian boy just grinned.

"How is it done?"

"You could call it magic."

Hans said, "The technology behind this place is impressive enough. You don't have to be childish and call it magic." Emile did not argue. France and Hans plied him with more questions, but since being forced into the wagon, he was no longer as talkative as he had been.

Winding about, turning this way and that, they eventually reached the north wall of the city. Everyone leaving Eternus had to submit to inspection by Republic troops. Legionnaires ringed the wagon when it was their turn. Leigh hid his blade in loose straw in the bed of the wagon.

"Where are you bound?" demanded an aquilifer bearing the marks of the III Legion.

"My father's farm," Hans said.

"Who are these men?"

Hans waved a hand casually behind him. "Papa sent me to the city to hire some new hands."

"And the girl?"

"My new wife." Julie batted her eyes and laid a fond hand on Hans's leg.

The Latin soldier made a notation on a wax-covered board. "Four departing: farmer, wife, and two laborers."

He let them through. With an enormous sense of relief, they drove through the great fortified gate.

"Strange, he said four departing, not five," France said.

"Slaves don't count," suggested Emile.

"Oh yes, they do. Slaves are valuable property. He didn't see you at all."

Emile shrugged. "How is that possible?"

"How is it possible to paralyze an entire building full of people?"

Outside the city, Hans urged the horses to trot. No one knew what might have happened to Jenny, Linh, and Eleanor.

Emile directed them. The Hill of Skulls was a mile from the north gate. Road traffic was thick for a while, but as they took three right-hand forks, fellow travelers became fewer and fewer. The terrain grew hilly and wooded, with the hilltops cleared of trees. They rode in silence until Hans reined in the team.

"What is it?" asked Julie.

Hans pointed. Vultures, circling a spot not far ahead.

"This is not wise," Emile said.

"If he says another word, hit him," was France's answer. Leigh agreed.

The paved road out of Eternus abruptly ended. Ahead was a rutted dirt track that wound between a pair of steep, grass-covered hills. Grass in the center of the path had been crushed recently by the passage of wheeled vehicles.

The horses balked, snorting and rearing their harness. Hans smelled it, too—the odor of death.

Leigh, Julie, and France piled out. Hans got down, too, tying the reins to a ring on the driver's box. Julie gave him the second sword they'd hidden in the wagon.

"Should we bring weirdo, too?" Julie said. Leigh doubled back and ordered Emile out. No longer grinning, he preceded Leigh up the road.

They heard voices. Someone was alive up there. With no plan but to save their friends, they walked straight up the road as it twisted around the hill. It truly smelled like its name—the Hill of Skulls.

France passed Hans. He reached the top a few steps ahead of the others. What he saw at the top of the hill made a sick taste rise in his throat.

There were bones all around. Not just human bones, though there were plenty of those, but cow and horse remains, too. The stench clung to France's face like a coat of paint.

At the center of the flattened hilltop rose a trio of marble columns. Atop these were statues—a man in Roman armor, presumably the First Citizen, a god wearing a winged helmet and carrying an oddly shaped rod, and a big, stylized perching eagle. Inside the triangle formed by the columns several men stood, stripped to the waist with shovels in their hands. A man in a toga stood by, watching, as did a woman in a long white gown with a veil over her head. Everyone was looking into a hole. The workmen were throwing shovelfuls of dirt into it.

France began yelling and running. The people by the hole looked up, startled. He ran right at the man in the toga, who had the smug look of a petty bureaucrat. Before he could protest or dodge, France slammed into him, hurling him into the deep hole he'd been standing beside.

The priestess screamed. One of the workmen swung his shovel at France, but he was parried by the timely arrival of Leigh, sword in hand. Leigh cut at the fellow, who dropped his tool and ran away, holding bloody fingers. The other three diggers offered no fight and fled.

France leaped into the hole. Standing close together in the pit were Jenny, Eleanor, and Linh. Dirt came up to Jenny's waist, Linh's chest, and Eleanor's armpits. They were gagged. Their hands were tied behind their backs.

France knelt in the dirt and tugged at Linh's gag. She was weeping with relief.

"We were going to die!" she gasped. "They were burying us alive!"

"I know, I know." He smoothed her hair and brushed the tears from her cheeks. On Linh's right, Jenny made annoyed grunts against her gag.

"Sorry." He worked the knot loose while Hans jumped down to free Eleanor.

They all began babbling at once.

"Kill us, the savages—"

"—no trial, just a sentence!"

"I thought I was dead!"

From above, Leigh threw down a pair of abandoned shovels. Hans and France dug the girls out. The man in the toga lay face down in the dirt. He groaned a little. France yanked the sword from Hans's belt and stood over him, blade held high.

"Don't!" Leigh called down.

"Bastard! Burying people alive!"

"It's the law," Emile remarked. "As it was in ancient times."

Disgusted, France threw the sword away. "This is not ancient times!"

They boosted the freed girls out of the pit. Julie and Leigh were guarding the priestess. Jenny identified her as Scipina, from the temple of Ceres.

"You have committed great blasphemies!" she said, nostrils flaring. "The gods will curse you forever!"

"Like I'm scared of stone mannequins," Julie said. When Scipina went on about curses and doom, Julie gave her a swift kick in the backside. Jenny offered to tie her up and gag her, as she had been. Julie happily helped her.

Linh had nothing to say. She had her arms around France's neck, and when they drew apart just enough, she kissed him.

Their friends found other things to look at. All except Emile. He watched them closely, finally remarking, "This is interesting."

"Get a life," Julie said, turning him away with force.

CHAPTER 23

With Scipina and the Latin official tied up and heaved into the pit, it was time to go. Out of earshot of the priestesses, they took stock of their meager assets: money, none. Weapons, a couple of swords. Food and water, none.

"It doesn't matter what we have or don't have, we've got to get out of here," Hans said. "The whole of the Republic will be on us like—like—" His Latin failed him for a metaphor.

"*Niveus in oryza?*" Leigh suggested. "Like white on rice?"

There was no argument. Julie said, "Which way do we go?"

"We know the barbarians of Ys live west of the Republic," France said. "Southeast is said to be an impassable desert."

"That's the way to go," Jenny said, arms folded. Leigh asked why.

"That's the way things work around here. People are told to do something, or not do something, and they just obey. If these Latin idiots say southeast is impossible, then let's go that way. Either it isn't really impassable, or else they won't chase us, because they think it is."

Her logic was unbeatable. Everyone looked ready to get going, but Julie pointed out an obvious problem.

"Which way is southeast?"

Nobody had a compass. Hans could make one with a needle, some thread, and a magnet, but he had none of these.

Linh squinted at the sun. It was still morning, so the sun was still climbing in the east. Pointing forty-five degrees or so to her left, she said, "That way must be southeast."

They set out—all but two. Eleanor stood by the pit, glancing uncertainly at the captives below. Emile actually backed away a few steps.

"What's the matter?" Jenny said. "Come on!"

"I fear the realm we're heading for," Eleanor replied.

"What do you know about it?' France asked sharply.

She sighed, still watching the rim of the pit. "It is called Heka, the Land of the Dead."

Julie laughed. "What is it, Zombie Town?"

Eleanor did not answer. Linh came back and took her firmly by the hand.

"Remember what Jenny said? Whatever you've been told by the Latins may not be true. We can't stay here—we'll all end up buried alive, or beheaded, or something awful like that."

Eleanor let Linh lead her away. That left Emile, slowly backing away from them.

"Come on, kid, don't be weird," Julie said. "We're in this together!"

"I cannot go," Emile insisted.

"Why?" several of them demanded.

"I-I made a bargain. A pact. I have given my senses to one who needed them to observe you newcomers up close—"

France said, "You're not Aemilius anymore, are you? I mean, you're in Aemilius's body and brain, but you're not the Belgian boy we came here with, are you?"

Emile slowly nodded in agreement. Julie gave a short, sharp snort of disbelief and signaled Leigh and Jenny to grab Emile. They approached on either side. Frowning, Emile dodged them. Leigh and Jenny closed in again.

"I cannot leave the Republic!" he cried. "Once beyond its borders, I will die!"

Jenny and Leigh froze. "Is that true?" Jenny said.

Emile insisted it was. To the others they asked if they should drag Emile along.

"No," said France. "Leave him. He may be telling the truth."

"He'll tell the Latins where we're going!" Jenny protested.

Emile didn't deny it, so they decided to bring him along for a while, when they were nearly out of the Republic (however and whenever that occurred), they would let him go.

They fled, south by east. Keeping out of sight by day and moving fast at night, they avoided farm roads. Several times they caught sight of armed patrols hunting them. Archers armed with the fearsome thunderbolt arrows guarded wells and fountains, hoping to keep the escaping teens away from water supplies. Cavalry scoured the roads, but they didn't stray into fields very far. Emile easily explained why.

"They think you are weak, city folk," he said. "They don't expect you to keep to fields and forest."

France had a disturbing idea. "Are you communicating with anyone?"

"How could he be?" Linh said.

"I don't know—mind reading?" That disturbed everyone, especially since Emile did not deny it.

"We could kill him and hide his body" was Julie's surprising suggestion. No one had the nerve for such a harsh deed, so the journey continued.

Four days after the girls were freed from being buried alive, the green, fertile lands of the Republic began to fade into arid, sandy terrain. A few pines and cedars took over from the cool woodlands. They saw snakes, and signs of more snakes—big ones.

"Not far now," Eleanor declared. "Life is leaving the land!"

They camped on sun-warmed boulders for the day. Everyone was hungry and thirsty. They'd gotten by using Hans's old Boy Scout tricks, like licking dew off leaves early in the morning and eating dandelions and other wild greens. One night they filled their pockets with chestnuts from a grove they passed through. Not daring to build a fire to roast them, they had to eat the nuts raw. The result was neither delicious nor digestible, but they carried on.

"Who would have thought it?" Leigh said as they sat on jagged rocks, watching the rising sun.

"Thought what?" Julie muttered.

"You. For sixteen years, pretty much, you lived plugged into Your/World day and night. I remember your fourteenth birthday, you watched your own birthday party on Your/World rather than see it for real—"

"Your/World is real," she said, annoyed.

"Not as real as this." Leigh held out his hands to the scene appearing before them as the sun rose. Even the sparse trees were becoming rarer, yielding the land to little more than rifts of sand, scattered boulders, and the strange squiggly marks in the dirt Eleanor insisted were made by poisonous snakes.

"You escaped from a brothel, broke into a palace, faced death, and worse." Leigh looked at his sister fondly. "I'm proud of you."

She was proud of him, too, but Julie did not mention his killing Ramesses. It was not an easy thing to do, and she knew it would haunt him for a long time to come.

Eleanor shivered, huddled against a boulder. Hans asked her if she was cold.

"This is the borderland!" she hissed through clenched teeth. "Beyond is the Land of the Dead!"

The land unrolled before them like a vast brown sandbox. It couldn't be compared with a beach because beaches always have water nearby. This enormous stretch of dunes looked as devoid of life as Mars. No, Mars had ice and microbes. The desert they faced looked as sterile as the moon. Heat rippled the horizon, and the sky was bleached of color by the dry air.

Hans and France had privately agreed that one of the strange powers of this island possessed Eleanor. She mentioned Apollo, but as with Emile's master, Mercury, they didn't believe Roman gods were lurking around them. Whoever the unseen masters of Hy-Brasil might be, they weren't marble idols or operatic deities. Eleanor did not seem to be as completely dominated as Emile, but she seemed apart from her friends, and she knew and said things their friend Eleanor could not know.

Emile stood on top of a large spear-shaped rock jutting point-first at the desert ahead. While Eleanor was distressed by the prospect of leaving the Republic, he seemed rather wistful.

"Why don't you go with us?"

France and Linh stood below him, holding hands.

"Can't," Emile said.

"Tell me one thing," Linh said

Emile smiled. "Only one?"

"Why did you help us? Why were we spared?" she said, indicating the others with a sweep of her free hand. "Everyone else from the *Carleton* became Latins and forgot their old lives completely. Why were we eight spared that?"

Emile fingered the edge of his grubby robe. "Sometimes a harvest yields too much, and the farmer has no place to store his surplus." He looked over his shoulder at the greener land behind them. "It is also true a herd is improved by bringing in new stock to blend with the old."

"Your examples aren't exactly flattering," said France. "Are we surplus wheat or a herd of wild bulls and cows?"

"You are newcomers. Let it be just that."

Emile twisted around suddenly. "Trouble," he said flatly.

Filtering through the thorny scrub and random juniper trees were many men on horseback. They wore the aluminum armor and scarlet cloaks of Republic cavalry.

Linh and France broke apart, running back to their friends with shouted warnings. Leigh and Jenny, the only two of them armed (with short, inadequate swords), called for everyone to get behind them.

Hans pulled Eleanor to her feet. She gasped, "Don't stand! Run! Go where they cannot follow!"

That didn't make sense. The land ahead of them was more open than where they were. The Republic cavalry could ride them down in empty terrain, but something about Eleanor's desperate state made Hans believe her. He shouted for all his friends to run, run into the desert.

Julie, Linh, and France took off. Hans followed, holding Eleanor up as he went. Jenny and Leigh kept their faces and blades facing the horsemen.

With a shout the nearest riders charged. They flowed around the big boulder where Emile stood. Leigh parried a spear thrust, and then dodged aside. Jenny—strong and tall, but not trained—swung wildly at her opponent. Her crazy cuts forced him back.

More riders fanned out to round up the fleeing teens. Linh and Julie ran ahead, sand pluming from their heels. France deliberately trailed them, hoping to fend off any horsemen who got too close. What with? He had nothing.

The sun rose higher. On open ground, it felt like fire was playing on their faces and exposed flesh. The Latin riders reined in. Given a respite, Linh, Julie, and the others ran on. They felt the heat, too, but it affected the Latins more.

Held tight against Hans, Eleanor's knees folded. He grabbed her around the waist and dragged her on.

Jenny had an idea. She flung her gladius at the nearest cavalryman. He wasn't expecting a missile, and toppled over his mount's rump when the substantial blade whacked him on the nose. With a triumphant yell, Jenny snagged the horse's loose reins. She meant to get on and ride, but the glaring sun drove the poor animal crazy. It reared and flailed its hooves until Jenny let go of the reins. Eyes rolling with terror, the horse galloped back into Republic territory.

Wincing and blinking against the sun's glare, the tough Republic horsemen withdrew. They cantered back past Emile, still observing the brief fight from his rock.

Leigh gathered up Jenny's thrown sword. He also found a spear dropped by the rider she had unseated. Walking slowly to his friends, bowed down by the heat, Leigh returned the sword to her.

"You're crazy," he said. It was a compliment.

She shoved the gladius through the sash on her priestess's gown. "We all are," Jenny replied. "No food, no water—how long can we last in this heat?"

"How long would we last back there?" The cavalrymen milled around among the trees and boulders, unwilling to cross the invisible border of the Republic.

Leigh saw Emile standing alone atop the boulder. He waved to the one-time weird kid in black, heir to a fortune in chocolate.

"So long!" he shouted through cupped hands.

Emile did not return the wave. He turned away and slowly descended from his perch. Leigh had the distinct feeling he would see him again someday.

Stumbling along in the deep sand, Hans suddenly lost his grip on Eleanor. She broke free of his grasp, slogged ahead a few steps, and then faced him with her hands on her head.

"You're the German guy," she said, her words slurred. "How did you get here? How did I get here?"

"Elianora? Is that you?"

"Who else?" she said crossly.

They others slowly converged on them. Hans held out his hand.

"Welcome back," he said. "We have a lot to tell you."

Sun and sand stretched to the horizon. How far did the desert go? No one knew. They made sunshades out of cloth torn from the hems of their garments and tied them around their heads. That done, there was nothing more to do but walk, putting a barrier of broiling desert between them and the strange, dangerous Republic.

CPSIA information can be obtained at www.ICGtesting.com
Printed in the USA
BVOW07*0052170914

366360BV00001B/1/P

9 781623 240004